D0805939

Jackie O
ON THE COUCH

Inside the mind and life of
Jackie Kennedy Onassis

Dr. Alma H. Bond, Ph.D.,

author of the *On the Couch* Series

bancroft
press

Although factual information forms the core of *Jackie O: On the Couch*, the book is a work of fiction, and is not necessarily a complete or historically accurate rendering of the life of the former first lady. The work draws upon some of the well-known details of Mrs. Onassis's history (*see Bibliography at the end of this book*), as well as speculations about her that have appeared in print. It is also based upon the author's impressions and analysis of Mrs. Onassis, whom Dr. Bond has admired from afar for half of her life. It is this great admiration that led to the writing of this book. It is emphasized that the author did not serve as Mrs. Onassis's psychoanalyst at any time.

Cover Design: Erika Saraniero
Interior Design: Tracy Copes

Published by Bancroft Press
"Books that Enlighten"
800-637-7377
P.O. Box 65360, Baltimore, MD 21209
410-764-1967 (fax)
www.bancroftpress.com

Library of Congress Control Number: 2011925901
ISBN 978-1-61088-021-3 (cloth)
ISBN 978-1-61088-025-1 (paper)
Printed in the United States of America

To my son Zane,
the sweetest man who ever lived
(Zane Phillip Bond, 1951-2007)

CONTENTS

PROLOGUE

You may wonder why I have shied away from writing my autobiography, a memoir, or a set of memoirs. It's pretty simple. Living my life has always been more important to me than writing about it. And, as you know, I have always valued my privacy. Now that I am terminally ill, I want to set the record straight, though only for my family. People have viewed me alternately as an icon, a role model to women all over the world who helped a grieving nation to heal, or a fool for putting up with Jack's outrageous philandering. Perhaps all of them are right.

Shakespeare asks, "What seest thou else / In the dark backward and abysm of time?" As I approach that "dark backward and abysm," I need to record my story as truthfully as I can. Most important, I wish to dispel the lies that have been published about me. Shakespeare also wrote, "Speak me fair in death." So before I die, I "speak me fair." Please listen . . . and believe.

Looking back, I see that everything I endured taught me a lesson about the kind of person I wanted to be and actually became. I want the world to know how I overcame my bad luck: a cold, distant mother; a womanizing father; their painful divorce; and at least one womanizing husband, to arrive at a place of contentment and fulfillment.

Now that I approach my mid-sixties, I see things from a much different angle, and want to point out how and where my points of view differ from those I had as a less mature woman. When I was young, I was angry. I felt the people close to me had cheated me of the love I deserved. Now, I have a greater understanding of why they were the way they were, and realize they probably could not have been much different. I hope my story will guide my family in finding their own inner peace. Writing this has certainly helped me.

I feel compelled to tell the truth, yet I do not wish to hurt my children. They are everything to me. I am taking a leap of faith that they will accept me, thorns and all. I am no saint, nor have I ever been. I am a flawed woman who, in some ways, perhaps, has given more to the world than it has given me. Ari seemed to grasp this, when he said in the midst of rage, "Whatever we think about her, we all know that Jackie is a good woman." I thank him for that gift. I would like this memoir to give Caroline and John permission to own their failings along with their virtues, as I have learned to do.

Chapter 1

M Y E A R L Y L I F E

I came into the world on July 28, 1929, six weeks late. I haven't been on time since. Weighing in at eight pounds, I was a healthy baby with dark, fluffy hair that curled slightly, a turned-up nose, rather thick lips, a rosy complexion, and the large, luminous eyes for which I was later known.

I was a precocious child. At four months, I already had four teeth. I spoke in sentences before I was a year old. My mother, Janet Lee Bouvier, said I was born talking. She used to joke that when my head emerged from her birth canal, I looked up at her and said, "My God, are *you* my mother?" All who knew me said I was a remarkable and beautiful child. One classmate described me as a little girl who looked like Bambi.

My mother was pretty and slim, and had a pleasant manner to those who didn't know her well. She was also a daredevil horseback rider. I began following in her footsteps at the age of five, when I won my first ribbon. Confident, aggressive, and independent, my mother was not a warm or emotional person. She sounded better than she was. In truth, she was a difficult woman to understand and even harder to please.

From observing her, I learned my famous "shit detector" skills

which proved so helpful to Jack in the White House. From the time I was a child, I would look down my nose at poseurs and pretenders and they would simply wither away.

Early on, I became aware that my mother's love of status and money virtually ruled her life. She related the story so often I think she actually came to believe it, telling everybody she was "one of the famous Lees of Maryland." Baloney! Her parents were lace-curtain Irish who left their homeland during the potato famine to seek their fortune in America. Though she lorded her "superior social status" over the Kennedys, her background was no better than theirs.

Janet's behavior, however, was not all social hypocrisy. At our dinner table, manners were everything. One thought before one spoke, and no interruptions or raised voices were permitted. My mother believed that good manners were respectful of human dignity. I agreed with her then and I agree with her now.

For her, not surprisingly, the name "Jackie" wasn't dignified enough. She wanted to call me "Jack-leen," but nobody listened to her. "Jackie" I was called and "Jackie" I remained all my life.

Much as I disliked my mother, and even hated her at times, she was the only person of importance who remained with me for decades. Her impact lasted a full sixty years, from the time of my birth until her death, and I believe she influenced the formation of my character far more than anyone else.

Janet Lee Bouvier Auchincloss—"Auchincloss" from her second husband, Hugh D. Auchincloss II—had a profound effect on every aspect of my life. She helped instill many of the qualities that would make me famous later on: her iron will and self-discipline in diet and grooming, her charisma and restraint, her love and knowledge of art, her talent for running an elaborate and complex household, and, perhaps most important of all, her incomparable taste. I would never have become a famous first lady if it hadn't been for Mummy. She was terribly strict and highly critical of me. People considered me reasonably well groomed whenever I left home, as did I, until my mother informed me, even as first lady, that my dress was too short, a seam was split, or the top button of my coat was hanging by a thread. Nobody could change my mood as easily as my mother. Her carping criticism probably did more to mold my perfectionist personality than anything else in my upbringing or in my genes.

For my first dinner at the White House, I invited senators and their wives, Jack's brother Bobby and sister-in-law Ethel and, fool that I was, my own mother. I was not sure yet that I had it all together as a hostess, but I had no doubt that if I slipped up, my mother would point out my error. To my delight, the dinner was impeccable, as was the service and even the music. I was bombarded with compliments from our guests. I grinned, thinking that even the genteel Janet Bouvier Auchincloss would have to admire my skills as a hostess.

"Isn't the record player broken?" she asked reproachfully in the middle of dinner.

"Goodness no, Mummy," I answered with as much sweetness as I could muster. "It's just Fred Astaire tap-dancing away!"

Mummy was difficult to understand. Although she constantly compared my sister Lee to me, and vice-versa, it was not always to my detriment. For instance, the same woman who was always judging my hems, buttons, etc., once said, "Jackie was always beautifully put together, but Lee regularly looked like she'd been deposited by a tornado." Then, smack in the middle of Jack's presidential campaign, forgetting her former assessment of my sense of style, she said, "Why can't you dress more like Pat Nixon or Muriel Humphrey?" *Pat Nixon and Muriel Humphrey?* Two greater frumps never graced the White House or Washington.

Nor did her criticism stop with my way of dressing. It extended into the most personal aspects of my life. She was furious with me when I began my affair with Aristotle Onassis. She didn't like him and found him vulgar in manner and appearance. She said he lacked the elegance I deserved and called him "a moral leper."

Janet would think nothing of swatting me across the face, even as an adult. When I was twenty-two years old, my mother was still arguing with me about which men I should date. Daring to stand up

to her for the first time, I replied, "Mummy, I'm grown up. You can't tell me who I can see and who I can't." Would you believe that Janet reacted to my self-assertion by slapping me on both cheeks? I stood there, too stunned to respond. A friend who witnessed the fiasco said Janet treated me like someone whipping a horse.

To my utter despair, I couldn't help acting like her sometimes. Years later, in almost a scene of déjà vu, little Caroline was playing with some friends in the White House. Somehow, they had gotten hold of my lipstick. When I came into the room and saw Caroline's smeared face, I slapped her over and over again, first on one cheek and then on the other, pushing her through the room until we reached the wall. Caroline sobbed, but the other children stood there as stupefied as I had been years before. I can never forgive myself for behaving like Janet at her worst. I hope Caroline has forgiven me, just as I, an older, wiser person, try to excuse my own mother, who, after all, was shaped by her own parents and her life, much as I was.

My similarity to Janet didn't stop with our methods of discipline. I was practically her mirror image in many ways, such as my proficiency at and love of horseback riding, my athletic ability and healthy way of life, my social skills, my reserve and, of course, my temper. Much of what people admired about me in the role of first lady simply duplicated Janet's behavior. Even my restoration of the White House into a work of comfort and beauty was modeled on Janet's renovation of the Auchincloss homes.

She also shaped my thinking about the role of women in society. Typical of the times, both my mother and I believed that making a good marriage was the only way for a woman to secure her future. Fortunately, she approved of Jack and even grew to love him (especially after he became president), and played a crucial part in arranging our wedding. I went right along with her philosophy that women could secure their future only through marrying well. I saw how wrong she was only after Ari Onassis died. I had always lived through men. I didn't realize until I lost him that I couldn't do that anymore and survive. For the first time in my life, I established an identity of my own, as an editor.

I can't blame Mummy for the fact that that I waited so long to grow up. Nobody says a mature woman has to keep on believing what her mother told her.

She and I both had terrible tempers. Once, Lee and I were fighting so ferociously that, in my rage, I actually kicked down her door. Janet's temper was even worse. When her stepdaughter, Nini, deigned to tell my mother that a fact she said she had quoted from the newspaper was incorrect, Janet, with long fingernails extended, ripped her face wide open until blood was running down her cheeks. In retaliation, Nini seized Janet's wrists and flung her to the floor. Hugh D. Auchincloss, standing up for his wife and not his daughter, threw Nini out of the house, informing her that she was now unwelcome at Hammersmith Farm. It is a moot question which lady should have been banished.

Despite her abusive behavior with her children, Janet could be extremely generous, especially after Jack was elected president. She was obliging about standing in for me at the scores of parties, teas, and ceremonies that bored me as first lady. My mother served as an important and face-saving substitute for me all during the White House years. I am an apolitical woman, and much about my husband's work didn't interest me. Although I loved Jack dearly, I cared little about the details of his administration. Before I met him, I had not even bothered to vote. By standing in for me at these official and semi-official functions, Janet helped to soothe the feelings of ruffled guests and smooth over all the fuss the newspapers made of my numerous absences. She helped me to remain myself during those hectic years. I will be forever grateful.

I had to attend the Inaugural Ball, even thought I didn't want to. I foresaw people milling around like mesmerized cattle, staring at me and watching my every move, but I was totally exhausted. As it turned out, I stayed long enough for everyone to admire my stunning Cassini-designed white gown and emerald necklace, and left as soon as I could. When I got home, I just crumpled. Jack, I am told, managed nicely without me.

Even Janet couldn't always help with my lack of availability. A post-inaugural party was held at the White House for the Kennedys, but I was still tired and refused to attend. Jack was upset about my absence, and apparently there were lots of disapproving looks and comments from the family. When asked "Where's Jackie?," Joe Kennedy growled, "She's upstairs resting, goddamn it!" Guests couldn't believe it when I announced a tea to honor my mother and didn't show up for it. (I guess I got back at her for those slaps after all.) When asked where I was, Janet said, "She's out walking her dog."

"Out walking her dog? When she's giving a party for you?" the amazed guest asked.

"Yes," Janet said. "She always walks her dog at this hour."

It is hard to say which aspect of Janet's mothering was more pronounced—her constant criticizing or her amazing helpfulness. One of the most important things she did for me as first lady was to stand in for me as area chairman for what later became the John F. Kennedy Center for the Performing Arts. Janet worked long and hard to make the Kennedy Center a success, and the fact that it is famous the world over now is due largely to her efforts.

From her, I guess I also inherited my ability to ignore what people think of me. One day, Janet, the journalist Tom Braden, Jack, and I were sitting in the Deck Room in Hammersmith Farm. She suddenly slid to the floor and started doing sit-ups. Neither Jack nor I paid her any attention until we noticed Tom becoming distracted by her movements. I laughed and said, "Oh, Mummy, stop it, will you?" Of course, she went right on with her sit-ups.

We had a complex relationship, one that Mary Barelli Gallagher, my secretary, labeled "push-pull." Sometimes I sought out Janet, and other times I was cool and unapproachable, depending on my mood and how she had behaved to me most recently. Furious that she had permitted a journalist to publish some of my personal papers, I got back at her where it hurt the most. I seated her and Hugh D. Auchincloss, who we called Hughdie, so far back on the reviewing stand during Jack's delivery of the inaugural address that they could only see the back of his head. To add insult to injury, I gave the front-row seats that had been reserved for them to their children, my half-siblings Janet, Junior, and Jamie. The children were thrilled, of course, and couldn't understand their good luck. Their mother never forgave me. Although I was happy about getting even with her then, now that Mummy is dead, I agree with her and think it was a mean thing to do.

My mother definitely had no respect for the privacy of others. My half-brother Jamie once said, "Mummy is the kind of person who opens your mail and bursts right into your room even though the door is closed. I told her once, 'Mummy, if you open another letter of mine, I'm going to take you to court. There are laws against doing such things.'"

"Did that stop her?" I asked Jamie.

"Of course not!" he answered. "She opened my mail the very next day."

"So, did you take her to court?"

"Nah. Hughdie would have thrown me out of Merrywood."

I laughed, but I understood Jamie's feeling quite well. Mummy was always barging into *my* room without an invitation. I objected strenuously, but it did no good. She kept right on coming in whenever she felt like it, even when I lived in the White House. I had to get the chief usher to keep her away. No wonder I'm such a private person! I feel good when I remember that, at the end of her life, I was a loving daughter to Janet. I took care of her when she was dying of Alzheimer's and supported her financially. I set up a million-dollar trust fund for her when Auchincloss funds ran out, and I took great pains to hire a devoted staff that escorted her to the activities she once liked, such as movies, plays, and concerts, even if she could no longer appreciate them. It was I, not Lee, who visited Mummy frequently during her long illness, and during her final days, I devoted a generous amount of time away from my work as an editor to spend it with her. I loved my father more than my mother, but Janet was the one I tried all my life to please. So now that she's gone, I guess I can

admit that my love for her was deeper than I knew. I can say in good faith that little Jackie Bouvier became America's queen in good part because of the efforts of Janet Bouvier Auchincloss, whom I loved after all.

My father's name was John Vernou Bouvier III, and he called himself Jack. I looked just like him, with my widely spaced eyes, snub nose, and dark skin, and I had many of his traits, both good and bad. My father was a thirty-eight-year-old stockbroker when I was born. Until his marriage, he had been considered one of New York society's most eligible bachelors. He was tall, with dark, wavy hair, an Adolphe Menjou mustache, and dark blue eyes. He resembled Rudolph Valentino, which gave him the nickname "the Sheik." He kept a becoming year-round tan, maintained mostly by the use of a sun lamp.

Most of all, he was known as "Black Jack," not so much for his swarthy color but for his reputation as a seducer of beautiful young women. When he walked into a room, most of the women all but threw themselves at him. But he was an eccentric man. No sooner had he won over a woman than he lost all interest in her. He would take a girl up to his bedroom, use her, and then toss her away like a discarded tissue. The next night, he would repeat the process with a different woman. Sometimes, he would have three or four in the same night. He was a man who measured his manhood by the sheer number of amorous conquests.

My analyst of later years said, "What you grow up with is normal to you." I guess the comportment of both Jacks in my life seemed to me the way all men behave, which is why I put up with my husband's philandering.

Black Jack went to Yale and, not surprisingly, considering his extracurricular proclivities, he graduated near the bottom of his class. My father squandered his money on gambling, drink, and nightly parties at his chic Park Avenue address. As his friend Louis Ehret said of my father and his money, he "pissed it away on women."

Black Jack had Dorothy Parker's philosophy: "Take care of the luxuries and the necessities will take care of themselves." The philosophy must have rubbed off on me. When a check came in, he used it to pay off his latest debt. Strangely enough, because of his uncanny charm, no one pressured him to pay his bills. He was a great teacher for someone like me who, I must admit, more than appreciates money. At one point, when he was on the verge of bankruptcy, he owned four cars, one of which was driven by a chauffeur dressed in a maroon uniform. He was warned by his father-in-law, who was subsidizing him, that he had to drastically cut down on his expenses if he wished the hand-outs to continue.

Infuriated at being told what to do, Black Jack defied his father-in-law and rented an elegant eleven-room Park Avenue duplex, where he remodeled the kitchen, added several bathrooms with gold-plated fixtures, built a new nursery, and equipped a gymnasium with the latest equipment. He also employed a trainer and a masseuse. He hired a cook, two maids, two grooms for his stable, and an English nanny for me. Then he took Janet on a second European honeymoon.

I never heard what reaction my grandfather had to his son-in-law's defiance, but from what I saw, it in no way put a damper on my father's spending habits. My own spendthrift ways, which I inherited *par excellence* from Black Jack, drove my mother, my husband Jack, and even the world's richest man, Aristotle Onassis, wild. I was just as defiant as my father, and all the tiresome lambasting from the above three had the same effect on me as my grandfather's threats had on Black Jack. I even topped him—I spent millions, while he spent only thousands.

My father was a vain man, and had no less than six photographs of himself hanging on the walls of his Park Avenue apartment. He spent a great deal of time and money maintaining his looks in his private gym and working out at the Yale Club. Besides keeping his tan year-round, he made a practice of sunbathing nude by a front window of his apartment. If he saw anyone looking at him there, he didn't

give a fig, as if to say, "God and the gym have given me a beautiful physique. If anyone enjoys looking at it, more power to them!" He wore perfectly tailored clothes, including gabardine suits and Brooks Brothers shirts, even while summering in East Hampton.

He was also a head-over-heels gambler, both at the races and on the stock exchange. Unfortunately, his addiction started quite early. He was expelled for gambling from Phillips Exeter Academy, his prep school.

Freud was right about the Oedipus complex. During my teens, I expected Black Jack to pick me up for a "date" every Sunday. I would stand at the door all afternoon, waiting for the sound of his arrival—the horn of his Mercury. I enjoyed his hugs and kisses as much as those of any man in my adulthood, and I got a thrill just holding his hand. The kind of intense love he had for me was more common in Europe than in the United States, and reflected the Latin quality in his personality. (No wonder I always felt at home in Europe.)

When he had to drop me off at Mummy's, I felt bereft. When I was with him, I tried to stay up at night until my eyelids drooped and he had to carry me off to bed. When Juliet said to Romeo, "Good night, good night! Parting is such sweet sorrow / That I shall say good night till it be morrow," I knew just how she felt.

When Daddy knew I was coming to visit, he would cancel all his previous engagements. Our love affair went on all during my childhood, and only began to yield in my late adolescence. I suppose I unconsciously knew that our reciprocal passion would interfere with ever having a man of my own, so I gradually lessened my involvement with him. I don't believe he ever forgave me for doing so. Yet I always remained first in his affections, and was the only female he remained faithful to all his life.

The Bouviers had quite the lineage. My grandfather, John Vernou Bouvier, Jr., distinguished attorney and graduate of Columbia University Law School, was so highly regarded by Supreme Court Justice Benjamin Cardozo that he was commissioned major judge advocate for the Army during World War I. He insisted on being called "Major" ever after, and would answer to no other name.

But even this great honor was not enough, for he sought ever greater social status, peppering his conversations among *la crème de la crème* of society with clichéd French phrases whenever he found the opportunity (and sometimes when he did not). His major aim in life was to entrench the Bouvier family firmly into New York society. He did this by joining every prestigious club in the area, dressing meticulously, and changing his address every time his fortunes increased. He moved from Nutley, New Jersey, to 247 Fifth Avenue, to 521 Park Avenue, and to 765 Park Avenue, a most elegant address right off 72nd Street. In the early 1920s, he also established himself as a summer resident of fashionable East Hampton, in Wildmoor on Apaquoque Road, and in a few years moved to an even more elegant home, Lasata, on Further Lane. He was, of course, a member of the swank Maidstone Club, as were all the Bouviers.

When he was sixty years old (he never gave up, did he?), the Major wrote and self-published a little book called *Our Forebears*, in which he traced the Bouvier heritage to illustrious French patriots and royal aristocrats. One Bouvier was described as a celebrated member of Parliament in 1553, while another was touted as an important Parliament lawyer in 1609.

The book, however, was a total fabrication, down to the invented coat of arms and adopted titled family. The Major traced his ancestral roots to a François Bouvier, who was born in 1553 of the noble house of Fontaine, but unfortunately, that gentleman had nothing to do with the Major's true ancestor, an ironmonger of the same name, whose wife was a simple domestic. My grandfather's imagination waxed even more eloquently in describing the Vernou family, which, according to him, was one of the most illustrious and ancient in the province of Poitou, which has been in existence since 1086. Lamentably, no one in present-day Poitou has ever heard of the Vernous of New York. I blush to admit that instead of titled forbears, my ancestors really were members of the bourgeoisie—tailors, shopkeepers, and farmers. The name "Bouvier" means "ox-herder" in French.

In me, the Major found an enthusiastic audience. He would sit me down with his book and explain every fine point in it over and over again. Eventually, even he grew tired of the story and fell asleep. But when he stopped, I would scream, "Wake up, Grandfather! Please don't stop. Read more!" In my mind, my true history was a noble one, and my real self belonged to the stuff fairy tales were made of, not the boring life I lived with my stern mother and frequently absent father. I grew up infused with visions of valor. Far back in the mists of time, at the juncture between history and myth, there came a man to lead his people to glory—a man named Arthur. I believed my ancestors were such men, and I daydreamed of finding a man like them for myself when I grew up.

The Major's imaginative revision of our ancestry had other ramifications for me. Until I was an adult, I didn't find out what a liar my grandfather was. I was told I was an aristocrat, believed I was an aristocrat, and behaved like an aristocrat. Perhaps that is why I was not surprised when I was treated like American royalty. It seemed my rightful place in the world. When I traveled to Versailles as first lady, or when thousands of women in Argentina shouted, "Ja-qui! Ja-qui! Queen of America!," I felt at home. All of my kin felt the same way. We had been told we came from nobility, we believed it, and we adopted the loftiest of principles. My father encouraged this fantasy. He told me once, "Jackie, don't ever worry about keeping up with the Joneses. We are the Joneses. Everyone else has to keep up with us."

The veracity of the book was first questioned by Francis J. Dallett, former director of the Athenaeum of Philadelphia, when I was already in the White House. I dare say it was one of the great shocks of my life, and I have rarely been so embarrassed. For weeks, I was so humiliated that I ducked around corners to avoid him at museum events, and I wouldn't go to art openings I thought he might attend. Fortunately, the good Mr. Dallett was kind to me and merely announced in *Antiques Magazine* that the book's many errors should be checked against other sources.

As for Black Jack, in my opinion, he was never in love with Janet, nor she with him. They were like oil and water, and they remained that way to the end of their lives. Everything in his life revolved around the bedroom (not hers) and spending money (not his), while Janet's life was wrapped around society, horses, and doing the proper thing.

In her growing-up years, Janet had played go-between for her constantly fighting mother and father. It was partly to remove herself from this unbearable situation that she married Jack Bouvier. She was to regret her solution for the rest of her days. After an East Hampton wedding touted as "the social event of the season," the new couple boarded the R.M.S. *Aquitania* for a five-week European honeymoon. Their difficulties started as soon as they walked up the gangplank. Jack began a flirtation with Doris Duke, the sixteen-year-old tobacco heiress known as "the world's richest teenager." He insisted it was entirely innocent. Janet apparently disagreed, and retaliated by smashing a large, expensive mirror on their stateroom door. Janet continued raging at him until they reached Paris—if she ever stopped.

People should have known they were a mismatch from the beginning. I would have, if I had met such a couple. Black Jack used to say he was "not cut out for marriage." Nobody disagreed.

Nor did he grow old gracefully. Though not yet fifty, he was already losing his good looks. He developed a paunch, and the ever-present sunlamp could not disguise the beginning of jowls. His slick, dark Rudolph Valentino hair was already graying at the temples.

Janet was completely different. On the surface, she was full of smiles and social charm, but underneath she had a core of steel. She had seen her own father's circumstances change dramatically, going from not far above poverty to great wealth. She was not an extravagant woman, but she liked nice things: plenty of servants, beautiful gardens, and linen sheets with deep embroidered hems. She didn't want to return to the days of penny-pinching. As she said, "I've been poor and I've been rich. Rich is better." Black Jack was a dreamer and Janet was a realist, and never the twain did meet.

I grew up rarely seeing signs of affection between them. My mother was not a demonstrative woman. I received few hugs or kisses from her. If I needed a sign that I was loved, I was much more likely to get it from my horse Danseuse, who taught me as much as my parents did. From Danseuse, I learned how to maintain my composure under the most difficult of circumstances, to maneuver carefully and not take unnecessary risks, to blend gentleness and strength, and when it was safe to ask for favors and when it was wiser to desist. But more about that later.

I grew up in a household in which I was surrounded by constant discord. My father often lay drunk on the living room couch, dressed only in shorts, socks, and garters. The drunker he got, the more he ranted and raved about people who did not appreciate him, in particular the "kikes," "wops," and "micks."

Not only did my father hurl abusive words at my mother, but he was physically violent toward her as well, and when drunk, bruised and battered her to the point of black eyes and bleeding wounds. I had to help drag him into the bedroom and undress him, and clean up the mess left by his vomit, urine, and semen. The next morning, I watched in humiliation as he begged Janet to forgive him and said he would never behave that way again. I feel rather bad now that I blamed Janet for my father's alcoholism, thinking that if she had made him happier, he wouldn't have had to drink. If I were his wife, I thought, I would know how to make him happy.

It's funny, isn't it, how I worshiped Black Jack? I never criticized him, no matter how revolting his behavior, and yet rarely gave my mother the admiration and respect she deserved. I was a child and didn't know any better. Freud (and Jack) would say it was because of my Oedipus complex.

But I was no happier than they. I had few friends, and spent my time reading or taking solitary walks along the beach.

I loved my father dearly, but he and my mother separated when I was nine years old, and they fought a tug-of-war over me the rest of their lives. I was distraught at their separation and divorce, and until my father died, I tried to get them back together again.

People think that different things are important to me than to the average person. That's not true. In my heart, I feel the same emotions as everyone else, especially in the passages of birth, marriage, and death. Like every other child, the most important thing in the world to me was to be surrounded by loving parents. That was not to be, and their hostility ruined my growing-up years.

Nevertheless, I adored my father with a passion that was not equaled until I married Jack Kennedy. Daddy was kind and loving to me, and bought me whatever I wanted, whenever I wanted it, at whatever the price. My few friends all loved him, too. He encouraged us to climb trees rather than be the little ladies our mothers demanded, and to ride without hands on our bikes, and to eat all the sweets we wanted, no matter how close it was to the dinner hour. He would take us out to lunch and let us order steaks and two desserts. I remember one friend saying, "I'm going to eat as much as he'll let me." He never complained, though we must have eaten him blind. He took us to Central Park in our play clothes, and even let us lick ice cream cones while sauntering down Park Avenue.

Sometimes, he would invite a number of my little classmates to lunch at Schrafft's, followed by a movie and a round of sundaes at Rumplemeyer's. He was extremely creative in his ideas of how to entertain little girls. For instance, on cold winter days, when Baker Field at Columbia University was deserted, he would take us to play on the outdoor rowing seats set up for the varsity team's sculling practice. Sometimes we went to the Fulton Fish Market, where my wide eyes opened even wider watching the fishes' heads chopped off with a huge carving knife. One day, he took me to the New York Stock Exchange gallery, where I was thrilled to experience the excitement of the shouting stockbrokers and to feel a part of my father's manly world. Lee and I were watching the brokers from the balcony when, suddenly, they all looked up at us and began to clap. It felt good.

Mummy, on the other hand, was stern, punitive, and harsh, and spent her life disciplining us. Suitable behavior and proper attire were de rigueur at all times. She enforced a code of ladylike reserve and aloofness in which public displays of emotion were taboo. There was one correct way to speak, to act, and to move—her way, and that alone was permissible. She wouldn't even let me grieve for my father after his passing. It was nothing for her to spank me if I cried for him. I would have been happy living with him, but she wouldn't even consider it. Criticized and punished by my mother, praised and pampered by my father, is it any wonder I adored him and couldn't have cared less about her? And is it any wonder I prefer men to women any day of the year?

I had my ways of getting back at Mummy's code of ladylike restraint and coolness. Like many children with strict parents they don't dare rebel against, I acted up in school. I became a mischievous and argumentative pupil, who had the distinction of being the naughtiest girl in the class. I could feel free to defy the teachers without worrying that Mummy would break out the hairbrush, and soon became a regular visitor to the principal's office. Of course, they eventually notified Janet, who said to me, "I hear you are often sent to the principal's office. Is that true?" I nodded. A look of horror and self-hypnotic eye-glazing came over her face. "What happens when you get there?"

Knowing I couldn't get away with it anymore, I thought I'd shock Mummy further by telling her the truth. "Well, here's the story," I said. "I play a trick on the teacher, like putting chocolate pie on her seat. The teacher sends me to Miss Stringfellow's office. She glowers at me and says, 'Jacqueline, I've heard some bad things about you!'"

Mummy's eyes opened even wider. "Oh?" she said icily, her voice turning up as she spoke. "And what happens next?"

"I don't know," I said. "I stop listening." Down came my pants and out came the hairbrush.

Miss Stringfellow, the principal, finally managed to get through to me by comparing me to a horse. She said, "I know you are a horse lover, and a thoroughbred yourself. You are intelligent, strong, and full of unlimited energy. But if a horse is the fastest racer in the world, yet won't stay on the track or stand still at the starting gate, what good is he? He is useless to his owner, who has no choice but to get rid of him. *You* are like that horse, Jacqueline. You have to harness your high spirits, or you, too, will be good for nothing." I had to admit that she made sense. After that, I began making fewer visits to her office, and eventually they came to an end altogether.

I grew up expecting to go to Vassar, which I did, but being a student there wasn't my forte. Though my grades were excellent, I hated the safe, isolated little world of the small upstate college, and wished I had gone to Radcliffe, where at least I would have had access to the cultural treasures of Boston. Although I received an A+ in some of Vassar's most difficult courses, such as the History of Religion and an English class in Shakespeare (wherein I recited the whole play *Antony and Cleopatra* by heart), I left the school after two years to go abroad and never returned. I finished my degree at George Washington University in Washington, D.C., which was more to my liking.

One of the most beautiful memories of my early life traces back to the summer I was seven years old. After their first separation, my parents had a brief reconciliation. I was so happy, I smiled all day long. The first night of their reconciliation, I lay awake in bed, too excited to sleep. My parents, about to go out on the town to celebrate their reunion, swept into my bedroom to say goodnight. How stunning they looked, the pair of them—like two movie stars! Mummy bent over me to kiss me, and I was enchanted by the smell of her perfume. When Daddy did the same, I almost swooned with delight. I grabbed onto him, and had to be pried loose by Mummy, who said, "Sweetheart, let go of your father. We're going out dancing tonight." They were going to the Central Park Casino to hear the great Eddy Duchin, she added. I reluctantly let go of Daddy.

If I had known how short-lived their reconciliation would be, I would have held on to him even longer. I soon learned the terrible truth—they were never going to reconcile, and I would never again have a full-time father. In 1940, when I was eleven years old, Janet sued Black Jack for divorce on the grounds of adultery.

Sometimes I think it's a miracle that I've fared as well as I

have. Of all the divorces I've ever seen—and I've seen many in my lifetime—theirs was the worst, because there was lengthy, relentless bitterness on both sides. From the time I was ten until I was twenty, both parents told me how awful the other was.

When my father left home, I felt he had forsaken me. I was eleven, and just about to enter puberty. It was a time when a young girl needs a father the most. Somewhere deep inside me, I will always feel like the girl whom men abandon. That is still how I see myself, and to some degree, that is what happened. Jack left me every day for any woman around, and even Ari had filed for divorce before he died.

When I became debutante of the year, my many beaus only momentarily changed how I felt. Until the next beau came along, I was still the girl no man could permanently love. My father broke my heart when he deserted me, and I don't believe I ever recovered. Every loss brings the pain back to me. The sudden absence of my father felt much the same to me as when Jack was killed, only when I was little, I believed that Mummy was the murderer.

My father was given visitation rights of alternate weekends, one day each week, and six weeks every summer, when he took us to a house he rented in East Hampton. I recovered each time I was with him and felt adrift again when I had to go back to Mummy.

It wasn't only my father that I lost with the divorce. Photos about the divorcing Bouviers and their children appeared in papers all over the country, with headlines that shrieked, "Society Broker Sued for Divorce." In those days, divorce was more than frowned upon, and children of divorce were pitied and taunted. Kids would follow us in the streets, yelling, "Your father left you! You ain't got no father!" The girls at Chapin giggled in my presence and laughed at me behind my back. At the sound of their laughter, or even the idea that they might be laughing at me, I blushed with shame. It got so I wouldn't leave the house alone, and became even more withdrawn and isolated. I've felt like an outsider ever since, infinitely preferring books to people. It was then I began to bite my nails, a habit I have never succeeded in overcoming. Later, I added continuous smoking to my list of nervous tendencies. The press was very much my enemy at the age of eleven. Is it surprising that I hated them the rest of my life?

In the battle for my affections, and those of Lee, my mother tried to outdo my father, which was difficult because of her strict personality and frugal ways. Our father had us on the weekends, which were reserved for gala events like the circus and the zoo, ice skating, pony rides in the park, the theater, movies, and expensive lunches where we could order anything we wanted. At Mummy's, we ate only healthy meals of steamed vegetables, which she made us finish to the last bite. Daddy lavished expensive gifts and clothes on us and instructed us what to wear, in contrast to Mummy, who would buy us just two or three respectable dresses at Best and Company every year. He hated the way she dressed us, saying, "We will buy you something very pretty to wear!"

I have to feel a bit sorry for Mummy now, because my father's generosity would be hard for anyone to match, let alone beat. When it came time to return home, we screamed and hollered that we didn't want to leave Daddy for a boring week of school and Mummy's harsh discipline. She often had to drag us away, shrieking all the way out to the limo. It didn't help. She never allowed us to stay with him a moment longer than the divorce papers specified.

Lee and I learned to manipulate them both to get what we wanted. Often, all we had to say was "Daddy lets us do such-and-such" for Mummy to cave in. When we complained about Mummy's strictness, Daddy would do something especially nice to prove to us how much better he was. We complained often. I would scream, "I hate my mother! I hate her, I hate her, I hate her!" Nothing made him happier than to hear that, and like as not, all I had to do was say it to have him buy me a beautiful new dress.

Daddy also taught us what a man finds attractive in a woman. He said a woman should cultivate an air of aloofness or inaccessibility. The more unreachable and unavailable a woman is, he said, the more attractive a man finds her. By being too eager, a woman scares a man off. A woman should offer a man only a little, then withdraw it, then

offer something else. This drives a man wild. He taught us to tease a bit, to be mysterious, and never to let anyone know what we were thinking. Daddy must have written the course for Psychology 101— his advice had the boys lined up wall to wall, to say nothing of the entire country, men, women, and some in-between, after I became first lady.

People sometimes said I had a split personality. On the one hand, I could be painfully shy and uncomfortable among strangers. On the other hand, when I entered a party exquisitely dressed in an outfit my father had bought for me, I moved about like some exotic princess. That's not so strange, when you think about it. In the former state, I was, in effect, Mummy's girl. In the latter situation, my heart belonged to Daddy. People often wondered which one was the real Jackie.

One of the great sorrows of my life was the fact that, as my father aged, he became a different man from the one I had idolized all my life. He was bitter and angry and felt life had treated him unfairly. He believed that Mummy had gotten the best of everything, including his daughters, whom he felt had deserted him. He was most unpleasant to be with, and perhaps I didn't visit him as often in his later years as I should have. At the age of sixty-six, he was stricken with cancer of the liver. Neither he nor I was told of the diagnosis.

On July 27, 1957, he experienced severe pain and was admitted to Lenox Hill Hospital for testing. Not knowing he was terribly ill and thinking he would be all right, I decided to spend my birthday with my mother in Newport. On the morning of August 3, I received an urgent phone call saying that he was in a coma. I rushed to be at his side. To my everlasting regret, I arrived an hour too late. His nurse told me that his last word was "Jackie."

I was terribly distressed and full of guilt that I had not been there to comfort him in his last hours, and had not been as attentive to him in his final years as I should have been. Despite my terrible grief, I took care of all the details, including the funeral service at St. Patrick's Cathedral and his burial. Before they closed the coffin, I closed his fingers around a link bracelet he had given me as a graduation present. At the service were seven or eight of his former girlfriends. They were all dressed in black and sat together at the back of the church, like the Black Widows Society. It seemed that once a woman loved Jack Bouvier, she loved him all her life.

He is buried in the Bouvier family plot at Most Holy Trinity Catholic Cemetery in East Hampton. It was my first experience burying a man I loved.

Chapter 2
LEE

I was almost four years old on March 3, 1933, when my sister, Caroline Lee Bouvier, was born. My father put her in my arms and said, "Here's your baby sister." I looked down at her puckered red face and thought: *A baby? Why do they need another one? Am I not good enough?* My father smiled and said, "Shall we keep her or send her back?" Without missing a beat, I answered, "Send her back."

Although I remained Black Jack's favorite all his life, my mother preferred Lee—she was always called Lee—and spent much of her time fussing about her. I got so used to hearing remarks like "Why can't you be more like Lee? Why aren't you as pretty . . . as neat . . . as well-behaved . . . as nice a girl as Lee?" that I stopped paying attention to Mummy. She could spank me all she pleased, but I still wouldn't listen. I was my own person even then, and nobody—not even Mummy with her hairbrush—could make me behave otherwise. Recently, I found some baby photographs of Lee and me in an old family album. Under mine, Mummy wrote, "Jackie." Under Lee's, in Mummy's scrawl, was "My Lee."

Later, I found some compensation for having a younger sister. She was the only one I could tell that I hated our mother and loved my father. In fact, I could tell her anything. Even when I was in the

White House, she was the only person I could say anything to without fear of it getting published. She was the only one with whom I could freely discuss Jack's philandering and how much it upset me. I knew she would understand because she had a philandering husband herself.

As the older and bigger sister, I made Lee do everything I wanted, like "Go get this. Give me that. Clean up the milk I dumped on the nursery floor." It was nice to have someone to boss around, although I got a little sick of her following me like a shadow and copying everything I did.

In our games, I was always the queen and Lee my lady-in-waiting. I had a gold crown my daddy gave me, and no matter how much Lee cried, I never let her wear it. When I became first lady and took her with me on a trip to India, we repeated our childhood game. I don't think she liked it any better then than she did when we were children.

Gore Vidal, who was related to us through his mother's previous marriage to Hugh D. Auchincloss II, always said that Lee and I had a sadomasochistic relationship. According to him, I was the sadist and Lee the masochist. I don't know about that, but I know that I often treated her cruelly and derived pleasure from teasing her. That may well be the source of my biting wit. We fought all the time, and though I always won, Lee gave as good as she got. She once hit me with a croquet mallet and knocked me out for two days. One day, she pushed me down the stairs. When I realized she could stand up to me, that was the end of our fighting—at least of the physical variety.

There were advantages in having a younger sister. Once, when I was six years old, I painted on our dining room wall a huge figure of an angry lady in a bright red dress. It ruined the expensive nineteenth-century wallpaper forever. No matter how many times Mummy had the wall re-papered, the lady's red dress bled through. Finally, she had the room painted red. But when Mummy was furious about it and pulled out the hairbrush, I said, "Lee did it." I don't think she believed me, but she was unsure enough to refrain from spanking me. Lee was too little to understand the situation. I'm ashamed to say I felt no guilt about it whatsoever.

One of my worst childhood memories of Lee still haunts me. I was supposed to play *The Blue Danube* at a piano recital. Whether it was because of my big hands or a lack of talent, I'll never know, but I just couldn't master the piece. Week after week, I pounded away, trying to knock it out as well as I could, and all to no avail. While there was a smattering of polite applause after I played at the recital, I have never been one to fool myself, and I knew it had been a disaster. I don't like failure and vowed never to touch the piano again.

Then, to my shock, the teacher came to the front of the hall and announced, "I have a surprise for you. Little Lee Bouvier has prepared a piece, too, and has asked to play it." Guess what the piece was? It was *The Blue Danube*, which apparently she had been practicing on the sly all the while. She zoomed through it like a pro. I was further mortified.

Lee and I were very different types. She was always the pretty one, although I like to think she wasn't as intelligent or as talented as I. I was tall, ungainly and, some thought, exotic. Lee, a pudgy and even plain little girl, grew up smaller, daintier, sexier, and more feminine.

For some reason, pretty as she was, people always paid much more attention to me. In one respect, however, I have to say she outdid me. Lee always wore dramatic colors, and wasn't afraid to appear in revealing outfits. At my coming-out party, when the other girls and I wore demure white gowns that might have been designed for *Alice in Wonderland*, fourteen-year-old Lee appeared in a tight strapless dress that wowed the stag line.

I'll grant that Lee may have been prettier than me, but she had a weight problem, and was jealous that I never seemed to gain an extra pound. When she first went away to boarding school, she wrote and asked me for advice on how to lose weight. I suggested that she smoke. Unfortunately, my mother saw the letter and wrote Lee a furious comment on the perils of nicotine. Mummy didn't know that Lee had picked up a cigarette practically when she put down her first rattle.

Lee probably had the better personality. She was more spontaneous and a warmer person, but she was not as strong as I. I've always felt a bit guilty about that.

We both preferred men to women—with our mother, can you blame us?—and had few female friends, so our relationship remained important for most of our lives. We often giggled together like high school girls. We had fun together, laughing about all the little things that had happened during the day. I found her friendship especially valuable during the White House years. The Kennedy sisters and I were always at each others' throats, and I relied on Lee for moral support. I don't know how I would have managed without her. I guess I have to admit that she was my best woman friend, and remained so until the late 1960s. I am grateful for her support. Without it, I probably would not have done as good a job as first lady. I appreciated her so much that I thought nothing could ever come between us, and am still surprised that it did.

I don't remember feeling greatly jealous of Lee. Although Mummy loved her more, I was Daddy's favorite, and that mattered to me more than anything else. I had less reason to be jealous than Lee had. Lee got married before I did—I'm sure she did it to beat me to the punch, because her marriage went on the blink a few years later. And then I walked away with the best catch in the Senate!

Lee was always crazy about Jack. She told Truman Capote she had a crush on him. *A crush?* Was she kidding? She was so nuts about him it made me sick.

Her envy was so great it poured over into her relationship with Truman Capote, whom she told all about it. "God, how jealous she is of Jackie!" he wrote about their "confidential" conversation, in which she told him, "She stole my life away. Jackie took everything away from me, including the areas in which I always was superior. *I* was always the one with the beautiful figure, who was chic and clever, and had fashion and decorating know-how. Yet it was Jackie who got the acclaim for my talents. I can't bear it! Will I ever be known as anyone besides Jackie's kid sister?"

I tried to help her, but she never could find satisfaction or happiness in anything she did. She could never get her life together, and probably never will. She starts a lot of different things, but can't follow through on any of them. I helped Lee whenever I could, sending her clients for her decorating business until she grew tired of the work. I asked all my friends to support her in her so-called acting career. I found couture dress designers who gave her discounts for being my sister. I lent her scrapbooks and photographs when she tried to write a book about her childhood. And I threw elaborate dinner parties at the White House honoring her.

Her ill-fated "career" as an actress is a case in point. She bombed in *The Philadelphia Story*, where the reviewers slashed her to bits, saying, among other things, that her performance remained at a uniformly wooden level. The best thing they could say about her was that she knew her lines. The other cast members, whom Lee evidently ignored on stage, didn't like her, either. Her leading man, John Ericson, complained that she had done the show solely for her own gratification, and that he had never worked with so rude and unprofessional an actor. Even our half-brother, Jamie Auchincloss, said she made an uptight, jittery Tracy Lord. A newspaper headline read, "Lee Radziwill Lays A Golden Egg!" (Lee was married to Prince Stas Radziwill at the time). She was so stiff and overly choreographed in *Laura* (a TV role Truman Capote got for her) that I was embarrassed to admit she was my sister. Her failure in acting left Lee distraught, and I doubt she ever got over the humiliation.

Next, she decided she would become a talk show host. With her extensive network of society and entertainment connections, she felt she could book famous, noteworthy guests. She asked her good friend William Paley, founder and chairman of CBS, to help her bring this about. He arranged for Sam Zellman, one of the network's news chiefs, to produce a pilot for a six-interview series called *Conversations with Lee Radziwill*. After the brief series ceased, Zellman said he did not consider Lee a born journalist—merely somebody with friends in high places. That is not how one becomes a journalist, he said. So much for Lee's television career.

Then, she was given a contract by Delacorte Press to write a memoir. But after finishing half the manuscript, the publisher told her it was unacceptable and refused to publish it. The problem, as I see it, is that Lee was reluctant to open up her real self and confront the truths she had hidden from everyone her entire life. You'd think she would have learned from the Major and his book about a fictional family. I am a book editor, and I never would publish such a book.

Somebody once came up to Lee at a party and asked how the memoir was going. Lee answered that she had finished it, but did not wish to have it published because it would offend certain people who were still living. She also said in an interview, "I am not a painter, although I paint; nor am I a writer, even though I have written a book." That's the most honest thing I ever heard her say.

She had long thought she would like to be a decorator. When she started a business as an interior designer (without going to school for it), she finally did something rather well, although she always spent more money than she made. But, par for the course, she got tired of working and, after just two years, gave up the only thing she showed a talent for.

Early in this career, because her income did not begin to cover her expenses, she was forced to sell her duplex and some of its beloved contents, including her collection of tortoise-shell card cases, her gorgeous gold Fabergé boxes, and a painting from Francis Bacon's valuable *Man in a Cage* series, and move to a much smaller apartment a few blocks away. This was the beginning of a downward slide for her that was to reach unfathomable depths. She was reduced to living in a tiny apartment with bare spots where furniture should have been. Gone was her gorgeous English Regency furniture. In its place was a plain wooden table. Even worse, she was constantly hounded by bill collectors. I had to co-sign her mortgage so she could purchase even this tiny apartment.

Losing her home and valuable possessions, as well as ending

her intense romance with Peter Tufo, a prominent New York City lawyer five years younger than she, set off a period of total turmoil for Lee. It was the first time anyone had dumped her—she usually did the dumping—and she took it hard. Having no one to turn to for emotional or financial aid (I had long since grown weary of bailing her out) and bored by her decorating career, she was lonely and sick, and following our father's example, she took to the bottle. Shattered and broken, she was often unable to work, and on the days when she could work, she made costly errors of judgment. After two years, she gave up her business altogether. Instead of taking care of her children, Anthony and Tina had to take care of Lee.

Although I wouldn't give her any more money, I knew something drastic had to be done to rescue Lee. So I insisted she join AA, and took her to a meeting at Saint Luke's Episcopal Church in East Hampton. I walked her into the meeting, where (for a change) she demurely took a seat in the back of the church, and then I waited outside in the car to make sure she didn't leave. I tried to ignore the stares of passersby looking into the car windows and shrieking, "Oh my God, that's Jackie Kennedy! Is she an alcoholic?"

Lee stayed in the church, and subsequently went to AA meetings there twice a week all summer, and to meetings in surrounding townships on other nights. I was told by a neighbor, who was also an AA member, that Lee was well liked by the group, and incorporated its essential values, perhaps for the first time in her life.

According to the neighbor, Lee did everything you were supposed to in AA, except stop drinking. She would go into the bathroom and take a few nips from the bottle she always carried. I'm told this is not unusual for alcoholics. Relapses are typical, and all they can usually accomplish is to stay away from liquor one day at a time.

After the first year, my sister gradually learned to re-establish her sobriety. Just as the 1970s were her drinking years, the 1980s became her years of recovery. It must have been most painful for her to get up in front of the group and say, "My name is Lee. I am an alcoholic." She had spent her life developing an idealized image of herself as a

beautiful, fashionable jet-setter, someone to be envied and admired. Now she had to prick that image and expose to a roomful of strangers just how broken a woman she was. I was proud of her. I don't know if I could have found the courage to do such a thing.

Her first and second marriages failed, as did her many love affairs. In my opinion, she was not a good mother. She neglected and bullied her children. Anthony looked to his father for emotional support, and Tina to me when her slender, pretty mother chastised her for being overweight and pimply. Tina would run away from home and come to my house, where she remained for some time. Lee never forgave me for that. She said I had no right to steal her daughter away, and we stopped speaking to each other altogether for a while. In January of one year, a friend asked me how Lee was. I said, "I have no idea. I haven't seen her since last summer."

Lee's first husband was Michael Canfield, who, rumor had it, was the illegitimate son of the Duke of Kent. Leave it to Lee to search out royalty, real or imagined. But Michael didn't have enough money for Lee, and after a few years, they divorced.

Her second husband, Stas Radziwell, was a real prince, both literally and figuratively, although his Polish title was not recognized in England. He was a big, affectionate teddy bear of a man who gave the warmest hugs of anyone I ever met. A delightful person with a sunny disposition who often laughed until the tears ran down his cheeks, he also could explode in bursts of rage. Lee refused to put up with his marital indiscretions, withdrawing from him sexually and freezing up like an iceberg whenever he came near her. She began an affair with Aristotle Onassis, which was the beginning of the end of Lee's marriage to Stas. They eventually divorced, but he and I remained friends to the end.

Was it passive-aggressive of me to remain friends with and take the side of a man who cheated on my sister? I always liked Stas very much, but in retrospect, I can see how my actions would have been hurtful to Lee. Was I trying to get back at her for being Mummy's favorite? Who knows? This is the kind of thing I ponder while tossing in my sheets at night. If I had it to do over again, I suspect I would think twice about maintaining that friendship.

I thought she was making a big mistake in divorcing Stas, and told her so. She never forgave me for that, and had the nerve to respond that she wondered how long my marriage to Jack would have lasted had he lived. From that time on, we grew farther and farther apart, until we reached the point where we were merely polite on meeting, and saw each other only at important family affairs.

I must admit that Lee's third marriage, to the film director and producer Herbert Ross, seems to be working out. Incidentally, Ross is Jewish. It's funny about the Bouvier women and Jewish men. Lee, Caroline, and I—to-the-manor-born Catholics—have all ended up with a Jewish man. I don't think there are many well-to-do men besides Jewish ones who are faithful to their wives. When Lee teamed up with Ross, a friend of theirs said, "Little Herbie from Brooklyn has found himself the classic *shiksa*." I've heard it said that the first time you marry is for love, the second for money, and the third for companionship. I don't know about that, but Maurice, my last, is the best of the lot—he is the kindest and most considerate to me. Caroline is smarter than Lee and I in that she didn't have to go through two bad marriages before selecting a good Jewish man. She is not carried away by glamour, good looks, and money, as her mother and aunt were. I think she is saving herself a lot of agony. Maybe she learned from my errors.

It was Aristotle Onassis who caused the big break between Lee and me. She badly wanted to marry him. But after Jack was killed, Ari, who always looked for the biggest catch, asked me to marry him instead. Lee never forgave me. When she heard about it, she supposedly shrieked, "How could she do this to me? How could she? I was supposed to marry him, not her!" Lee insisted that she had introduced us after my baby, Patrick, died.

Lee's suspicions were first aroused when Ari gave me a magnificent diamond and ruby necklace. "All he dug up for me were three dinky little bracelets not even Caroline would wear to school," she said.

Of course, that's not what my sister told reporters. What she said was, "I am happy to have brought my sister and Onassis together. I'm sure their marriage will bring her the happiness she deserves."

But after that, whenever she could say anything mean about me, she did. She told a reporter, "When Jackie wakes up in the morning, the first thing she asks for are the newspapers. She examines them all thoroughly, looking for any that mention her. If she finds one, she circles it in red and cuts it out, but if there aren't any, she throws away the papers."

The worst thing she ever said about me was after Ari died, and a picture of me following his coffin appeared in the papers. Lee said, "That's my sister, the professional widow, for you! She has been waiting for years to walk again behind the coffin of a dead husband." That will sting until the day I die.

I must admit that I could be just as mean to her. I once told her that everything she had was because of me. She answered, "Oh, yeah? Well, it's because of me you found Onassis and got twenty-six million at his death. You owe me a finder's fee!"

Now that I'm older, I have to wonder if my "stealing" Ari away from Lee when I knew how badly she wanted him was my way of getting even with her for all the mean things she had said about me. In self-defense, however, I badly needed Ari at the time, and felt getting out of the country was a matter of life and death for my children and me. But more about that later.

I've missed Lee since we became estranged. No one else understands what we went through together as children. But it must be difficult to have a sister who was first lady of the nation when you're a nobody. I felt sorry for her when we visited India. She was always seated a few elephants behind me. The papers all reported that "also along was Mrs. Stas Radziwill." I would not like to be tagged as an "also along." I tried to make up for it by hosting a special dinner-dance for her at the White House, to which seventy-eight of Jack's and my friends were invited. I said to Mary Gallagher, my secretary, "Let's invite her friends." Then, after I thought about it, I said, "Does she have any friends?"

I held a second party for her, and it was a party to end all parties. This time, eighty-nine people were invited, including celebrities and many socially prominent people Lee had been dying to meet. You'd think she would have been thrilled to have such a party given in her honor, but no—she went into the ladies' room, stayed there a long time, and came out with red eyes.

But angry as I often am with her, when I needed Lee desperately, as when Jack died, she was always there. It was Jack's brother Bobby who called Lee and told her the terrible news. She was on the first flight she could get to be by my side. When a friend of Jack's told her it was nice of her to be there, Lee turned on him in fury and said, "Nice? Nice? How dare you say that? Would you expect me not to be here?" Before going to sleep that night, Lee wrote me a lovely note telling me how much she loved and admired me and attached it to my pillow with a safety pin. She remained with me for several weeks after that, and was a great comfort to me. Her actions made it clear she loved me, and I became aware I loved her, too, and always would. In similar manner, when Bobby was murdered, Lee quickly rushed to my side. For all her competitiveness and hostility, when I needed her, I had a sister.

Remembering how comforting she was to me, I am conscious of the destructive forces in our lives that made her the way she is. While many people are able to overcome the circumstances that shaped them, I am sad to say that, other than in the instance of her alcoholism, my sister was never able to find it within herself to do so. I tried to help in all the ways I could, but it seems that all my efforts came to naught. She is still the person she was. I guess Lee is one of the hitherto unacknowledged tragedies of my life. When I think about it, I cry.

Chapter 3

HORSEWOMAN EXTRAORDINAIRE

I 've loved horses since I was a tiny girl. My mother put me up on my first horse when I was just a year old. When I was only two, I won my first horseback-riding contest. Riding was a love my mother and I shared, but, as in every other aspect of my life, she didn't let me enjoy it. Once, when I was very little, I fell off my horse Buddy. I climbed back on immediately, and all the spectators applauded—but not my mother. "Jackie, you remounted the wrong side of the horse!" she yelled. "That's not the way to take care of a horse." Mounting on the left side has been a tradition since the days of the knights, who wore their swords on the left side. But my mother was oblivious to the fact that I was not wearing a sword, and that the right side was as good as the left for a little girl remounting the horse who had thrown her.

I went to all the horse shows in East Hampton from the time I was a small child and soaked up every detail. Always dressed in jodhpurs and paddock shoes, I loved every minute of it. People couldn't get over the fact that I knew the name of every horse and its records, and were always bothering me to recite them. I have a great photograph of me sitting on a rail at the annual horse show when I was six years old, totally oblivious to the adults around me. My body

is leaning forward, the better to see the competition, and from the expression on my face, it's clear I'm totally absorbed in the horses and riders. Knowing Lee was not as good at riding helped keep horses *my* passion. Of the two of us, I followed most closely in my mother's footsteps. Janet was a brilliant equestrian who won one prize after another, and her superior ability was touted in all the newspapers. It took me a little while, but I am delighted to say that I eventually matched her accomplishments.

One of the most prestigious events for riders under seventeen is the ASPCA Horsemanship Championship. Many winners of this prize have gone on to earn Olympic medals or win major jumping events. When I was only twelve years old, I finished in a qualifying class at the Southampton Horse Show and became eligible to compete in the national finals at Madison Square Garden, where the jumps were three and a half feet high. I competed on November 8, 1941, for the benefit of the USO. It was one of the high points of my life. Strangely enough, one of my competitors was Ethel Skakel, later to become my sister-in-law, the wife of Bobby Kennedy.

Unfortunately, I was not among the final twenty chosen by the judges for the afternoon ride-off, but, win or lose, competing in Madison Square Garden is always a thrill for any rider. I loved being in the National Horse Show and often returned as a spectator with my children.

When my parents separated, my horses were the only constant in my life. Thank goodness they were always there. When Janet and Black Jack briefly attempted to reconcile and our home atmosphere became unbearably irritable and tense, I was able to find comfort in horses. I even did well enough to win a blue ribbon at the annual horse show that summer, where I won first prize riding Pinto Dance Step in a contest for riders under nine years old. A neighbor tells me I was a nice rider among the East Hampton crowd, and was always well turned out. It was important to me even then to be well dressed for the occasion. I might not have cared so much how I looked (or smelled) around the house in those days, but I was always sure to bathe and put on fresh riding clothes when I was going to a show. Years later, when my life was again in turmoil, I again had my horses to turn to for comfort, and took pleasure in knowing I was perfectly dressed to ride.

I said before that Danseuse was the love of my life. When she saw me at the gate, she would neigh with joy and trot happily up to me. A graceful, beautiful animal with a distinguished head and large, expressive eyes, she exhibited a fiery spirit whenever I rode her. She proudly pranced around me with arched neck, head held high, and nostrils flaring, and had an uncanny ability to soar through the air with incredible grace and power. Yet, when I called her with a loving word, she transformed herself, almost by magic, into a docile, gentle creature. She became an obedient horse with a burning desire to please me, never losing for one moment her proud bearing and elegant presence.

She was a joy to ride, with her soft, broad back and lively gait. Every day, I brushed her coat until it gleamed, and her mane and tail were almost as smooth as an elegant lady's coiffure. Her powerful hindquarters allowed her to move with a natural balance. Whatever the pace, she had an inborn sense of rhythm and maintained an even tempo without requiring constant rider adjustment. With an unlimited confidence in my ability to handle her with a light hand on the reins, she understood what I wanted without words, as no human being ever has before or since.

She gave me the marvelous sensation that I could have asked her to do anything I wanted—that all I needed to do was think of something and she would carry out my wishes. With her, I felt in absolute harmony. Unlike some horses, she was extremely calm— not easily upset under saddle. She did tend to be a little bossy in a motherly way, but learning to handle my mother taught me the techniques to keep Danseuse, or Donny, in line. Once I knew for sure that Donny understood what I wanted, whether it be on the ground or under saddle, I asked only once. If there wasn't an immediate, obedient response, I administered an appropriate discipline, in her

case a firm, well-placed smack of the whip. I did it only when I felt it was necessary.

One time, I was galloping over the countryside with Danseuse, daydreaming about Jack and what I was going to do about his womanizing. I was so into my fantasy that I neglected to see or hear a rapidly approaching train. A frantic Danseuse bolted right up to the tracks, which were enveloped in a thick, long, black column of smoke. I yanked on the reins with all my might and firmly held onto the bit in Danseuse's mouth. I pressed my legs into her body with all my strength to let her know I was there with her and to remind her of the obedient relationship we had built up over the years. I was not at all sure my initial actions had any effect. Would I be able to contain the powerful mare? For a few horrendous moments, I was afraid I couldn't. However, after pulling frightfully hard on the bit, Danseuse came to an abrupt halt. It seems that her need to obey her beloved mistress was stronger than her panic. Incredibly, she continued to stand there motionless while the brightly lit monster rumbled closer and closer and sounded louder and louder, until the wind of its swift passage circled around our heads. Danseuse stood still as a monument, and with my legs pressed to her flanks, I felt her trembling. What a valiant animal! How I loved her! What a priceless gift of loyalty and friendship she bestowed on me! Her great love for me saved both our lives.

I think Daddy loved Donny as much as I did, and we were never more contented than when the three of us were together. When Daddy died, I made up a scrapbook of letters we had written to each other, and at least half of them were about the horse and our plans for her. It helped me deal with his loss that I still had Danseuse. When my mother married Hugh D. Auchincloss, my life changed forever. For me, the best thing about their marriage was that it opened up more riding possibilities. I began attending the Holton-Arms School in Georgetown, not far from the Auchincloss estate, which was called Merrywood Farm. I was able to ride every single day of my life, both at school and at Merrywood. I was in heaven! Next to being with my father, it was my greatest source of pleasure. I am grateful to Hughdie for that, if nothing else.

Our extended family now spent summers in Newport, Rhode Island, at Hammersmith Farm. When I was thirteen, I attended the horse show in East Hampton for the last time, as a participant in the costume division, where I wore jockey silks. My figure, now more womanly than ever before, looked great in the silks. I had finally caught up to Lee in the body department.

When I was fifteen, I was enrolled at Miss Porter's School, in Farmington, Connecticut. I missed Danseuse dreadfully, and wrote to my grandfather Jack, begging him to pay the twenty-five dollars a month it would cost to stable my horse at Miss Porter's. He said he would pay for Danseuse if I would write him a poem a month. It was a bargain. He got his poems, and I got my horse and my first paycheck as a member of the literary world. I spent every spare moment grooming Danseuse, and was much less homesick after she arrived.

At Miss Porter's, Danseuse was kept in a box stall between the stalls of two other horses, both of whom were adorned with similar, beautiful blankets. In fact, all the horses except Danseuse were bedecked with the same style of cover, and I didn't have enough money to buy her one. It just wasn't fair. One frigid winter day, I worried that, sans blanket, Donny would freeze, so I yanked a blanket off another horse and covered Danseuse with it. Because all the blankets were alike, the owner of the stolen blanket never knew what had happened to it, and Danseuse remained warm and comfortable all winter. I regret to report that I never gave the theft another thought, until now.

I also bought a fifty-year-old sleigh and attached it to Danseuse. Aboard the sleigh, Nancy Tuckerman (later to become my social secretary at the White House) and I had wonderful outings on the ice and snow. Years later, I purchased a similar sleigh for Caroline and John to be pulled around the White House lawn by Caroline's pony, Macaroni. The children whooped and hollered and had as good a time as Nancy and I did at Miss Porter's.

One of the great tragedies of my life was Danseuse's death of old age at twenty. I went into a deep depression, and didn't leave my bed for days. I got up only after I thought of the idea of making a scrapbook about her—the first of many I was to make to help me mourn—in which I pasted photos, newspaper accounts of her competitions, and notes and poems about her. It was a way to keep her alive. She was an elegant lady, and I loved her. She had a soft, pink spot at the end of her nose that I loved to kiss, and she would sniff her nostrils gently when she knew I had an apple waiting for her. To make sure she always had one, I planted my own little apple orchard. When I stood in front of her with an apple and said, "How about a kiss?," she performed a cute little trick. She would curl her upper lip and kiss me. I didn't even mind when she slimed all over me. She would never, ever bite—she was too much of a lady for that. I will always miss Danseuse, the horse love of my life. All I wanted was to be alone with Danseuse in the country, and for people to leave me alone.

Unfortunately, my summers in the Hamptons soon became a thing of the past. In 1943, I was devastated to learn that the East Hampton Horse Show grounds had been sold, to be developed as a farm. I still visit the property in my dreams, where they remain show grounds forever.

There is one story about Jack that always makes me smile, although I must say it didn't when it first happened. Danseuse and I were about to leap over a fence when she caught a foot in a rock and came to an abrupt halt. I went sailing over the fence. I wasn't badly hurt, and if you ride all the time, you have to expect a few falls. Unfortunately, a photographer "just happened" to be close by and took a most unflattering picture of me as I sprawled ungracefully on the ground. I was told that the photo would be published in the papers the next day. Furious, I complained to Jack, "You are the president of the United States. Can't you do something to stop them from printing the picture?"

He laughed and said, "I'm sorry, Jackie, but when the first lady gets thrown on her ass, that's news!" The photo was published all over the world. It hurt me much more than the fall.

One note about another beloved horse—one that the whole country revered. Incredibly, his name was Black Jack. He was the jet-black riderless horse who led Jack's funeral procession, gallantly trotting sideways on his way to Arlington Cemetery. A sixteen-year-old quarter-horse and Morgan cross, he was strong enough to carry a heavy saddle with empty boots facing backwards. Black Jack became a national hero, and subsequently rode in the funeral parades of Presidents Eisenhower, Hoover, and Johnson. Visitors by the dozens trooped in to see him. The year he reached the age of twenty, fifteen hundred people came to visit him, one bringing him a 180-pound butter pecan birthday cake. After my husband's funeral, I received a letter from the secretary of the Army asking if I would like to have the horse for my own. I thanked him for his gracious thought, and answered that, in my opinion, it would be more appropriate for Black Jack to continue in the military service. I didn't tell the Army secretary this, but I think I couldn't have borne the daily reminder of Jack's funeral procession.

Black Jack was humanely put down after twenty-four years of distinguished service. He was given a full military funeral and buried on the Fort Myer parade grounds at Summerall Field. His stall continues as a shrine, still visited by hundreds of fans every year.

I can't leave this discussion of horses in my life without mentioning my passion for fox-hunting. I am frequently asked, "How can you go on fox hunts and kill defenseless foxes?"

I want you to know that people have the wrong idea about fox-hunting in America. We don't *kill* foxes, we *chase* them. In fact, the sport of fox-hunting is sometimes called fox-chasing in the United States, because our aim is not to kill the animal but to enjoy the thrill of the chase. The only foxes we catch are too old, sick, or crippled to run away. On a recent hunt, hours of sweaty galloping resulted in the death of only one fox, a decrepit old animal with three legs. People assume there is a choice—either hunt the foxes or leave them to grow to ripe old age. But that is not what happens in the real world, where

many foxes are killed every year. If fox-hunting were made illegal, the number killed in other ways would rise, and many more foxes would die slowly and cruelly in snares, or be killed by the wild shooting of amateurs.

The key is to find a way that involves the least cruelty to the foxes. When I go fox-hunting, I am not being cruel, but am in fact doing the foxes a service by preventing them from dying a crueler death. My conscience doesn't bother me at all.

Contrary to public opinion, American fox-hunters are generally kind-hearted people (and I consider myself one of them). We are in favor of land conservation to support fox populations, and even provide food for them in the winter. I don't know why most people refuse to understand that hunting is a sport that brings out the best in people—love of animals, each other, nature, sport, and happiness. It allows me to lose myself in the excitement of galloping behind baying hounds in pursuit of elusive quarry.

People make such a fuss about the fact that I like to hunt, you'd think I was the only occupant of the White House who ever enjoyed the sport. My distinguished forebears include George Washington and Thomas Jefferson, who both kept packs of foxhounds before and after the Revolutionary War, and Ronald Reagan, that standard-bearer of good taste.

What do I like about it? When I fox-hunt, I like to gallop as fast as I can. I love to race the wind and to watch the scenery pass swiftly by. It is man against nature, and I love it when man (or woman) is the winner. Flying over the landscape makes me feel like Tinker Bell, and no matter how long I've been riding, I hate to come down to earth. Every day you ride is an exciting adventure in which you can never tell what will happen next. In *Oliver Twist*, Charles Dickens wrote, "There is a passion for hunting, something deeply implanted in the human breast." I know what he meant. There is no joy greater than entering the chase world, the time apart that fox-hunters experience while engaging in our life-enhancing hobby. I love those mornings when the earth is warm but the air is cold, the scent lies thick and low, and the smoke rises from village chimneys and floats down to lay across the ground. Heaven itself could not make me more ecstatic.

Another reason I love to hunt is that it's a joy to watch hounds and huntsmen working together as if they were one being. I've never had that happen with a human. Has anyone? It takes great skill and artistry to hunt live quarry, and it is a beautiful thing to see the hounds, by scent alone, follow the trail of a fox. The excitement gets into your blood, and once you have participated in a hunt, you yearn forever to repeat it. Chasing foxes takes you to beautiful parts of the country that people ordinarily are not privileged to see. My dear friend C. Z. Guest once said of me that no one else who came to visit her in Virginia could stay up so late at night and still get up early enough to be on horseback by 7 a.m. We had wonderful times together, and she told everyone I was not only an elegant lady but a great sport. Who else do you know who was called both elegant and a great sport by C. Z. Guest?

As everyone knows by now, I adore fine clothes almost as much as horses. It pleases me that I am known worldwide for my sense of style. But however lovely the gown or renowned the designer, I am never so comfortable as when wearing hunting clothes, which I think are more becoming to me than any other kind of apparel. I love the black hunting coat with colored collars that women wear while fox-hunting, the white shirt with white stock tie, the canary vest, the beige breeches, the tan or string gloves, and the patent-topped black dress boots. Despite my general dislike of hats, I love the black protective hunt cap, with the chin strap the sport requires. The clothing is most practical for riding a horse across the countryside. Unlike most modern attire, tradition and safety, not fashion, govern what it is correct to wear during a hunt. The dress is appropriate and comfortable, and has withstood the test of time.

Believe it or not, that is what I like in clothing. Forget gowns, forget designer clothing, forget couture fashion. I love wearing a riding habit, and am never so at ease in any other type of garment. In fact, if you want to know the real Jackie Kennedy Onassis, just think of me on a horse.

Chapter 4
J A C K

J ack was gorgeous, Jack was rich, Jack was brilliant, Jack was charming. He certainly charmed me, although I am known for seeing through people. I think that, in a sense, he charmed people, and especially women, out of necessity. He had been a lonely, emotionally neglected child. To begin with, he was born only a year after his retarded sister, Rosemary, who took up most of his mother's attention. As a result, poor Jack was allowed to be the baby for much too short a time. This fact, which has never been commented upon by any of his biographers, may explain why he so desperately needed the attention of all the women he could get.

To make matters worse, Jack was brought up in the era of Dr. Emmett Holt, the author of *The Care and Feeding of Children*, who looked askance at parents openly displaying affection and love to their children. If they were to be kissed at all, it was to be done chastely on the cheek. Otherwise, Dr. Holt advised, the horrors of tuberculosis, syphilis, and other grave diseases would be passed from parent to child.

"My mother never hugged me—not once," Jack told me in a rare vulnerable moment. "I went to sleep at night hugging my dog and pretending it was my mother."

What the good doctor did recommend was smacking children if they misbehaved, and like my mother, probably even if they didn't. Jack resented his mother Rose's absences, and when he was six years old, he told her, "Gee, you're a great mother, going away and leaving your children all alone!" She thought the remark was cute, and didn't see the pain inherent in it, thus sparing him at least one resounding smack. Nevertheless, the psychological hurt smarted as long as he lived.

When Jack was a student at Choate Rosemary Hall, a boarding school in Wallingford, Connecticut, she never came to visit him. Although he begged her to write, she did so only rarely. He told her the trouble with coming home for Thanksgiving was that you get home just long enough to see what you're missing. Only when Jack received last rites in London in 1947, on what was thought to be his deathbed, did his mother come to his side. Jack told a friend, "My mother? She's a nothing." I guess he meant nothing as a mother.

Nor was Rose sympathetic to the minor tragedies of childhood. If a child fell down, he or she got no sympathy from Rose. "Get back on your feet!" she commanded. "Stop that sniveling and behave the way a Kennedy is supposed to!" Jack used to say she didn't so much raise her children as manage them, and called her "the drill sergeant." Underneath their bright smiles, the Kennedy children were all sad and lonely, abandoned as they were by their parents for months at a time. A friend of Jack found their house strange and creepy. She said the parents were never there, unless a party was going on. When the children came home from boarding school, they didn't even have a room of their own where they could hang posters and keep their treasures on shelves, but were stuck into any place that happened to be available. Jack would ask his mother, as though it was a normal request for a child, "Which room do I get today?"

Another situation that scarred Jack forever was the fact that Rose favored his older brother, Joe, Jr. Rose thought Joe, Jr. was much brighter than Jack, and that it wasn't possible for there to be two intellectually gifted children in a single family. So Jack decided that if he couldn't have love, he would get people's attention, one way or another. In college, he did this by being a slob. A slovenly dresser, he never picked up anything, whether clothes or wet towels.

But he was also better read than his roommates, with a superb feeling for literature well beyond that of most of his peers. His roommates were impressed with how many of the questions on the radio program *Information Please* Jack could answer correctly. Someone once asked him how he managed to accumulate so much knowledge. Every day he read *The New York Times*, or *Time* magazine, and repeated to himself and analyzed the information he picked up. (I do that, too, but I think Jack was better at it.)

Jack wanted to be a football hero like his brother Joe, Jr., but didn't weigh enough to make the team. At six feet and less than one hundred fifty pounds, he was painfully thin. The football coach called Jack a great big stringbean. After playing a few games on junior varsity in his sophomore year, Jack dropped the sport, but not without being deeply disappointed in himself. I believe he would rather have become a professional football player than president of the United States.

In place of athletic stardom, he developed the best sense of humor of anyone I've ever known. Some of our best times together were spent joking. He and I could banter for hours. He amused his classmates by pointing out the absurdities of everyday life and the difference between people's pretensions and their behavior. He also learned to disguise his rage with wit, to never sound angry or indignant, and to get his revenge by mocking his foes.

Still, all his life, whenever Jack was depressed, he stopped eating, and there was many a meal where the only food he ate was dessert. He was close to anorexic, which kept him thin even in middle age. I once told him he looked like a pumpkin attached to a broomstick. I thought it was funny. He didn't.

Neglected as he was as a young boy, it is not surprising that, from birth on, Jack was constantly sick, with many of his illnesses, I believe, of emotional origin. He was by far the frailest and sickest of

the Kennedy children. If I hadn't gotten it from Jack himself, I would not have believed the list of illnesses. In addition to lifelong back problems and severe Addison's Disease, a hormone disorder causing weight loss and weakness (among other serious problems), he suffered at various times from colds, mumps, hives, fallen arches, swollen glands, a knee injury, German measles, bronchitis, blood poisoning, appendicitis, urethritis, prostatitis, duodenal ulcer, gastroenteritis, hepatitis, malaria, anemia, asthma, allergies, low blood pressure, and zooming cholesterol. Before he was three, he had developed scarlet fever, measles, chicken pox, and whooping cough. Oh, I forgot—from the youthful age of fourteen on, he had to wear reading glasses, which he made sure never to be seen wearing in public. He endured such unbearable pain from irritable bowel syndrome when he was a boy that he often had to be hospitalized. Of course, his mother never came to visit him in the hospital then, either. Feeling unloved and in constant competition with his big brother, a rivalry he always lost, it is interesting that Jack never again suffered from irritable bowel syndrome after Joe, Jr. died.

Rose wrote in her autobiography, "We used to joke that a mosquito better not bite Jack, or his blood would surely kill it." You'd think she would have taken his illnesses more seriously and acknowledged that, had she been a better mother, Jack might have been a healthier boy.

Despite all this, Jack refused to see himself as a chronically ill man, but only as a strong, robust person who just happened to be sick much of the time. Perhaps his denial of the true state of his health served him well. Otherwise, how could he have done all he did in his lifetime?

Jack was, I believe, the world's most charismatic human being. Both men and women fell in love with him. And politics, his chosen career, is a business that glorifies charm and considers seduction praiseworthy. "He's an artist who paints with other people's lives," said Polly Kraft, the wife of Joseph Kraft, one of the presidential campaign's speechwriters. "He raises the spirit of a room. 'Come along with me!' he says—and we all skip along after him."

Most of his friends called him "Johnny," but I called him "Jack." It made him mine. It's funny—lots of women I know rename their husbands. A friend of mine married a man everybody, including his mother, calls "Jim." His wife calls him "James." The new name means a new beginning—that he belongs to us like a newborn.

My Jack was incredibly vain. I had to laugh when I saw him take out his small Ace comb and fluff his vital, exuberant hair a thousand times a day. He also went to the hairdresser almost daily. He started to turn gray in 1955. Of course that was unacceptable to John Fitzgerald Kennedy, so he had his hair dyed. Unfortunately, the art of hair-coloring had not yet been perfected, and the color came out differently each time. Some days it was reddish, some days brown, and some days, in the sunshine, he looked almost blond. His favorite was brown with reddish tints, and the hairdressers eventually got pretty good at producing it. I guess he had every right to be proud of his hair. No president in history had a head of hair as gorgeous as his.

The bane of his existence was that he was the unproud possessor of rather excessive mammary protuberances for a male, especially a male as macho as Jack. Someone once took a picture of him in his bathing suit. When he saw it, he was appalled. "Look at those Fitzgerald breasts!" he cried out. "Get rid of that photo!"

Jack came a long way from his slovenly college days. After his adolescent rebellion ended, Jack developed scrupulously hygienic habits. He took a bath or shower anywhere, three to five times daily, and after each one, he put on a different suit. He wore increasingly expensive, handmade, two-button suits, and only custom-made monogrammed shirts and exquisite narrow ties—selected, I must add, mostly by me.

He owned dozens of dark handmade shoes, in which the left shoe was fitted with a special lift, because his left leg was a half-inch shorter than the right. He once bawled out his valet, George, for telling a reporter that he, Jack, had twenty-five pairs of shoes. George couldn't understand what was so terrible about that.

"How many pairs of shoes do you have, George?" Jack asked.

The valet replied, "One."

"Well," Jack said, "don't you think that all the other people who own only one pair of shoes will resent my owning twenty-five?"

A friend broke in, "How many pairs *do* you have, Jack?"

"I haven't the slightest idea," he said.

He knew he was special, but he didn't like to advertise it. A weary miner covered in coal dust once said to Jack, "Are you the son of a very rich man?" Jack had to admit he was.

"And have you always had everything you wished for and never wanted for anything?" the man asked. Jack nodded.

"And never done a day's work with your hands in your life?" Jack reluctantly agreed that the man was right.

"Well," the miner said, "let me tell you something. You haven't missed a thing!"

Even more revealing was Jack's comment after his father bought him an airplane, the *Caroline*, to campaign with. Jack said to a reporter, "I don't know how anybody could run for president without having his own airplane."

Jack loved to meet celebrities. There is a story about him and Tennessee Williams that I adore. It seems Tennessee was quite taken with Jack, and told Gore Vidal, "Jack has an attractive ass." Vidal, of course, repeated the comment to us. To my surprise, macho Jack grinned, cocked his head, and said he found the remark exciting.

It was typical of him to examine photographs intently, spending hours looking at himself on glossy papers before deciding which ones the public might see. I don't blame him for that. He was that rare kind of person whose image is improved by the camera. In his photos, he always looked younger than he was and in radiant health. He had every reason to be gratified by his appearance. He was the most gorgeous man I've ever seen. Besides Jack's beautiful features and marvelous physique, he had a skin that shone like gold when he was deeply tanned, making him look like a Greek god.

Jack had Addison's disease, the illness that killed Jane Austen at the youthful age of forty-one. Jack certainly would have followed in her footsteps had it not been for cortisone, the first of the "miracle drugs," which was discovered just in time to save his life. One of the side effects of Addison's disease is causing the patient's skin to shine like burnished gold when tanned. Jack, like my father, always made sure he had a tan. Added to his magnificent face and figure, the golden tones of his skin made Jack a stunning man. The color didn't show up on black and white photographs, but in person, onlookers sometimes gasped at his beauty. A friend of mine, on seeing Jack for the first time, raved, "He was bigger, his hair was redder, and he was handsomer than I'd ever imagined."

Jack didn't lack self-confidence in other areas. When an interviewer asked him, "Mr. President, don't you think you have a very big job?" Jack answered, "Sure it's a big job, but I don't know anybody who can do it any better than I can."

I was often furious with him because he was shameless in exploiting Caroline and John, Jr., letting them hog the space reserved in newspapers for photos of local children. I always tried to protect our children from the constant glare of the photographers and raise them as normally as one possibly can in the White House. Jack didn't give a damn about doing so, and thought only about what would bring him the most votes. Or maybe I'm being unfair. After all, as president, he did have the weight of the world on his shoulders. If it made him happy to see photographs of his children in the newspaper, maybe I should have just let it go.

An incident early in his 1960 primary campaign in West Virginia upset me, when he appeared on television to make his victory announcement. At that point, I was completely unknown. He was enjoying his greatest moment of triumph, smiling his white toothpaste smile at everyone in the hall, as they all stamped and chanted, "Jack! Jack! We want Jack!" Though I stood nearby, he ignored me. Feeling completely superfluous, I quietly slipped out into the car, where I sat alone and in tears until he was ready to fly home. I doubt if he even knew I had left the room.

I didn't like the language he often used. Because it came from a highly literate man, a man who gave some of the most beautiful presidential speeches in history, I found it to be disgusting. He was always talking about "balls" and "grabbing his nuts." "Prick," "fuck," "bastard," and "son of a bitch" were part of his daily vernacular. He thought he was being manly. I think he was being gross.

But I guess I'm not one to talk about nervous habits. Famous for my poise, I bite my nails until my fingers bleed, and I used to smoke at least two packs of cigarettes a day—well, maybe three. Worst of all, I'm a sensitive sleeper, and can't sleep at all unless I wear an eye mask and ear plugs.

Although he, too, looked cool as a cucumber, it was only a pose with Jack. He had a lot of nervous tics. He was always pulling up his socks, drumming on those beautiful white teeth, or patting his pockets—why I don't know, as he never carried any money in them and mooched off everybody he knew. Then, too, his hand was always going up under his jacket to push up the corset that supported his back. He couldn't sit still for more than half an hour, and had to get up and walk around for a while, even at dinner or the movies.

There was one habit of his I especially couldn't stand. He would always walk a few feet ahead of me, as if he were a king and I were his slave. It was humiliating. Pierre Salinger, his presidential press secretary, said to him, "Jack, you better stop that. It looks terrible." Jack said, "Tell Jackie she should walk faster."

Cool as he seemed, he was really an emotional man. His hands shook when he was under pressure, he was easily moved, and he wept easily. Once, when a stray dog looked pleadingly at him, Jack's eyes filled with tears.

He could be irritable, too. Usually, but not always, his victims were women, and such incidents weren't pretty. Jack himself told me the story about a stripper, Temple Storm, who was one of his conquests. One night, on coming out of a nightclub to meet Jack in his car, she stopped to talk for a few moments with the club manager. "Goddamn it," Jack shrieked at her, "you made me wait for you!"

Nor did I always escape his wrath. Jack was lying in the bathtub gossiping with his friend, Chuck Spalding, about people who lived in New York. Passing by, I overheard the names of a couple I knew and stopped to listen to more. Jack leaped up from the tub, yanked open the door, reached over, and pulled my hair. "You son of a bitch!" he screamed. "Don't you ever eavesdrop on me again!" I thought that was pretty rotten of him. Just because he was president of the United States didn't excuse his being a louse!

Although you wouldn't always know it, Jack was proud of me and my accomplishments. One Christmas, he bought me a palette, an easel, some oil paints, and some canvases. But then he expropriated them to begin painting himself. He mostly painted little houses with smoke pouring out of their chimneys, like the ones he had seen in Ireland. I didn't think they were so great, although I didn't tell him that. But he thought they were wonderful, and challenged Teddy to a painting contest, which Jack had every confidence he would win. The Kennedys were selected to serve as judges. The winner was—Teddy! Jack was mortified. It served him right for stealing my paints!

Jack thought he'd had a difficult childhood. Not everybody bought that story. He told his friend, Dave Powers, the state senator who was the manager of Jack's Boston campaigns, that he was born in a house smaller than the one in which Powers was born and had come up the hard way. "Oh, yeah," Powers said. "You really had it tough. They forgot to bring you your breakfast in bed one morning." Jack howled, and reused the line every chance he had.

"You must be willing to die daily," Emmet Fox, the influential author/lecturer, once said. That's how Jack lived. He once told a friend, "They keep giving me chemicals for my disease. They'll kill me by the time I reach forty-five. You have to learn to live every day as if it were your last. That's the way I do it." He had the sense of not being well, and always wondered how much time he had left. He kept asking his friends, "How do you expect to die?" When they, in turn, asked how he thought his life would end, Jack answered, "In a car. An automobile accident."

Once, when he pressured a staff member to answer the same

question, the man reluctantly replied that he thought dying of old age was the best way to go. "Oh, no," Jack vehemently responded. "The best way to die is in war!" He pictured himself dying an early, violent death, which he much preferred to dwindling away in a hospital bed.

You have to remember that, in the 1940s, when Jack was a young man, he never knew when he would be called up to serve in the armed forces, or if he, like his brother, wouldn't return home alive. He couldn't plan what he was going to do with his life, and in a way was just marking time. There was no point in beginning to study for a lifelong profession, he felt, when he didn't know if he would be around to practice it. Jack was a prescient person who always knew he would die young. That's why his favorite poem was Alan Seegar's "I Have a Rendezvous with Death":

> I have a rendezvous with Death
> At some disputed barricade.
> When Spring comes back with rustling shade
> And Apple blossoms fill the air
> I have a rendezvous with Death
> When Spring brings back blue days and fair . . .
>
> But I've a rendezvous with Death
> At midnight in some flaming town,
> And I to my pledged word am true,
> I shall not fail that rendezvous.

He would recite the poem at the drop of a hat. Much as I love poetry, I guess I could be excused for getting tired of it. Now I feel bad that I moaned, "Oh, Jack! Not again!" each time he repeated it.

Jack drove me crazy with his absentmindedness. He was forever forgetting his keys, where he parked his car, and even engagements we had made. All his friends were angry with him at times and, if they dared, told him so. He thought his forgetfulness was funny. I didn't. I think he inherited this annoying trait from his mother, who had to pin little notes all over her clothes to remind her of things any normal person would remember.

He was eternally leaving behind briefcases, clothing, and papers in airports, trains, and hotels, so his staff was forever flying from Washington to Hyannis or Palm Beach to pick up stuff urgently needed at some important meeting or other. He once sent the *Caroline* to pick up his dog, Fallon, whom he had forgotten to bring back with him.

In his early years, Jack was not an outstanding student. He had no patience for courses that did not interest him, and threats, no matter how powerful, did not move him to do work he did not want to do. He was always late to classes and did not apply himself to his studies—he was too busy reading books that interested him rather than those assigned him. He busily pursued a merry social life. He was engrossed by many fields and activities, but did not stick to any of them for long, and rarely gave all of himself to anything. He liked reading in various specialties, he liked sports, he liked roughhousing, he liked to play football and golf, he liked girls, and he liked to visit New York. He enjoyed bugging people and enjoyed watching their reactions.

Known as a devilish cut-up, he was extremely popular with his classmates, who thought he was captivating. Tall and skinny, he looked like you could blow him over with a strong breath. His classmates called him "Rat Face," considered a term of endearment, because of his protruding ears and slender face. Unfortunately, his teachers did not love Jack—they found him a trial.

At Choate, Jack and ten other boys started a secret club which met regularly in Jack's room. They named the club "the Muckers" (although when they referred to it among themselves, I'm afraid they changed the first letter of the name), and had little gold charms made up for members in the shape of a shovel engraved with "CMG," for "Choate Mucker Club." "Mucker" was a word used by the headmaster to refer to boys not living up to the school's high standards. Jack, of course, was the club ringleader.

The boys weren't really bad, but they snuck out at night to buy milkshakes and engaged in a lot of roughhousing. Unfortunately, their "secret" trips leaked out to the authorities. The headmaster wanted to expel the club members, and got up in chapel and denounced them as bad apples in the bushel. Jack's father, Joe, was called to school to talk with the headmaster.

Strangely enough, shortly after Mr. Kennedy's visit, two fine movie projectors showed up for the school's weekly Saturday-night movie. The boys were punished by losing three or four days of their Easter vacation, but despite their misbehavior, they were allowed to graduate in June. Jack finished sixty-fourth in a class of one hundred and twelve boys, but was elected most likely to succeed. They couldn't have been more right.

We all know that Jack was a devil, but do you know that he was also an angel? While he was traveling abroad as a college student, he met a sculptor, Irena Wiley, the wife of John Cooper Wiley, a career foreign service officer. She was then in the process of designing an altar for a church in Belgium, and chose Sainte Thérèse of Lisieux as her theme. The altar consisted of a statue of Sainte Thérèse and twelve panels dramatizing the highlights of her life. Irene was quite taken with Jack's curly hair and serenity and asked him to be a model for one of the panels. When the Nazis overran Belgium, Irena sent the altar to the Vatican, where anyone today can observe Jack's angelical early likeness on one of the panels.

Jack's senior thesis at Harvard was called *Appeasement at Munich*. His objective was neither to condemn nor absolve English Prime Ministers Stanley Baldwin and Neville Chamberlain, but to draw a lesson for America from Great Britain's failure to keep pace with Germany's military might. The American people were starved for information about the war and how it started in Europe. Jack's thesis promised to satisfy that hunger. His advisor, Bruce C. Hopper, re-read it four years later and was amazed by the maturity of his judgment, and pronounced it well beyond his years.

The exploding world crisis (as well as his lifelong ambition to be a writer) convinced Jack to turn his thesis into a book with a new title, *While England Slept*, which he (and Daddy, of course) did everything possible to promote. Joe phoned Henry Luce from London and asked him to write the foreword, which convinced both *The New York Times* and the Time-Life organization to publicize the book's publication. *While England Slept* was phenomenally successful, receiving excellent reviews and selling quite a few copies, although Harold Laski wrote Joe Kennedy that no publisher would have even looked at the book had Kennedy not been U.S. ambassador to the United Kingdom. As Jack graduated with a B.A. in international affairs *cum laude* from Harvard University in June 1940, a year behind his cohorts, the book established him as a deep thinker with great political potential.

It is said that birds of a feather flock together. That is nowhere more evident than in Jack's choice of college roommates—Torby Macdonald and Ben Smith. Including Jack, one ended up a congressman, one a senator, and one president of the United States.

Jack was comfortable in the presence of intellectuals, although he neither was one nor wanted to be one. He appreciated the historical significance of artists and thinkers, and understood that works of genius are a nation's greatest treasures. Along with me, he believed that artists are pivotal figures in the life of a nation. Thus, he invited famous authors, Nobel Prizewinners, scientists, and actors to dine at the White House. He (and, I must say, I) somehow fit in with the culture of the 1960s, and represented it. With his movie-star charisma, his sexual license, his use of drugs, and his love of celebrity, he was the epitome of everything new and exciting about the era. Although his moral values were not mine, and that caused me considerable grief, I have to say that Jack lived out the fantasy of every American male and changed the culture forever.

Whatever his shortcomings—and there were many—he was a great man and a great president. Humanity will never know what heights he would have reached had he lived. Of everything he ever said, I love this remark the most: "The problems of the world cannot possibly be solved by skeptics or cynics whose horizons are limited by the obvious realities. We need men who can dream of things that never were."

John F. Kennedy, the dreamer, was the love of my life. Nobody realizes how much of me died with him. Despite having had another husband and a wonderful male companion, there isn't a day that goes by when I don't think about Jack. I will miss him as long as I live.

Chapter 5

INGA-BINGA

A lthough it pains me to do so, I ought to tell you something about Jack's first love, who under different circumstances could have turned out to be his last. When he was a mere boy of twenty-four, he fell passionately in love with a stunning, twice-married woman of twenty-nine whose name was Inga Marie Arvad. He called her Inga-Binga. When it comes to women, some men are grown-up at twenty-four, but not Jack. Like all the Kennedys, he was late to mature, and late to marry.

Inga was an aggressive, sophisticated woman who was much more sexually experienced than Jack. No doubt she taught him plenty. She herself said, "He's got a lot to learn, and I am happy to be his teacher." He was mad about her, as only a youth can be with his first love, and he wanted to marry her. Joe, Sr. didn't like the idea at all, and said he hoped with all his heart that Jack would realize that such a marriage would abort his political career before it had even begun, and that he should reconsider his decision. Jack and Inga flew to Palm Beach to plead with him, and the old man (who sometimes had a heart) went so far as to contact officials in the Catholic Church to see how much it would cost him to get a papal annulment of Inga's marriages. For reasons to be discussed later, Joe was able to keep his money.

It was rumored that Inga had been the mistress of Axel Wenner-Gren, an international billionaire capitalist, a close friend of the Duke of Windsor, and a known Nazi sympathizer. Inga, a former Miss Denmark, had acted in German movies and even been briefly married to the Hungarian film director Paul Fejos. She had been a journalist for a Danish newspaper in Berlin and interviewed Hitler, Göring, and other top Nazi officials. She wrote about Hitler, "He is not evil as portrayed by the enemies of Germany, but simply an idealist."

I never met her, but according to all reports, Inga was a beautiful girl. Even Hitler thought so. She was sitting in his box at the 1936 Olympics when he said of her, "Now there is a perfect Nordic beauty!" Her career in the movies was interrupted by the war, and Inga came to the United States, where she enrolled at Columbia University to study English. She then went to Washington, where she, like me, obtained a job at the *Times-Herald*. She wrote a column called "Did You Happen to See?" She and Jack's sister, Kick, became close friends, and Kick introduced Inga to Jack.

She (again, like me) wooed him by writing a column about him, opining that he was a boy with a big future. He fell for her right away, finding her a gorgeous and sexy woman. She was animated and intelligent, had a wonderful sense of humor, was great fun, and someone with whom he could talk seriously. Inga, who had an effervescent personality and a happy smile, was one of those people who enjoyed whatever life brought her.

Finding him brainy with a clever Irish head, she firmly believed that one day he would be president of the United States. And though he was given much more than his ancestors, she said, he had retained the rugged hide of an Irish potato. And she apparently knew how to satisfy Jack sexually. If he had married her, it is entirely possible he would not have had to stray from the marriage bed. Or perhaps it was not so much her sophisticated sexual techniques that turned him on, but the fact that he was *in love* with her.

I know Jack loved me dearly, but there is all the difference in the world between loving and being *in love*. They say that being *in love* is the best aphrodisiac, but we'll never know if that was true about Jack, will we? Maybe if I'd had honey-colored straight hair that didn't require de-kinking, a complexion like peach ice cream, eyes as blue as a velvety morning, long legs that began at my shoulders, and a D-cup bra like Inga, Jack would have been *in love* with me instead of her. But I didn't and he didn't, and therein lies the tragedy of his life and mine.

It has been said that with every couple, there is always one who loves and one who is loved. With us, I was the one who loved, who did all I could to make Jack fall in love with me. He never put himself out as much for me, though I know that, in his own way, he loved me. With Inga and Jack, however, Inga was far less interested in Jack than he was in her; hence, he was always chasing her. Jack was a man who always said he enjoyed the chase more than its spoils. As a result, he never ceased to be enamored of Inga. I believe she was the love of his life, and he never got over losing her. Sometime after that, when he was marching his platoon, one of the sailors whispered loudly, "How's Inga?" Jack hissed at him under his breath, "You son of a bitch!"

I think he would have liked to have had five yellow-haired children with her, grown old with her, and died in her arms. Under other circumstances, they might well have done that. He kept her love letters to the day he died. I would have read them if he hadn't kept them under lock and key. I searched his pockets for the key when he was asleep, but never managed to find it. He must have swallowed it. I did manage to get a peek at one of the letters once when he was in the bathroom and had neglected to lock his cabinet. Knowing her, he wrote, was the brightest part of his exceedingly bright twenty-six years. When I read the letter, I went into a depression that I never completely overcame until years later, when I went into psychoanalysis. I still don't like to think about it.

One night, he called out "Inga-Binga" in his sleep. I woke him and asked, "Why did you call out Inga-Binga? Were you dreaming?" He answered, "Jackie, *you* are dreaming!" Another time, when we were making love, he called me "Inga." Needless to say, that marked the end of that love-making session.

At the end of World War II, Inga married Tim McCoy, a retired cowboy movie star who operated his own rodeo and wagon show. They bought a horse farm outside of Nogales, Arizona, and raised two sons. The McCoys lived together, presumably happily, until she died of cancer in 1973 at the age of sixty. After I became a book editor, the scuttlebutt was that she had been offered an enormous sum of money to write the story of her affair with Jack, but turned the publisher down. Not many people would do that, as I found out from dreadful experience. Maybe she really did love him.

When Jack heard about her marriage, he walked around glumly for weeks, locked himself in his bedroom for hours at a time, and emerged with red eyes. Of all the women in his life, she was the only one I would have traded places with.

The problem with Inga was that there were a lot of rumors that she was a German spy, and Joe, Sr. began to get worried. Jack, in the Navy at the time, was stationed in Washington in a job where he handled restricted material. His captain was concerned that Inga was using Jack to find out all she could about the Department of the Navy and the Department of Naval Intelligence, and wanted to retract Jack's commission and have him discharged from the Navy. It's a good thing he didn't, because if he had, it might have ruined Jack's political career. Gossip columnist Walter Winchell, at the instigation of FBI Director J. Edgar Hoover, published an article that said one of Joe Kennedy's sons was being wooed by a Washington journalist who was applying for a divorce from her husband. Hoover then sent a warning to the senior Kennedy that his son was in big trouble, and Papa should yank him out of Washington immediately.

The next thing Jack knew, he had been plunked down at a naval Siberia—Charleston. "They shipped my ass to South Carolina," he admitted, "because I was going with a Danish blond they thought was a spy!" He was put to work at a non-sensitive desk job in which he instructed workers how to protect defense factories from being bombed. Jack loathed the job and said it bored him to death. Rant and rave though he did, the Navy would not reassign him. Jack and

Inga paid a visit to J. Edgar Hoover and begged him to write a formal letter saying there was no evidence that Inga was a spy for Germany or anyone else. Hoover answered that, although that was correct, he could not sign such a letter, because if Inga later decided to become a spy, his neck would be on the chopping block.

All his life, Jack had deferred to his father's wishes. For example, although Jack lacked religious convictions, he attended Mass weekly. He told a friend, "It's just one of the things I do for my father." Despite Joe, Sr.'s manipulations of the highest order and his insistence that his son dump Inga, Jack, for the first time in his life, did not submit to his father's will.

A close friend of Jack's told me that his father blew up over Inga and yelled, "Get rid of her or else! You can't marry a non-Catholic divorced and remarried woman with a checkered past and be elected President!" Jack walked around for days with a whitish, almost disembodied look on his face, and staggered about as if he were about to faint. Then he made the decision that led to his becoming the man I married.

The two men had a final talk about the potential marriage. The Kennedy patriarch insisted on saying no, but Jack made up his mind to continue the affair, regardless of the political consequences and his father's wishes.

After that, Jack regularly went AWOL and came up to visit her in Washington, and she came down to Charleston on weekends, registering in different hotels under assumed names such as Barbara White. Unfortunately, the FBI continued to keep files on Inga and Jack, maintaining that, on at least one occasion, she stayed at the Fort Sumter Hotel and engaged in sexual intercourse with Ensign John F. Kennedy. According to tapes the FBI made of the lovers, she called him "darling," "sweetheart," "honey," "honeysuckle," and "honey chile," among other terms of endearment, and told him, "I love you." Much as I loved Jack, I was never able to call him the affectionate names Inga did. It just isn't my style.

A friend of ours told me something I never cease to marvel at.

To his astonishment, he said, when Jack stood up to his father, Jack underwent a transformation that he, the friend, had never seen before or since. Jack's color changed overnight from deathly white to a rosy glow, as if he were so full of electricity that he'd glow in the dark, and people could almost see the blood coursing through his veins. He had found the courage to confront the father he had feared all his life, and it made a man of him. It was the turning point of Jack's life. As a result, he became infused with a magnetism that never left him, and put him in the center of every room he entered. His courage then foreshadowed his heroism later as a naval lieutenant, his exhausting four-year campaign for the presidency, and his election to the office of president of the United States. No wonder he was able to write *Profiles in Courage*. He belonged in it himself.

But fortunate or not, depending on your point of view, the Jack-Inga love story didn't end as in a fairy tale, and the couple was not fated to live happily ever after. Only one thing in Jack's life was stronger than his passion for Inga. He wanted to become president. When J. Edgar Hoover warned Jack that public knowledge of the affair would ruin his career, he knew that no matter how much pain it caused him, he had to end the relationship if he was to become what he was born to be. He dropped Inga-Binga, who seemed to concur with his decision, writing him:

> We are as well matched as any two people could be, but because I've been guilty of some foolhardy things in my life, I realize I must now say "No." I don't want to harm you, dear, and alienate you from your father. If I were only eighteen years old, I would fight like a tigress to keep you, but I am not eighteen and am much wiser.

And perhaps richer. It is known that Joe Kennedy could buy his way out of anything, and it is possible he paid her off to end the relationship as quickly and quietly as she did. She soon got herself married to Tim McCoy. Jack, I believe, missed her all his remaining life.

Chapter 6

MY UNHAPPY MARRIAGE

J ack and I met three times before we clicked. Our mutual
friends, Charlie and Martha Bartlett, insisted with admirable
persistence that we meet at a dinner party given at their home
in June 1951. It was pleasant enough seeing the handsome
young senator in person, but he did not seem particularly interested
in me—I never believed so handsome and rich a man would ever find
me attractive—and I wasn't all that interested in him.

I had inherited my father's exotic looks, with his square face,
wide-apart eyes, indelicate features, large bone structure, and dark
skin. My mother despised my big, masculine hands and feet, my
broad shoulders, my kinky hair, and my low hairline. My looks were
unfeminine, according to her, and if I didn't change them, no man
worth having (i.e., someone rich) would ever want to marry me. That
my own mother found me physically revolting was not something
I could easily get over. Bit by bit, criticism by criticism, she had
destroyed my self-image. There was nothing too grand or minor that
I said or did that didn't bring down her wrath. If she saw me walking
on water, she would say, "Jackie can't swim." I grew to hate her for it,
but even worse, to hate myself.

Because she was not particularly bright, she also disliked my

mind. Women didn't have to know anything, she said, besides how to make a man feel important and how to run a pleasant, efficient home. She said men don't like women with intellectual inclinations, and they disliked women who didn't reflect their opinions. She disparaged everything that made up my identity—especially my love of books and learning, and my passion for French culture and history.

When I think about it, I'm amazed that I've managed to stay out of an institution. I listened because it was Mummy talking, and I learned to keep my intellect hidden from everyone but myself. I even developed a whispery voice I thought was sexy, as well as the habit of looking so deeply into a man's eyes that he felt he was the only person in my world.

The Bartletts were determined to get Jack and me together, and invited the two of us to the wedding of Charlie's brother, David, in East Hampton. After the ceremony, Charlie shouldered his way into the thick of the crowd, grabbed my hand, and pulled me toward the corner, where Jack was talking animatedly with a beautiful blond. We managed to get halfway through the room when we were stopped by the former heavyweight champion of the world, Gene Tunney. The boxer, a friend of Charlie's father, began to regale us with stories of his fights. When Charlie finally extricated me from Tunney and got me to the corner where we had seen Jack, he and the blond had disappeared. It would take the Bartletts another two years before they could get us together again.

Just before I was scheduled to leave for a vacation financed by my stepfather to my beloved France, I accepted an invitation by the unstoppable Bartletts to dine at their charming brownstone. Jack, of course, was invited, too. They made sure we sat directly across from each other at the dinner table. I looked into Jack's broadly smiling, inquisitive face for the first time and knew at that moment that he would have an overwhelming, even destructive influence on my life. I was terrified, and realized immediately that a relationship with this man could only mean heartbreak. But, with just as much certainty, I felt that the joy would be worth the pain.

Jack had a different recollection of our meeting. After we were married, he said, "I leaned over the asparagus and asked you for a date."

"No asparagus was served that night," I said coolly.

He said he had known from the start that I was the right woman for him, but needed to wait a while to get married. "Now it's up to you," he said, in what was his idea of a marriage proposal.

I said, "That's very big of you!"

When we dated, we had a lot of fun together. He told a friend, "Jackie is wonderful in her personal life, but do you think she will ever amount to anything in her political life?" I cut in, saying, "Jack is wonderful in his political life, but do you think he will ever amount to anything in his personal life?" We all laughed hysterically.

Later, I thanked the Bartletts for their "shameless matchmaking." By the time we finally met at their home, much in my life had changed. I had won a contest in *Vogue* magazine, which awarded me a six-month position in their Paris office. Because of my low self-regard at the time, I didn't think I could do the job well and turned it down. My stepfather then found me a job at *The Washington Times-Herald* as their inquiring photographer. I'd ask questions of people on the street and take their photos, which were published in the paper with their answers. I had a good time working for *the Times-Herald*. I asked only those questions that interested me, such as, "Do you think a woman should let a man know she is smarter than he is?"

Jack Kennedy figured prominently in office gossip, and I was treated to daily stories about the handsome, charming, rich young congressman. He was a war hero, had already published one bestselling book, was determined to run for the Senate, and was audacious enough to say he was going to become president of the United States someday. In the meantime, in my rush to prove Mummy wrong in her estimation of my attractiveness to men, I became engaged to John Husted, a nice, solid, boring young stockbroker. When I saw Jack again and remembered all I had heard about him at the office, I couldn't help but compare him to Husted, and broke our engagement by unobtrusively dropping my engagement ring into his coat pocket. He recovered quickly enough to get married the next year.

It was on the ensuing vacation to France, financed by my stepfather, that I lost my virginity—to John Marquand, Jr., the son of the famous author. After a night of club-hopping, we took the elevator to his apartment. He reached out with one hand and "stalled" the lift, a maneuver I heard he had used before. He then pushed me against the wall with his other hand, yanked up my skirt, ripped down my panties, and stole my "virtue." After it was over, I said to him, "Is that all there is to it?"

When I came home, Jack called me from Massachusetts to make a movie date for the following Wednesday. As I heard the clinking coins dropping one by one into the phone, I knew I would accept.

Jack already had a deep hold on me that was to last all my life. He was a gracious, wealthy, charismatic young man pursued by movie stars, famous writers, heiresses, and their ilk. Although I had heard much about his womanizing, he always treated me differently than any other woman he dated. Not once during our courtship did he propose that we go away for a weekend or that I spend a night with him. When I asked him about it later, he answered, "You are the kind of girl a man marries." If so desirable a man wanted me, saw something special in me, and singled me out from all the other women in his life, surely my mother was wrong in her opinion of me. He proved to be the magician who was to heal years of Mummy's abuse.

My mother had always struck me as leading an empty and stifling existence. I knew I wanted something different—a big life full of meaning. I believed I could build that kind of life with Jack. Before long, I found myself desperately in love with him.

In 1953, two years after we met, Jack and I were married in Newport. We had an ecstatic honeymoon in Acapulco, and I returned to Washington anticipating that I had left behind forever my years of misery. I couldn't have been more wrong.

Back in Washington, Jack behaved as if he were still a young bachelor who thought nothing of leaving Georgetown parties with other women, abandoning and humiliating me. Jack's friend Lem Billings had warned me of what I was getting into by marrying a thirty-six-year-old womanizer, and I'd had the experience of my father and his lady friends as a model. Nevertheless, I was shocked and devastated by the depth of Jack's craving for other women.

I had entered into our marriage deeply scarred from Janet's years of attacks on my self-esteem. Expecting sexual validation, I met only further destruction. When Jack began cheating on me, it ripped the scabs off barely healed wounds and reinforced everything Janet had drilled into me over the years. Having been brainwashed into believing that no man would ever want me, I blamed myself for his philandering. A real woman would have been able to satisfy him, I told myself.

Unfortunately, about the same time, my first pregnancy ended in a miscarriage, further tarnishing my loathsome self-image. A real woman, I thought to myself, would be able to deliver a live baby.

Much as I love Jack, I have to say he was a terrible husband the first few years of our marriage. (Someone who shall remain unnamed once called him "the world's worst husband.") In addition to his womanizing, he worked night and day trying to bolster his chances for the vice presidency, and was away practically every weekend giving speeches throughout the country. I went to one luncheon for him and found myself seated five or six seats away. I said to the senator next to me, "This is the closest I've come to having lunch with Jack in months. In fact, I haven't seen him at all since Labor Day." Jack made a joke about his agenda, too: "Every time I get to the middle of the day, I look down at the schedule and see there's five minutes allotted for the candidate to eat and rest." I didn't think the joke was at all funny.

In fact, he never got home at night before 7:45 or 8 p.m., and often arrived later. When he did get home, he generally was so tired that we could only go out, or have people in, once a week. And that was on a good week. Sometimes, he was so wrapped up in his work, I might as well have been in Timbuktu. On the rare occasions he came

home for dinner, the damn phone would ring all the time, and he insisted on answering it. When I said, "Oh, Jack, why not just let it ring?," he would get mad and we would have a fight. Politics was my enemy as far as my husband was concerned.

Being president is one thing, but running for office is an ordeal that any sensible person would wish to spare her loved one. You anxiously watch your man run himself into the ground and wish you could rescue him, but, of course, you can't. I once thought that if I ever wrote a book, I'd call it *The Poison of the Presidency*. Many presidents agreed with me. John Adams said, "If I were to go over my life again, I would be a shoemaker rather than an American statesman." The great Thomas Jefferson, whom Jack loved, felt even more strongly about it. "Politics," he said, "is such a torment that I would advise anyone I love not to mix with it." He spoke of the presidency as "splendid misery." Even Herbert Hoover, who is not someone I ordinarily quote, said, "This job is nothing but a twenty-ring circus—with a whole lot of bad actors."

My home life with Jack was practically nonexistent. It was the loneliest time of my life. I grew more and more depressed, until all I did was lie in bed and read bestsellers.

I also resented the fact that we were never alone together. His buddies were practically a fixture in our house. Not only that, but they ruined my meticulously furnished household, stubbing out their foul-smelling cigars in my Sèvres ashtrays, dropping ashes in my antique Chinese vases, and plopping their muddy boots on my elegant white silk couches. Again, I thought it was all my fault that Jack needed so many people besides me, and asked myself what these men supplied that I lacked.

Shakespeare knew what life was about when he wrote, "My way of life has fallen into the sere, the yellow leaf." Yours and mine both, Will! Sometimes, when I was honest with myself, I felt my life was one vast emptiness. I tried to cover it up with projects like decorating our house, giving dinner parties and dances, and so forth, but nothing I did had any meaning. My life stretched out like an endless field of straw. Nobody was in it except strangers about whom I couldn't have cared less. I found myself talking to Jack's friends and thinking we were communicating, only to discover that we were on completely different tracks—they hadn't understood me and I hadn't understood them. And for all the French cuisine we ate, even the food seemed tasteless. What I really like to eat are salads. Sometimes, I thought I had been better off as the inquiring reporter.

Besides his constant absences, Jack didn't hesitate to say what was on his mind, and it wasn't always flattering. He enjoyed describing me as a person who had "a little too much status and not enough quo." His sense of humor didn't make his quips easier to take. The entire Kennedy family got together once to think up ways to make the shy, artistic, literary Jackie more palatable to the Democratic ticket. In front of everybody, Jack said, "The American people aren't ready for somebody like you, Jackie, and I don't know what we're going to do about it. I guess we'll just have to run you through subliminally in one of those quick-flash TV spots so no one will notice." It was worse than a slap in the face, and I ran from the room in hysterics, mortified by the whole incident. Despite his intellectual brilliance, Jack was not great at empathizing. He never did understand why what he said so upset me.

I am not the only person who found Jack insensitive to the feelings of others. A friend related a time when he was telling Jack a story, and Jack kept interrupting. The friend said to me, "If I had told Jack he'd hurt my feelings, he honestly would not have known what I was talking about any more than if he had stepped on an ant."

I have to admit that one of the peak joys of my later popularity was that it proved to the whole Kennedy crowd how wrong Jack had been in his assessment of me and the American people.

I am a perfectionist. You would expect my husband to know that, wouldn't you? But he showed up one morning at 11 a.m. and said, "What are you planning for the forty guests coming for lunch? They're expected at 1 p.m." Nobody had told me a thing about it. Trembling, I tried to think up something quickly that forty people could admire and then eat. I decided to go to a nearby Greek restaurant and order Greek salad, and cheese and fruit for dessert. The meal turned out to be delicious, and nobody suspected I hadn't made it with my own big hands.

It took me a long time to recover from that occasion, if I ever have. But I did adjust. After that, I made sure to be prepared at all times for unexpected guests. Freezers were just coming into common use. I bought one, packed it with all sorts of goodies, and told Jack I could now serve 647 people on short notice.

We were incompatible in many other ways. I like small, elaborate dinner parties, where I could show off my elegant silver and Sèvres china by candlelight. I enjoy lingering over a daiquiri after dinner and discussing ballet, foreign films, and art. But this kind of conversation bored Jack, and he would go upstairs to bed. Whatever his gifts, elegance was not among them. One night after he was elected president, when I had the White House chef serve *quenelles Nantua*, a concoction of egg whites, sole, pike, heavy cream, and lobster sauce, Jack said, "For God's sake, Jackie, I'm the president of the United States. Can't I get a simple hamburger in this house?"

I said, "Sorry, Jack, but I'm not going to run the White House like a hash house!"

In truth, Jack liked to guzzle beer, gorge on steak and potatoes, smoke foul-smelling cigars, and talk politics long into the night. When I served the tasteful dessert of cheese and fruit at the Greek lunch, he embarrassed me by sneaking into the kitchen and coming back to the party with a huge bowl of vanilla ice cream and chocolate sauce.

This was not uncommon. As a child, Jack snuck into the kitchen and stole forbidden goodies like ice cream, chocolate syrup, pancakes, and cheese sandwiches. Everything he put in his mouth had to be creamy, sugary, or both. He couldn't drink coffee without dumping three spoonfuls of sugar into it.

Generally, Jack could be a real pig at the dinner table. I tried to disguise my disgust, but after being brought up with the impeccable manners of the Auchinclosses and Bouviers, my husband's lack of refinement was a constant irritant. Some of his friends were even more vulgar. One of them—and I won't mention any names—would actually pick his nose at the dinner table. I was horrified, having never seen behavior like that before. My own mother, whatever her flaws, had always made sure I was faultlessly mannered.

Even when Jack tried to be nice, we weren't on the same wavelength. I had written and illustrated a little story for my step-sister Nina. Without my knowledge, Jack, who thought it would please me, sent it to a New York agent. I wasn't pleased at all. In fact, I was furious. I had always written and painted for the family, but didn't kid myself about the value of my "art." I was embarrassed by the story I'd written and thought the rest of the world would laugh at it. So I was quite happy when the agent was unable to find a publisher and returned the manuscript.

Jack and I were also different in our need for company. He could not bear to be alone. Perhaps it was because he was brought up in a household with a neglectful mother and eight brothers and sisters. His relationships were largely superficial. Bill Walton, a close friend, or at least one who was always around, said, "You'd never bleed in his presence, nor would he in yours."

Unlike Jack, I am perfectly comfortable alone. I like nothing better than to take solitary walks by the seashore, or to spend hours in my bedroom reading, painting, or writing. I might speak with a few friends on the phone now and then, but I am not one for long, drawn-out conversations. Bunny Mellon is a dear friend, and there are a few others. But I do find men more interesting than women. Maybe it's because, in our society, men usually have more interesting jobs. At least they did when I was married to Jack. Just look at the powerful, brilliant, and appealing men surrounding him in the White House. Unfortunately, Jack had not been raised to take women seriously enough to give them important appointments in his administration. Perhaps if he had, I might have enjoyed their company as well as that of the men.

Jack and I did like movies, but our tastes were so different it's difficult to believe we enjoyed the same art form. Jack loved westerns, particularly anything starring John Wayne, while I get pleasure from foreign films and art movies. When I brought *Jules and Jim* into the White House, he fidgeted for five minutes, then got up and left the room. I love French singers like Edith Piaf and Charles Trenet, but his favorites were Broadway tunes and Irish ballads like "Danny Boy." I like them, too, but how many times in a day can a person listen to "I'll Take You Home Again, Kathleen"? I kidded him by saying, "I know what your favorite song is: It's 'Hail to the Chief.'" He did not smile, much less laugh.

I love horses; he was allergic to them and couldn't stand being around them. I insisted he accompany me to the 1961 Washington horse show. It was a big mistake. He hated it, and yelled, "Get me out of here!" After a half hour, he departed, leaving me to watch the rest of the show with the Secret Service agent.

He loved the family compound at Hyannis Port, but I hated it, and demanded the family chauffeur take me elsewhere.

He said, "Where do you want to go?"

I answered, "Anywhere at all. Just not here."

I loved Wexford, our country house in Virginia; Jack wouldn't even go there. Everybody knows about my passion for and appreciation of art, but Jack liked only the most obvious art and lacked all ability to understand the soul of the artist. The list could go on and on, but it makes me too sad. It's good we both loved the children.

I don't like to think about it, but I guess Jack also had his dissatisfactions with the marriage. Once, he was asked, "If you had to live your life over again, how would you change it?" He answered, "If I had my life to live over again, I would have a different father, a different wife, and a different religion." Wow to all three!

And, again, there was the matter of Jack's infidelities. Among the wealthy upper classes, adultery was (and is) not just an accepted transgression, but a mark of sophistication. To the Kennedy men, infidelity was no more significant than grabbing a cup of coffee at a corner drugstore. Not that Jack was such a great lover. A "quickie" was the only sex that interested him. He went too fast and then fell asleep. One woman, asked about his sexual prowess, said, "It was a great seven and a half minutes." Marilyn Monroe explained his lack of sexual talent to a newspaperman: "Jack said the reason he didn't do foreplay was that he didn't have the time."

Later in our marriage, I went for counseling and learned to tell Jack what would please me sexually. Jack improved his technique, but it was too little too late.

Everyone wondered if I knew about Jack's numerous dalliances. There were so many that a member of his staff said, "It was a regular revolving door at the Kennedy White House. Women had to battle each other to get in line." Of course I knew about his behavior, and said as much to my sister Lee, a few intimate friends, and even Adlai Stevenson. At that time, divorce was unacceptable for politicians, especially Irish-Catholic ones, and would have ruined Jack's career, so I never let it slip in public that I knew about his playmates. A journalist asked me one time if I minded that so many young women went into a frenzy around Jack.

"Of course not," I lied. "Women are idealistic and respond to an idealist like my husband."

I even tried to be a sophisticate and made fun of his ability to turn on the charm and dazzle women. "You are absolutely incandescent," I teased, calling him "magic." It didn't help me feel any better.

One time, in despair, I asked him why he acted like his father and played around with so many women, when it easily could have destroyed his presidency. He looked down at the ground and, like a sad little boy, said, "I really don't know. I guess I just can't help it." At that moment, I actually felt sorry for him. I did love him, and we were both heavily invested in his going down in history as a great president. To me, putting up with his weakness was worth being part of a great man's life. Besides, Jack was the world master of sweet talk, and could usually manage to deflate my anger, for the moment anyway. It reminds me of an Abraham Lincoln line—that people who have no vices have few virtues.

Despite all my attempts to live with his infidelities, I frequently found myself unhappy and tearful. My tears were close to unendurable to Jack, yet left him unmoved, irritable, and puzzled. He usually tried to talk me into feeling better, pointing out all my blessings. Sometimes that worked, sometimes it didn't. When it failed, he got into a terrible mood himself. After all, Kennedys were not supposed to cry. His mother didn't, nor did his sisters. What was wrong with me? Why should I?

By and large, despite the depression it brought on me, Jack's womanizing was a cross I chose to bear, although it remains a festering wound to this day. Here is a secret I've never told anyone, except my analyst: I think as Jack got older, he became less and less able to perform, and turned to ever more desperate methods to keep himself aroused—like threesomes. I suspect that is why he took hallucinogens and smoked grass with Mary Meyer, a so-called friend of mine. (I'll tell you more about that later.) But toward the end, even these drastic attempts sometimes failed and left Jack flaccid and embarrassed. At these times, he was at his gloomiest, and nothing I could do or say could cheer him up.

Anyway, isn't every choice a person makes in life a trade-off? You put up with what you don't like in order to enjoy the glorious parts. For me, what made being Jack's wife worthwhile was, among other things, meeting historical figures like Winston Churchill, Nikita Khrushchev, and Charles de Gaulle, and even becoming a small part of history myself. I've traveled the globe over many times, visited exotic lands, and been privileged to see the great wonders of the world. I never could have done or seen all that if I hadn't married Jack. I've always liked power, and I must admit I enjoyed the prestige of being the wife of the president of the United States. Without him, my life would have been a wasteland, and I would have been aware of the emptiness all along the way. And he did give me two marvelous children, whom I wouldn't have hurt for the world by leaving their beloved father.

But that doesn't mean his indiscretions didn't sting—and sting badly. In the privacy of my bedroom, many a pillow was soaked through with tears. But publicly, I determinedly ignored his promiscuity. On the good side, this developed certain aspects of my personality which otherwise might have remained dormant. As I did with my mother, I found subtle ways of exacting revenge. Jack's compulsive womanizing left me free to go my own way and, much as it upset him, spend time fox-hunting, squandering as much money as I pleased on designer clothes, jewelry, art, and decor, and jet-setting all over the world without experiencing any guilt. It served him right, I figured, if he spent more time on my budget than the U.S. government's.

After examining my monthly account once, he looked up at me quizzically and asked, "Is there such a thing as Shoppers Anonymous?" The senior Kennedys complained, too, but I didn't let that bother me, either. *If they approve of my habits*, I thought, *fine. If not, the hell with them!* According to Aristotle, "It is the mark of an educated mind to be able to entertain a thought without accepting it." Or better yet, as the equally astute philosopher Dorothy Parker said, "I shall stay the way I am because I do not give a damn." If I worried all the time about what they said about me, I'd never be able to get out of bed in the morning. What could they do about my behavior, anyway? In the face of my spending habits, they were as helpless as I was about Jack's philandering. It felt great to have the shoe on the other foot for a change.

Sometimes, when I was feeling particularly loving toward Jack, I'd think, *He has the weight of the universe on his shoulders, a matter of life and death for all of civilization. He has to handle this incredible burden while in excruciating physical pain. As a good wife, shouldn't I support anything that gives him the strength to hold up under the load?* Well, I thought that once in a while, anyway.

One of his mistresses even made me laugh. Marilyn Monroe, asked by Hollywood columnist Earl Wilson what it was like to have sex with the president, said, "Well, I think I made his back feel better." I should have had her to the White House more often.

Despite my dissatisfaction with Jack, I tried my best to be a

good wife and did everything I could to make him love me. Although I wasn't the type of wife to ask, "What's new in Laos today?," I straightened my hair, got an Audrey Hepburn pixie cut, wore elegant dresses from Paris, exercised hours every day, and ate lettuce leaves for lunch in an effort to build a beautiful body that would win his love. He hated me to wear brown or flowered clothing, so when he told me he didn't like a particular dress of mine, I never wore it again. I did little things for him that only a woman in love would do, like leaving him funny little notes all around the White House to cheer him up. He would open them and burst out laughing. I'm told I'm a great mimic, and loved to amuse him by imitating the mannerisms and accents of some of the world leaders with whom he dealt. It always broke him up.

He also relied greatly on my "shit detector" skills and on my insights into foreign leaders and United States politicians. I seemed to have a sixth sense that enabled me to distinguish between people who were serving Jack and those who were self-serving. I was particularly good at picking out phonies who concealed their lack of knowledge behind an impressive pseudo-intellectual front. Jack always asked me what I thought about so-and-so, and usually adjusted his behavior accordingly.

While he was shaking hands and giving speeches, I entertained the boring wives of local politicians and smiled until my cheeks ached. When his buddies protested that I looked "too rich" and "too New York," I even took off most of my make-up and wore simplified styles with little jewelry, none of it real. Lee understood what a sacrifice that was. And worst of all for a compulsive smoker, I never took out a single cigarette in public.

Every night before falling asleep, Jack liked to hear his favorite records, such as *Camelot*, on his old Victrola. In the freezing winter, I was the one who crept out of our nice warm bed to play the records for him. For a while, I confined my reading to books about history and politics that Jack could use in his campaign speeches. He incorporated them into practically every speech, and grew famous for them.

During his devastating back surgery, I probably kept him alive. I conducted research for his book, *Profiles in Courage*, and even brought the manuscript to Jules Davis, my history professor at George Washington University, for corrections and suggestions. I was a good wife.

If you will forgive the cliché—Jack wouldn't; he hated clichés—it seems that even the horrible cloud of his back surgery had a silver lining, and a very silvery one at that. The time he spent in bed reflecting on deep political issues and reading the works of great men in political history changed Jack and permanently deepened him. The JFK who fought for the leadership and control of the Democratic Party in 1956 was much stronger and tougher than the charming young man who had successfully run for the Senate in 1952. If it hadn't been for his terrible back problems, I don't believe John Fitzgerald Kennedy would have become the man and the great president he was.

Brilliant as Jack was, he needed all the help he could get with languages. One of my favorite stories involves his famous Berlin speech. No doubt trying to emulate my success in speaking French to the French people, he thought he was saying, "I am a Berliner." But he didn't know that in German, *un Berliner* and *Berliner* mean two different things. So what he really said was, "I am a jelly doughnut." I get hysterical whenever I think of it. Everyone thought it was hilarious—everyone but Jack.

Although nobody knows this, he also turned to me for advice whenever a world crisis occurred, such as the Bay of Pigs, the Cuban Missile Crisis, and the rise of the Berlin Wall. I always steered him away from the Cold War and toward peace and nuclear disarmament. He respected my political instincts and listened to me.

Yet, in spite of all I did for him, none of my efforts changed him in the least as far as his women were concerned. Jack continued to womanize to his heart's content, telling his friends that if he didn't get his "daily dose of sex," he would suffer from headaches.

I loved a lot about Jack. I loved the way he warmed me up when we cuddled in bed. I loved his fresh Irish smell and the feel of his smooth skin. I loved his height, his bearing, and his handsome, open face. I loved that we laughed a lot together and had a lot of fun. We both enjoyed gossip, the more salacious the better, particularly stories about which movie stars and politicians were sleeping with whom. As Alice Roosevelt Longworth said to Jack, "If you haven't got anything nice to say about anybody, come sit next to me." I also loved his wit, as when his sister Eunice said, "Jack, some of your speeches could use more fire," and he said, "Eunice, some of your speeches belong in the fire." We were both expert at games, but Jack didn't like that I won them all the time. Once, when we were playing *Scrabble*, he said, "For God's sake, Jackie, can't you lose once in a while?" I said in a naive tone, "But Jack, I thought the Kennedys enjoyed being competitive!"

Sometimes, we reveled in each other's intellectual interests, and Jack was delighted that we filled in the gaps in each other's knowledge. I tutored him in art history and he taught me about making movies, which he had learned about from his father's mistress, Gloria Swanson. We exchanged ideas about de Gaulle, whom I adored, and Winston Churchill, all of whose books Jack was familiar with. We both loved poetry and memorized each other's favorite poems. We relished each other's company, and I was never happier than when we were together.

But all human beings have their shortcomings. The worst of Jack's appeared during my second pregnancy, and nearly ended our marriage. After Jack lost the Democratic nomination for vice president, in an attempt to cheer himself up, he left for France to vacation with his parents. I was in my sixth month of pregnancy. To my despair, a month before the baby was due, I developed such severe cramps that I fell to the floor and had to scream for help. Jack was contacted, but continued on his vacation. I was quickly rushed to Newport Hospital and forced to undergo a premature emergency Caesarian section. It was not successful. The fetus of the little girl, whom I had already named Arabella, was stillborn.

When I regained consciousness, it was Bobby sitting by my bedside, telling me about the baby's death, and it was Bobby who arranged for her burial. Jack still refused to come home. "What good would it do?" he said. "Arabella is already dead." Can you believe a man could be so insensitive to the emotional needs of his wife? The next day, the newspapers headlined, "Senator Kennedy on Mediterranean Trip Unaware His Wife Has Lost Baby." The papers said I lost the baby because of the nervous tension I had experienced during the Democratic convention. I blamed Jack. I still do.

It didn't help that his mother told Jack, "She shouldn't have been doing all that water-skiing."

Mother Teresa once said that the hunger for love is more difficult to root out than the hunger for food. I agree. Although I knew he cared for me in his own limited way, I yearned for him to love me in an all-consuming way. Jack didn't, and he never would. He just was not able to love that way, at least not at this time of his life, and not me. Sometimes I found my longing for Jack's love so painful it was all but intolerable. I remember talking with Bobby's wife Ethel about it. I said, "I don't want to stay married to such a selfish person. He makes me miserable. I want out." Ethel laughed, and said, "Are you kidding? Grandpop [Joe Kennedy] would never let you leave the marriage."

"Really?" I said. "Don't be so sure!"

Ethel must have betrayed my confidence, because I soon got a call from Joe Kennedy inviting me to lunch with him at the elegant French restaurant Le Pavilion. I had always loved Joe, and he loved me dearly. In spite of all his faults—or maybe because of them—he reminded me very much of my father.

Joe assured me between bites of Chicken Polanaise that divorce was not possible for me and Jack, because it would ruin his political career. Then he asked if we couldn't work something out that would compensate me for my marital unhappiness and suggested I consult his lawyer. I was skeptical that anything could make up for such deep unhappiness, but out of curiosity, I consented to meet with him. To my surprise, he made me an offer that was too good to refuse.

After my parents divorced and my mother married Hugh D. Auchincloss, I spent my adolescent years at Merrywood, a land of WASPs, old money, and society. You'd think I would have felt secure, surrounded by all that wealth. But I didn't. I was raised *as if* I were rich, but I had no money of my own. Growing up among rich relatives, I always felt inferior to my mother's new family—Mummy shunted Lee and me aside in her new role of stepmother until we felt like little orphans. Five of the seven children at Merrywood received trust funds from their Auchincloss grandmother. Compared to them, Lee and I were the impoverished relatives.

Having money adds sweetness to the soul. It brings a kind of grace to living and sets wealthy people apart, although I realize from bitter experience that it doesn't necessarily make them better people. Having money gives the rich a kind of control over their world and bestows poise on women and a heightened sense of who they are. Money causes an inner light to shine through everyone's face, whatever their nationality, size, or shape—a light that even old age cannot extinguish. From my youth onward, I felt I lacked these essential attributes and was terrified that my future children would be as bereft as I was. I determined that someday I would marry somebody richer than my stepfather.

Joe was a shrewd man and knew the way to get what he wanted from me. His lawyer said that Joe had offered to set up a trust fund of a million dollars for any offspring Jack and I might have in the future. If I had no children in five years, the million dollars would revert to me. In addition, I wanted it added to the contract that if Jack were to bring home any venereal disease from one of his women, my price would go up to twenty million dollars. The lawyer informed Joe of my terms. He agreed, laughingly adding that if I thus contracted a sexually transmitted disease, I could name my price. As I said, it was an offer too good to refuse. The money brought my standing among the Kennedy siblings up to theirs, and for the first time, I no longer felt like the poor relation I was as a teenager in Merrywood.

I also said that I wanted a new car as part of the bargain, and asked for a Thunderbird. Joe said, "The Kennedys drive Buicks." I got a Buick.

There is an amusing afterword to this story. When Ethel heard I was getting a trust fund of a million dollars for any children I might have, she was furious. She said, "I already have five children. Why can't I get a million dollars for each of them?" Ethel nagged Bobby until she got him to report her complaints to Joe. As a result, he set up a trust fund of one hundred thousand dollars apiece for Ethel's and Bobby's children, the principal of which each would receive upon reaching the age of twenty-one. But Ethel was still not happy about the matter. She grumbled, "Only a hundred thousand dollars apiece? How come her kids get a million and mine only one hundred thousand?" Bobby convinced her to drop the matter, saying that if she didn't, Joe was likely to withdraw the offer altogether.

I probably made a mistake accepting Joe's offer. Afterward, I became more and more depressed. I felt isolated, friendless, and ignored by my husband, his family, and the staff. Since losing the baby, my unhappiness had become unbearable. No doctors were able to help me feel better.

I had entered into the marriage with every hope of living a long and happy life with Jack. I had lived up to my part of the bargain as well as any woman could, but I was dreadfully disappointed that Jack failed to give me the things I needed: his love and the affirmation of my physical self. It wasn't fair. But as Jack himself said, "Life isn't fair."

Chapter 7

RESTORING THE WHITE HOUSE

On entering the White House as a new tenant, my first reaction was one of horror. The so-called "People's House" was, in my view, the world's greatest monument to bad taste— seemingly a place no one had ever loved. In fact, I'd seen nicer barns. Worst of all, I could find absolutely no trace of its formidable past. I knew I couldn't live there for four years without gagging, and determined to do something about its dreadful state as soon as I could.

The White House, I thought, should exhibit the wonderful heritage of our country. For instance, we had an extraordinary flowering in the eighteenth century, but nobody would know it to look at the White House. I would have felt terrible if I had lived there for four years and did nothing to set it right.

First of all, I asked the Library of Congress to send me everything they had on the White House and pored over the material for days, taking notes as I read. I threw out all the junk that looked as if it was bought at a Grand Rapids furniture sale. As far as antiques were concerned, there were two white pottery dogs on the mantelpiece in the East Room. Some antiques! They couldn't have been more than ten years old. I got rid of the Pullman car ashtrays (Caroline had made prettier ones in nursery school) and painted over Mamie Eisenhower's ghastly pink walls. Her motel-modern decor, seasick-green curtains, and dime-store ornaments also had to go, as did the Victorian mirrors, which were hideous. I couldn't bear to look at them for even a day and immediately banished them to the basement. The ground floor hall looked like a dentist's office, and the East Room resembled a roller skating rink after a teenager's all-night party. What was particularly painful for heavy readers like Jack and me was that there wasn't a decent reading lamp in the entire White House. Hadn't the Eisenhowers done any reading there? Before my head hit the pillow on our first night in the mansion, I began planning to restore the White House to what it should have been, with authentic eighteenth- and nineteenth-century antiques.

I decided to make this my major White House effort. I am a person who chooses my projects carefully, and then I throw myself into them heart and soul, working night and day to achieve my goals. Because I suffer from insomnia and often can't sleep at night, I am in the habit of getting up and writing down my thoughts. Insomnia has benefits that nobody ever discusses. It gives me more working time and, therefore, more ideas than most people enjoy. In the silence of the night, while my dear husband was snoring away (I was always envious that he fell asleep the moment his head hit the pillow), there was not an ashtray, a vase, or an andiron that did not come under my scrutiny.

I thought long and hard about where to put chandeliers and had them moved from room to room. I constantly had walls painted and repainted until the painters hid when they saw me coming, and I rearranged furniture and paintings every day to find the positions where they could be shown off to best advantage. It enraged me when other members of the White House Restoration Committee (I will not mention any names) slacked off. I wrote them many an angry note, but it seldom changed their behavior, and I should have known. To paraphrase Gertrude Stein, "A slacker is a slacker is a slacker."

Unfortunately, Jack did not see it my way at first and was afraid

I would waste the taxpayers' money. "Come off it, Jackie," he said. "I don't want you tearing up the White House, pitching out everything you see, and rearranging every object in sight! The public is still in an uproar over the South Portico balcony President Truman added to the White House, and I don't want anything like that to happen in my administration." I understood his concern. He hadn't been in the Oval Office one hour before carpenters began to tear it apart as painters mixed paints, electricians rewired, and plumbers reworked pipes.

Jack was not the most knowledgeable person about interior decorating. When we were first married, he didn't know the difference between a pretty room and an ugly room. He actually bought our Georgetown house because he liked the door knocker. But when he saw that I knew what I was doing, Jack sang a different tune and began to cooperate with me, even convincing Congress the restoration was necessary to make the White House the superb historical monument it deserved to be. He was particularly delighted when I found him a desk carved from the timbers of an old British warship and presented to President Rutherford B. Hayes.

I brought in famous New York designer Sister Parish to redo our living space, and requested that she bring in loads of chintz to lighten up the old dump. Not quite trusting Sister, I snuck Stéphane Boudin, head of Maison Jansen, the famous Paris firm, into the White House behind Jack's back. Hiring a Frenchman to help decorate America's primary public mansion was strictly verboten, so I asked that he keep his presence a secret. This turned out to be about as possible as keeping a hurricane from public knowledge, and the media had a field day with it and with me. When they interviewed me about it, I lied and said that Boudin was "merely a consultant" to the committee that was doing all the work. Do you think anyone bought that story? Of course not. But I had *mon décorateur* to help with the restoration, and that was all that mattered.

Along with my New York and Paris decorators, I hired curators, historians, and scholars, and had Jack formulate legislation to smooth

our way. I solicited contributions from anyone I thought likely to contribute, and from some who were not. You'd be surprised at how often I was wrong about who would turn out to be generous. I organized platoons of fine arts experts from all across the country to help, and got quite good at convincing private donors to contribute their historic furniture. I shamelessly got manufacturers to donate their products, and practically forced museums from all parts of the United States to give over 150 priceless works of art. In just one year, my committee transformed the White House into a national monument worth over ten million dollars.

The project did not go off without a hitch, however. I had ordered some chairs for the family dining room. They were lovely, but turned out to have certain shortcomings. Every Tuesday morning, Jack held a breakfast meeting for congressional leaders. Promptly at 8:45, Lawrence O'Brien, special assistant to the president, entered, pulled out a chair, and sat down. Under his weight, the chair fell apart and he fell to the floor. The speaker of the House, John McCormack, picked him up and said, "It's a good thing it wasn't the president." Then Jack came in and everybody rose. As he took his seat, a menacing cracking noise was heard. McCormack and Mike Mansfield, the Senate majority leader, grabbed Jack's arms and prevented him from sitting down, thus saving his dignity. This aspect of my renovation project was the subject of some heated discussion at our dinner table that night.

Jack then reverted to form and became furious at how much money I was spending. He practically had a stroke when he learned that the wallpaper I had installed in the Diplomatic Reception Room cost $12,500. He became angrier when someone leaked my further restoration plans to the newspapers, and they ripped me (and him) to shreds. What really got them going was that I had the "Scenic America" wallpaper from the nineteenth century steamed off a historic house in Maryland instead of purchasing new paper of the same design at considerably less cost.

In my own defense, I felt—and still feel—that the most historically significant residential building in the United States deserves to be outfitted in wallpaper actually made at the time the building was erected. The White House is worth the real thing, and not an imitation. When I told that to Jack, he said, "I don't give a damn how much it's worth—$12,500 is an obscene amount to pay for wallpaper!" Jack was so stingy. He deserved a wife more like Abigail Adams, who hung laundry to dry in the East Room of the White House.

He rarely mentioned (to me, anyhow) that in the three years of his administration, 240 pieces of furniture and art were given free to the White House thanks to my efforts. And I myself discovered in the bowels of the White House several dust-covered paintings of the great French impressionist, Paul Cézanne, important portraits of American Indians and, as my *piece de résistance*, some of Abraham Lincoln's china. In a long-unused men's room, of all places, I was flabbergasted to discover marble busts of George Washington and Martin Van Buren. Nearby, one of Christopher Columbus lay hidden.

After the disclosure about the wallpaper to the press, I swore my committee to secrecy to avoid any further publicity. It didn't help. Just a few days later, *The Washington Post* ran a story saying that I planned to have the historic Blue Room done over in white. "It won't be blue anymore," the paper wailed. *Newsweek* took photographs of the silkmaker, Franco Scalamandré, standing in front of the looms producing sixty thousand dollars' worth of white-on-white silk he had promised to donate to me. I was pleased to have his services—he had been making silk fabrics for the White House since Herbert Hoover's presidency. Jack was irate when he heard the supposed news, and shouted, "Herbert Hoover be damned, I won't have that bloodsucker Scalamandré in my White House!" He insisted that the magazine not publish the photos. "One thing nobody can accuse Jackie of is having an overdeveloped social conscience," he told his buddies. *He* should talk about conscience!

I coolly ordered handwoven twenty-five thousand-dollar raw silk curtains from France. Then I instructed my committee to scour antique shops and warehouses across the country to find exactly what

I had in mind. In this instance, nothing else but what I had in mind would do—certainly not the dreary imitations you can find in a third-class hotel. I ordered the painters to redo one single room seven times until they got the exact wall shade I wanted. The beautiful blue and white fringe I needed for the draperies in our bedroom cost over fifty dollars a yard. Everything had to be just right. Anything less would have spoiled my vision. Would you call that being a perfectionist, or is it just that I knew what I liked and wouldn't settle for anything less?

Jack let me have it. "Good God, Jackie!" he yelled. "There isn't a corner of the White House you've left unturned." He complained that the poor Blue Room was now white, the Red Room cerise, and the Green Room chartreuse. He complained that every couch, footstool, and ottoman had been re-upholstered in crushed silks and hand-painted brocades. "I can't find my way to the bathroom without tripping over some expensive new piece of furniture!" he said, and with my five thousand-dollar chandeliers and thirty-five thousand-dollar eighteenth-century carpeting, he insisted I'd exhausted in a few weeks the entire yearly amount allocated for the restoration. "When is this going to stop?"

I said, "Stop worrying, Jack. I'll come up with some way of paying for it."

"Yeah," he said, "and I'm the man on the moon."

When I was a little girl of eleven, I took my first tour of the White House and remember complaining to my mother, "They don't even have a book telling us the history."

My mother said, "Of course, if you were president, you would run the White House better, Jackie." Her remark upset me, and ruined the White House tour for me. It wasn't an isolated experience.

In thinking of ways to pay for the restoration, I returned to the idea I had as an eleven year old. I decided to publish a souvenir guidebook for tourists. I myself would write the foreword and sell the book for one dollar to people taking the White House tour. People rushing through the place in fifteen minutes couldn't possibly remember what they had seen. The book would remind them of their tour for years, and the publication would finance the restoration. It could be reprinted with every new administration, incorporating any new material.

Saying it sounded to him like commercializing the White House, Jack objected. He grumbled that the taxpayers would never approve. I found myself wishing I had been married to Thomas Jefferson, because he would have known how important my work was. But with Jefferson no longer around, I got together a group of museum experts and made Henry Francis du Pont, a Republican no less, the head of the committee. The octogenarian du Pont was the country's leading expert on American furniture. Jack, who knew as much about period furniture as I know about football, was reluctantly persuaded by the committee that all historic houses sold such books. The way I worked it, nobody would dare criticize his decision.

The book turned out to be a tremendous success. The first printing of 250,000 sold out in three months, there were two more sold-out printings in 1962 and, though it has gone through many revisions, it is still being sold and has sold well into the millions. *The New York Times* admired the fact that raising money for the White House restoration this way removed the burden from the shoulders of the taxpayer.

There was another way I saved money for Jack's administration. The White House really needed some beautiful paintings, so I borrowed a number from leading New York art galleries and invited my committee to tea. When the members arrived, they found the paintings propped up all around the room. I informed the guests that if they liked any of the paintings enough to donate them to the White House, they would earn the country's eternal gratitude. By the end of the afternoon, not a single painting had to be returned.

While I was obsessed with my personal privacy, I did want to get as much publicity as possible for the restoration. I knew that media coverage would increase interest in the White House and encourage private gifts. So I made personal appearances, posed for photographs, smilingly signed autographs, and wrote thousands of letters. I also did

a lot of verbal lobbying in magazines like *Look* and *Life* to let people know about the project and to solicit donations from the public. I was delighted when a vice president at CBS, Blair Clark, contacted me to ask if I would like to conduct a televised tour of the White House to show the nation the results of the restoration. He suggested a one-hour program. When I felt a bit overwhelmed at the idea and hesitated, he added, "The network is planning to donate one hundred thousand dollars to the restoration project." I quickly accepted the deal.

We had to evacuate the White House for a whole weekend so that the network could bring in the necessary five tons of equipment. I spent all day Saturday and Sunday going over my notes so I would know their contents by heart and not have to read on camera. I hate it when people read speeches—if someone is going to address an audience, she owes them the courtesy of knowing the material well enough to speak spontaneously. For the show, I knew I could ad-lib whenever I thought of information I believed would interest the public.

I showed up for the taping wearing my favorite red two-piece suit and my signature pearls. Thinking it would be more than enough time, I allotted three hours for the taping. To my dismay, I was told it would take all day, and I would be lucky if we were finished by then. I protested, saying, "I can't possibly do that. I'm planning to go fox-hunting." But when the network people stressed how important it was to finish the taping, I sighed and reluctantly agreed to forego the foxes.

More than forty-six million Americans watched the show as I strolled through the Lincoln Room, the State Dining Room, the Reception Room, the Blue Room, the Green Room, and the Red Room of the restored White House, mentioning the names of the private donors as I proceeded. Passing through the stately rooms, I pointed out such items as sofas, desks, clocks, lamps, wallpaper, china, silverware, and portraits, and spoke about their history. I was proud of myself that there wasn't an ashtray or armchair I couldn't identify or describe in detail. At the time, I realized I was probably the world's greatest expert on White House furnishings, and was deeply gratified when I won an Emmy award for my television tour. For one brief shining moment, I felt on top of the world.

But of course, not everybody agreed with the Emmy voters. Norman Mailer, who I used to think was my friend, had the nerve to write that I moved like a wooden horse and sounded like an aspiring but totally untalented actress. In fact, I had been in many plays at Miss Porter's boarding school and always received fine notices in the school paper. Besides, his criticism made utterly no sense. Talking about the White House restoration wasn't an actor's role at all! I got even with him by telling my secretary to remove him from all future guest lists at the White House. Anyway, forty-six million people thought enough of the program to stay tuned. And more important, Jack said he was proud of me, and even briefly appeared at the end of the program and said so.

By the time the taping ended, I was so exhausted that I told Janet Cooper, the secretary for the Fine Arts Committee, I wouldn't take any more questions on the restoration for at least a week. "In fact," I said, "I don't care if the whole White House goes up in flames!" Then I retracted that statement and told Janet I would see her when I recovered, "if I ever do. I think I may have smallpox."

Later that year, Doubleday wanted to do a book based on the show. At first, I objected because I had wanted to do my own book on the restoration, co-authored by the photojournalist David Douglas Duncan. My potential co-author insisted that to do his part satisfactorily, we would have to close down the White House for two days. I asked Jack if we could do it, and he roared, "Absolutely not! The last time the White House was closed up was when the British burned it down in 1812." So that was the end of my book, and Doubleday proceeded to publish theirs, which, like the TV program, was called *A Tour of the White House with Mrs. John F. Kennedy*. I have always regretted not being able to do my own book on the subject. If I had to do it over again, I would go ahead without Duncan.

Another White House project that worked out well was my effort to preserve the ancient Egyptian temples that otherwise would have been flooded after the construction of the Aswan Dam. I saved the monuments from destruction by getting Congress to appropriate funds and by raising money privately. To awaken public interest in the project, I arranged for an exhibition of Tutankhamun treasures at the National Gallery in Washington, along with the public announcement that fifty million dollars was needed to preserve the monuments. To my great surprise, I raised most of the money from private donors. To demonstrate their gratitude, Egypt shipped the Temple of Dendur, stone by stone, to the United States, where it rests to this day next to the Metropolitan Museum of Art in New York. I feel gratified every time I look out my Fifth Avenue windows and see the temple. In a further demonstration of Egypt's appreciation, President Gamal Abdel Nasser presented me with a recently excavated limestone statue of a noble from the fifth dynasty. It was said to be worth over $250,000. I felt entitled to keep it.

My other arts-related project, the National Cultural Center in Washington, later to be named the John F. Kennedy Center for the Performing Arts, was also a great success. The Center, a wonderful memorial to Jack, presents theater, ballet, dance, jazz, orchestral, chamber, popular, and folk music, as well as multimedia performances for people of all ages. It's the nation's, possibly the world's, most ambitious performing arts facility, hosting thousands of performances a year for audiences numbering in the millions. Touring productions and television and radio broadcasts originating at the Center are seen or heard by millions more. A leader in arts education, the Center produces and nurtures developing artists, resulting in hundreds of theatrical productions and innumerable new ballets, operas, and musical works.

I am particularly proud of the fact that it was in good part my influence on Jack that brought about his interest in funding the project. Before he met me, he wasn't the slightest bit interested in the arts.

Not all my efforts were as successful as the restoration. I tried to arrange for the enlargement and restructuring of the White House library. I planned to fill the library with books of significant American writing that have influenced American thinking—books by presidents (including *Profiles in Courage*, of course), great statesmen, and famous writers. Whenever possible, I wanted first editions in their original bindings. Such books are extremely expensive, and unfortunately for us and the country, the project has never been completed.

When Jack and I left for Dallas in November 1963, only three items on my restoration agenda were left undone. The golden fabric for the drapes ordered for the East Room had taken longer to weave than planned, upholstery for the State Dining Room chairs had not yet been completed, and I was still waiting for the ground-floor chandeliers to arrive. Nevertheless, I knew I had done well, and wrote Clark Clifford that the White House restoration was all it should be, and everything I had ever dreamed of. I left for Texas glowing with satisfaction.

When I look back at my life at this late date, I feel most gratified by the restoration of the White House. My work changed that great building, and perhaps the taste of Americans, forever. Although Nancy Reagan took down the plaque I had placed in our bedroom— the one that said, "In this room lived John Fitzgerald Kennedy with his wife Jacqueline—during the two years, ten months, and three days he was president of the United States"—there was nothing she could do to remove my imprint on every room in the White House. I believe it is everlasting.

Chapter 8

THE RAH RAH GIRLS

The Kennedys were not a family; they were a tribe. The siblings rarely had any separate interests and they rarely did things on an individual basis. When you saw one Kennedy, you saw a troop. They traveled in packs. When they went sailing, for instance, you saw them descending en masse on the yacht club and taking it over. Jack's terrible childhood illnesses had their silver lining: At least he became absorbed in reading books. Otherwise, he might have just marched along with the rest of the gang.

The best (or worst) example I can think of is the Christmas I bought Jack an expensive set of oil paints and canvases and gave it to him at the annual Hyannis Port holiday celebration. No sooner did Jack open the package than his brothers and sisters grabbed the paints and began to splash blobs of color on the canvases. As they dabbed at their "masterpieces," the paint flew left and right until their clothing and the surrounding furniture were as splattered as the canvases. All the while, they screamed and hollered for their siblings to come and rave about their "works of art." Personally, I couldn't tell one painting from the other. I turned my back and went to my room. I was horrified.

The Kennedy girls and I never really clicked. I like art and culture.

They liked touch football, which they played as competitively as their brothers. I tried it once and broke my ankle; that was the end of my football career. Ethel's little joke was that I wouldn't play because I was afraid I would smear my make-up. They laughed at me behind my back and called me "the deb," and later, "the widder." I called them "the rah rah girls." We were nice to each other in public, but that's as far as it went.

Like her mother, Jack's sister, Eunice Kennedy, was extremely religious, some thought to a fault, and it would have surprised no one had she decided to become a nun. I think all the Kennedys should have been born boys, especially Eunice, who was the most intelligent of the bunch. Her father said, "If Eunice had balls, she'd be the president of the United States." In many ways, she was a carbon copy of Jack. He himself said that Eunice was a lot like him. Some even commented that she looked like Jack Kennedy in drag.

Yet she was not a girl whom boys sought. Her words spurted out in bunches, as if she were afraid she would never be able to get them all out. I suspect it was because nobody at the Kennedy dinner table was interested in what girls thought, and poor Eunice, fifth in line of the Kennedy children, had to eject her words in a continuous staccato voice to prevent herself from being interrupted. She was a gawky stringbean of a girl, thin as a rail, just like Jack. The family called her "Puny Eunie." And like Jack, she, too, was unable to sit still for more than a few minutes at a time. When told she resembled Jack, Eunice was ecstatic. Jack was stunning; Eunice was not. In my view, what was gorgeous in Jack was not attractive in a woman.

Eunice was Jack's favorite living sister. I thought of her as the leader of the rah rah girls, a role she maintained all the way to the White House. She and the other Kennedy women gave tea parties for women all over Massachusetts, and then the country, and contributed greatly to Jack's successful campaigns.

Later, I was most displeased with her when she refused to support my marriage to Aristotle Onassis. Asked by a reporter how she felt about it, her response was a stony, "No comment!" And although I received congratulations and best wishes from all the other Kennedys, only an icy silence emanated from Eunice. I also detest the fact that she opposed abortions and fought in every way possible to prevent them. Like a good reactionary, she had once dated Joe McCarthy. It was a good match.

Despite my personal dealings with her, I must admit that there is much to admire about Eunice. The only Kennedy sister with a superior academic record, she earned a degree in sociology from Stanford, having spent her first year at Radcliffe. She was the only member of the tribe, male or female, who didn't abandon their retarded sister, Rosemary, but visited her regularly in the convent where she was kept hidden away. In 1968, she established and chaired the Special Olympics for mentally disadvantaged individuals. More than one million children and adult athletes now take part in Special Olympics programs in more than 150 nations. Participation in the Special Olympics is free for those who qualify. Events accommodate various levels of ability so that contenders can compete with others of similar capabilities. The Special Olympics is a wonderful and lasting accomplishment for Eunice, and for the world.

It is interesting that the Special Olympics oath is "Let me win. But if I cannot win, let me be brave in the attempt." It certainly conflicts with Joe, Sr.'s well-known adage, "We don't want any losers around here." I admire the fact that Eunice dared to defy her father and stand up for what she believed in. In that way, she was a woman after my own heart.

Her actions were also a source of pride to Jack. Even President Reagan agreed and, in 1984, awarded her the Presidential Medal of Freedom, the nation's highest civilian award, for her work on behalf of the mentally retarded. Giving back much good to the world, she was truly Jack Kennedy's sister.

Jean Kennedy, the eighth of the nine children of Joseph and Rose Kennedy, was the shyest and most guarded of the Kennedy children. This is not surprising when one hears the story of her birth. Joe was trying to figure out what to give Rose to celebrate the new baby's arrival. A friend said, "What can you possibly give a woman who has had her eighth child?" Joe glumly answered, "A black eye."

Rose said of Jean, "She was born so late she only experienced the family's tragedies, not our triumphs"—nor much of their love and attention, either. Jean was a quiet, lonely child who would have benefitted from the special care of her mother. She often appeared lost in the rowdy games and sports of her older siblings, and was usually overlooked amidst the clamor. In compensation, this sweet-tempered child turned to Kico, a warm and loving nursemaid who gave Jean what her mother could not or would not. Yet, when the family accompanied Joe, appointed ambassador, to England, Kico was left behind, and Jean never ceased to mourn her absence.

Jean also had a snotty side. Because she received little acclaim from being herself, she stressed her superiority in being born a Kennedy, and frequently bragged of her position as a family member. From the age of nine or ten, she often measured her wrists and ankles and took pride in their slimness. "Yours are not slender enough to be an aristocrat," she told a young cousin. Jean was also known to brag about how rich her family was, and how she would have to be careful in choosing her friends and potential husband to avoid those primarily interested in her money.

In 1956, in the small chapel of St. Patrick's Cathedral in New York, Jean married Stephen Smith, a businessman who later took over the Kennedy family finances and became a political advisor and campaign manager for the Kennedy brothers. The Smiths maintained a lower profile than other members of the Kennedy family.

Both Stephen and Jean Smith were present at the Ambassador Hotel in Los Angeles when Jean's brother Bobby was shot and fatally wounded by Sirhan Sirhan the night Bobby won the 1968 California Democratic presidential primary. Neither Smith ever fully recovered from the shock. Nor have I.

In 1993, Jean Kennedy Smith was appointed by President Bill Clinton to be U.S. ambassador to Ireland, and continued the legacy of diplomacy begun by her father, the ambassador to the court of St.

James during the Roosevelt administration. Smith did far better in the post than her father. As ambassador, she played a pivotal role in the region's peace process.

In 1974, Jean Kennedy Smith founded the Very Special Arts, a nonprofit organization which promotes the artistic talents of mentally and physically challenged children. She also sits on the board of the John F. Kennedy Center for the Performing Arts. Rose and Joe must have done something right. Their girls really are competent women.

As I think about it, I'm reminded just how accomplished Jean is. Strange, isn't it, how some people stay in your mind and others, no matter how often you see them, simply don't exist for you? Jean has some nice traits and is a good person, but she just seems to fade into the woodwork, as she did among the Kennedy siblings, so that I, too, don't think about her much one way or the other.

Patricia Kennedy, the sixth of the Kennedys' nine children, was different from the family's other females in that she was the only one who was not ambitious, a "deficiency" that greatly bothered her mother. A pretty girl, Pat didn't understand the family emphasis on winning. For her, and not her siblings, it was the joy of playing, not the victory, that mattered. Thus, she wasn't an object of great interest to the rest of this family of "winners." In fact, they often forgot about her, although perhaps in her values, she was at the head of the pack. She also was widely considered the best-looking and classiest of the five sisters, carrying herself with the aristocratic bearing of her mother.

At school, she was popular and worldlier than her classmates, one of whom said, "Pat was quite sophisticated, but always struck me as being as lonely as she was reserved." Fascinated with Hollywood because of her father's adventures there (romantic and otherwise), Pat wanted to be in the movies, but considered it inappropriate for a Kennedy to be an actress, so she settled for the production side of things and became an assistant for singer Kate Smith's radio show. Like the other Kennedy women, Pat worked for all of Jack's campaigns, and after his assassination, she continued to campaign for her brothers.

Pat was a romantic who spent much of her time daydreaming. Given her father's passionate love affair with Gloria Swanson, it's not surprising that Pat married a movie star. Poised as a princess, as befitted a Kennedy woman, athletic (she was a champion tennis player at college), and supple, Pat is best known as the Catholic schoolgirl who defied her domineering father by marrying Peter Lawford, a graceful, gentlemanly British actor.

"If there is anything worse than marrying an actor," Joe blasted, "it is marrying a British actor!" Jack didn't agree. He and Peter became pals, and Jack the politician used to ask Peter the actor for advice on how movie stars wooed their audiences so he could learn to do the same for voters. Apparently, Lawford's advice took. The actor Robert Stack wrote in his autobiography that he had known many actors, but few had Jack Kennedy's charm for women. All he had to do was look at a woman, Stack wrote, and she'd tumble.

In 1966, after eleven years of marriage, the still-defiant Pat divorced Peter, the first divorce in the very Catholic Kennedy family. She was unwilling to tolerate her husband's heavy drinking, extramarital affairs, and gradual addiction to drugs. Good for her! But because she was a devout Catholic, she never remarried. After the divorce, she had her own battles with alcoholism and suffered a bout with cancer.

My favorite living Kennedy woman, albeit by marriage, is Joan, Ted's first wife, who is both drop-dead gorgeous and a lovely person. I could relax with her. I don't always like to talk, and Joan often didn't say a lot. To show how much I thought of her, in an unofficial will written ten days after Jack announced his bid for the presidency, I stipulated that if Jack and I were killed, she and Ted should raise Caroline as their own child.

Joan and Ted had a terrible marriage, and she would frequently come and discuss it with me. Ted usually ignored her and was often unkind to her, but she was particularly upset about his womanizing. I told her that was just the way Kennedy men are, that it was nothing personal, and that she would have to decide if it was worth it to stay with him. They seemed to have little in common, and I wondered why he had married her in the first place.

Unfortunately, in my opinion, she decided to stay with him, and became a severe alcoholic. Unfortunately, too, she was the least extravagant of all the Kennedys. Joe, Sr. said that she and Ted were the only ones in the family who lived within their means. Personally, I think Joan would have been better off spending than swilling.

Joan clearly was a desperate woman. She couldn't cope with the Kennedys. Although she tried hard to fit in, she just wasn't able to. I didn't fit in either, but I had the stamina to hold my ground and fight the family's destructive forces. Perhaps she sought me out to borrow some of my strength. I helped her out whenever I could. When she had her first child, she didn't have a home, clothes, or any preparation for campaigning with Ted. So I found them a fully furnished house two blocks away from me, hired an Irish nursemaid for the baby, and lent Joan some of my chic Balenciaga and Chanel clothes to wear while campaigning.

It was me she came to for help when she realized how serious her drinking problem had become. She also turned to me after her divorce, and following the sudden death of an investment banker she had planned to marry. I invited her to visit me after his funeral, and she came for a week. She fell apart as soon as she saw me. "The heartache never ends, Jackie," she said, sobbing. "I finally meet a decent man, and he's ripped away from me. It's not fair!"

I put my arms around her and held her like a baby. After she had calmed down, I said, "After all we've gone through, can you still expect life to be fair?" I told her we had to take whatever happiness we could find, and we had to keep marching on. After all, we had children.

The most outrageous media gossip was that Teddy and I were lovers. It bothered me because I liked Joan and didn't want to upset her, and she had enough problems without that. Anyway, although I always liked Ted and am grateful that he was there when I needed him, to me he was always Jack's little brother. Besides, I always liked older men, and he was about my age.

I am happy to say that late in her life, Joan overcame her alcoholism and went back to school to get her master's degree in music. I'm proud of her. The thought that I may have helped Joan regain her mental health is most gratifying to me, and helps me get through my own dark days.

The one Kennedy woman I think I could have been friends with was Kathleen, or "Kick," who was killed in an airplane accident before I met Jack. She was his favorite sister, and he adored her. They spent a lot of time with each other and often traveled together. Although she wasn't beautiful in the conventional sense (her nose was too big), she had an incredibly magnetic personality like her brother Jack, and people were drawn to her like ants to a picnic. When Kick was in a room, she was always the center of a crowd, many pushing and shoving to get close to her. Like Jack (and, with all due modesty, me), no matter the number of people present, she had the ability to focus all her attention on the person with whom she was speaking, and thus make each one feel that he or she was the most special individual in the world.

She also had a marvelous sense of humor, which was much like Jack's. Years after she died, men would talk about her with tears in their eyes. One man, who spoke of her with a longing expression in his eyes fifty years after her death, said she was the most sensuous woman he had ever met. Jack said I reminded him of Kick. Knowing how much he loved her, I consider that comment one of the nicest things he ever said to me.

Kick figured in Jack's life well after her death. Jack always had a hard time sleeping. His friend Lem told me that Jack found it easier to sleep with a woman by his side. He would imagine the woman was a friend of Kick's and that, the next morning, they would all three have breakfast together. Then he was able to fall asleep.

Kick loved England and, for all ostensible purposes, abandoned America to become an Englishwoman. She was fresh, presumptuous, and daring, and the British loved her for it. Only Kick could have gotten away with calling the staid Duke of Marlborough "Dukie Wookie" and coming up to some young earl or lady and asking, "What's new, kid?" Unlike most debutantes, Kick wasn't intimidated when presented to the king and queen in a room full of princesses and daughters of diplomats. Behind the sovereigns' backs, she was not above calling them "Georgie Porgie" and "Lizzie." Nevertheless, for days, she practiced the curtseys she had learned from the nuns at the convent. Like Jack (and me), she was uncomfortable revealing her feelings, and pushed away those who dared to be intrusive. In this sense, she fit in perfectly with the British aristocracy.

When she was only seventeen or eighteen years old, she became a friend of Lady Astor. Kick, daughter of the most fervent Catholic woman in the United States, ignored the fact that Lady Astor was notoriously anti-Catholic. Told that Kick often went to Sunday Mass, Lady Astor muttered, "How do you bear all the mumbo-jumbo?" Kick made British society her own, and it was whispered about her that she belonged at the center of the country's upper-class as surely as if she had been born to it.

Kick dared to defy her Catholic mother, even though threatened with disinheritance, and married William John Robert Cavendish, marquess of Hartington, a Protestant and the eldest son and heir of the tenth duke of Devonshire. (I always knew I could have loved that girl.) Unfortunately, after a few ecstatic years together, Billy died in an airplane crash. Kathleen was devastated. Rose, her dear mother, told her grieving daughter that Billy's death was God's way of punishing her for leaving her church. Just what a person in deep mourning needs to hear!

A few years later, incredibly, Kathleen was also killed in an airplane crash. Jack was utterly destroyed. He burst out crying when he heard the news, and sobbed, "My heart is broken. My heart is broken." Then he holed up in his room for weeks. He never stopped missing her.

Her death made Jack increasingly conscious of life's fragility, and

that any one of us can be wiped away in a second. From then on, he decided, he would live each hour, each minute, to the fullest, in what Martin Luther King, Jr. called "the fierce urgency of now." By the time Jack was forty years old, he had already squeezed in a lifetime of activity. How sad that he lost so many loved ones at so young an age. The losses changed him, and came close to ruining his life.

Chapter 9
JACK'S OTHER WOMEN

I never understood why Jack couldn't find enough satisfaction in our bed to meet his sexual needs. He always seemed to enjoy making love with me, but yet, this essentially kind and caring man didn't seem bothered by how dreadfully he hurt me each time he had sex with another woman. I can only blame his father, who, by example and encouragement, distorted Jack's values terribly. He taught Jack that his own pleasure came before everything else and that he needn't feel guilty about it. Much as I loved Joe, Sr., I'll never forgive him for that.

Joe was an outrageous philanderer who slept with his mistresses, including the great screen actress Gloria Swanson, right under his wife's nose. One or another of his women frequently lived in the Kennedy house, and Joe was known for his uninhibited attempts to seduce the friends of his daughters and the wives of his friends. When Joe and Rose traveled on a steamer to Europe, he took Gloria right along with them. Even Gloria wondered how Rose could put up with her husband's boorishness.

But Rose had been raised to believe that self-sacrifice, self-denial, and self-renunciation were crosses women were designed to bear, and she pretended not to notice that these "friends" of her husband were

sleeping with him. She graciously treated them as honored guests. Her daughters were not embarrassed by Joe's shameful treatment of Rose, but, in fact, seemed proud of her submissiveness. One can imagine the humiliation Rose must have kept locked up inside herself. I certainly can.

And yet, there is another side to the story that one rarely hears about. Rose, a stalwart Catholic, believed that copulation, even among married couples, should be only for procreation, and kept her husband at a distance save for the once every nine months it took to make a baby. And even those rare sexual treats were curtailed with the birth of Teddy. At age forty, Rose decided not to have any more children.

One has to feel a bit sorry for this naturally lusty man deprived of marital privileges by his wife, so perhaps it was not all Joe's fault that he felt forced to turn to other women for sex. His sons did not criticize their father's treatment of their mother, but rather admired his sexual behavior, considering it sophisticated and the essence of manliness. It doesn't take a psychologist to understand how natural it was for them to follow in Joe's wanton footsteps. Just as Joe took his mistresses to Hyannis Port, Jack brought them to the White House. Passing women around and bragging about their sexual conquests was typical of Kennedy men. Only Bobby, who adored and respected his mother and shared her religious bent, was different—at least I thought so, until I heard rumors of his affair with Marilyn Monroe. But in general, he didn't challenge his father's behavior, nor did he emulate it. As a result, he was excluded from his brothers' carousing and was labeled a puritan by Jack. Perhaps that is why Bobby married at age twenty-five and had the only good, lasting marriage of all the Kennedy sons.

Many women would have walked out on so philandering a husband as Jack. But my mother had pointed out my feminine shortcomings my whole life, brainwashing me to the point where I regarded Jack's sexual behavior as proof of my inadequacy as a woman. It wasn't that I didn't want a faithful husband. It was that I didn't feel I deserved one. I told myself I was lucky to have anything when I could so easily have had nothing at all.

In my decision to stay with Jack, most important of all was not what his father offered me, but the fact that I grew up with a father every bit as much a philanderer, and it didn't keep me from loving him one bit. Black Jack used to regale me with stories of the women he had slept with. I would point out a beautiful woman, perhaps the mother of one of my classmates, and say, "That one, Daddy?" I would quiver with delight when he would answer proudly, "Not yet, but I will," or, "Oh yes, that one."

Looking back now, I can see that I served as an enabler, and that my father may well have enjoyed showing off his sexual prowess to me as much as he did engaging in activities with the ladies. Was I somehow as proud of Jack's attractiveness as I was of my father's?

Besides, although it pains me to admit it, when Jack's plans to be president were no longer just a grandiose fantasy, I had no intention of giving up my wish to live a life of historical significance.

When Jack became president, you'd think he would have protected his interests by refraining from any action that might have jeopardized them. Anyone who thinks that simply didn't know Jack. The more reckless the activity, the more it excited him, and he engaged in behavior that had every possibility of derailing his presidential career. The summer after she was born, I took Caroline up to Cape Cod. Jack, then a senator, took advantage of my absence to begin an affair with Pamela Turnure, a receptionist in his Senate office who everybody said looked like a miniature version of me. He spent many a late night in her apartment. I had to wonder why he needed Pam when he had the real Jackie in his bed. I also questioned his need for Pam so soon after Caroline was born. He adored

Caroline, and being a father seemed to validate his sense of self, just as being a mother did mine.

Pam's landlady, Florence Kater, infuriated by the idea of a potential president cheating on his wife, launched an attack against Jack, including letters to the newspapers, to Jack's father (hah!), and even to such important figures as Eleanor Roosevelt and Boston's Cardinal Cushing. Fortunately for Jack, journalists at that time customarily refused to publish information about the sex lives of politicians.

Apparently unworried that they would break with journalistic tradition, Jack continued his outrageous behavior. He slept with every woman available and some who were not.

As you have gathered by now, I am a great lover of Dorothy Parker's wisdom. Another quip of hers fits Jack to a T: "If all the girls who attended the Harvard-Yale game were laid end to end, I wouldn't be a bit surprised."

In Washington and on the road, Jack's buddies provided him a revolving White House wheel of sexual partners. On the rare occasion when none was available, he could always turn to willing staff members, of whom there were plenty. Someone was always lying (or should I say laying) in wait for my charismatic husband, the most powerful man in the world. I've heard that the duke of Devonshire remarked, "Jack did for sex what Eisenhower accomplished for golf."

I had my ways, flimsy as they were, of coping with his scandalous behavior. With most of my friends, I pretended not to know the truth, and preferred that they consider me naive rather than pity me. With some of Jack's friends who helped him obtain his floozies, I indicated that I knew quite well what was going on but simply didn't care. In any case, it helped a bit when he was on the road, when I didn't have to view his muck right under my nose.

Looking back now, I realize what I didn't in the early days of my marriage: By being chronically late, I was trying to punish Jack for his dalliances. I could have sworn I just "needed the time" to look my best. But now, in my older years, I know better, and try to be more open, honest, and forthright about my true feelings.

As Jack emerged into the spotlight, his behavior became more and more risky, and did not escape the notice of at least a few insightful others. After he was elected president, one of his Secret Service agents said, "Kennedy is the kind of guy who runs through fires holding a full can of gasoline."

In 1960, a month after I became pregnant with John, Jack began an affair with Judith Campbell, to whom he had been introduced by Frank Sinatra. Soon after, Sinatra also presented her to the Mafia boss Sam Giancana. Even columnist Arthur Krock, a family friend, warned Jack that he had better be careful or a newspaper exposé would bring down his presidency. Joe, Sr. informed Krock that Americans didn't give a damn how many times Jack got laid.

Americans *do* care how many times Jack got laid. They want their president to be a man they admire and look up to.

In the first year of his presidency, Jack made a grave error of judgment that left him devastated. At the end of President Dwight D. Eisenhower's second term, the CIA began training a company of anti-Castro Cubans in Guatemala. Jack had been informed of the plans to land the force in Cuba and to try to assassinate Castro. Not wanting to seem a sissy to Khrushchev, Jack ordered the Defense Department to proceed with the invasion and attempt the overthrow. The success of the plan to establish a non-Communist government depended on support from the people of Cuba. Unfortunately, we didn't get it. Our forces were put ashore at the Bay of Pigs, where they were easily captured by Castro and his troops. Failure to assess correctly the loyalty of the Cuban people was almost the swan song of Jack's presidency, scarcely before it had begun.

The next day, *The New York Times* wrote that the invasion's failure had shaken other countries' trust in the United States. "Kennedy has lost his magic," a newspaper headline blasted. A humiliated Jack was more deeply depressed than I had ever seen him. Some of the invading exiles escaped to the sea, while more than one hundred were killed, and almost twelve hundred surrendered and were taken prisoner by Castro's forces.

These men on the beaches, having set off with great hopes and having fought courageously, disregarding the danger to themselves, had been shot down like dogs or imprisoned by Castro. The images flooded Jack's mind. The only other time I'd ever seen him cry before then was in the hospital when his back wasn't healing and he was sure he would never get well. I had watched helplessly as tears filled his eyes and poured down his cheeks. Now, again, this time in the bedroom, he buried his head in his hands and sobbed, and allowed me to take him into my arms.

The prisoners remained in captivity for twenty months as the United States and Castro negotiated terms for their release. Castro finally agreed to accept fifty-three million dollars' worth of baby food and drugs in exchange for the prisoners. The Bay of Pigs failure had a lasting effect on Jack's reputation and, indeed, on the conflict between the two nations.

Don't tell anybody (and I never would have told him this), but I blame Jack at least partly for the catastrophe. Jack was arrogant. Nobody could tell him anything: He always knew it all. Although he had inherited a growing invasion force from President Eisenhower, Jack allowed it to keep expanding at a fast pace. He could have called off the attack at any time, as General Maxwell Taylor, whom Jack himself had appointed to teach him the ropes of conducting an invasion, had advised. When Jack planned the attack on Cuba, did he consult with Robert McNamara, his secretary of defense, General Eisenhower, or the joint chiefs of staff? Of course not. Although Jack's experience in warfare was limited to commanding a PT boat, he was supremely confident that he knew better than these experienced, died-in-the-wool soldiers how to conduct an invasion. Many experts could have told him, had they been consulted, that an amphibious nighttime landing on an unknown beach would be practically impossible for a well-trained army, let alone the Cuban exiles who had received only a few months of training.

Nor did I ever hear him consider whether it was ethical or moral for one government to assault another; he only thought about how to make the attack more successful. But bad as it was, the failure was far from a total calamity. In all likelihood, it helped the United States avert a much greater disaster—a nuclear one—eighteen months later when Jack managed the Cuban Missile Crisis with much greater consultation.

Broken up as he was about the situation, I love that Jack never lost his sense of humor. When asked, "What do you think about the Bay of Pigs?" he answered, "I think about it as little as possible."

When caution was most necessary, however, Jack again jeopardized his presidency with an extremely foolhardy act. You'd think he would have learned from the Profumo scandal in England, which ruined Prime Minister Macmillan's career. But he seemed to feel that no such thing ever could happen to him. Not ten minutes after I left for our Glen Ora estate in Virginia, Jack had Judith Campbell brought into the White House—*the* Judith Campbell, whose close association with the Mafia, if publicized, almost certainly would have brought down Jack's presidency. He walked this woman, who looked and talked precisely like the moll she was, through my beautiful, meticulous bedroom and the adjoining closet I had built for him so he wouldn't have to stoop to open his drawers or pick up his shoes, and then to his bedroom, which I had furnished so lovingly. A few hours later, his limo was en route to Glen Ora to see me, and Campbell was on her way to Chicago, where she rejoined Giancana.

Jack took no security measures with the women he was intimate with. Any one of them could have had a listening device to record their shenanigans, a poisoned-filled syringe, or a knife or bomb in her purse. I doubt if Jack knew of Campbell's association with criminals, although the fact that they had been introduced to each other by Sinatra should have been enough of a heads-up. Nor, in all probability, was he aware that Giancana had been recruited by the CIA to assassinate Castro after the Bay of Pigs fiasco. Even Jack wouldn't have been that foolish. Nevertheless, news that the president of the United States was sharing a woman with a Mafia kingpin secretly hired by the U.S. government to kill Castro surely would have destroyed Jack's presidency.

Of course, another of Jack's notorious affairs was with Marilyn Monroe. He did not love her—she was just his biggest celebrity "lollipop." They first met at a party at Peter Lawford's Santa Monica house, and first had sex on a trip he took to California in 1961, when they spent a lot of time in the hot tub together. They had sex again when Peter smuggled her into New York's Carlyle Hotel in a brown wig and dowdy dress. For their next meeting, Peter brought Marilyn to Bing Crosby's estate in Palm Springs, California, where Jack was relaxing after delivering a speech on morality at the University of California at Berkeley.

Everybody in the movie business, including Peter, knew how disturbed Marilyn was. Jack also knew, and had just been warned by the FBI to take care or he would lose his presidency, but that didn't deter him one bit. After her marriage to Arthur Miller had broken up the year before, Marilyn had been confined to the Payne Whitney psychiatric hospital in New York. On her discharge, she regressed to her drug and liquor addictions, was discovered at least once in a drug coma, and began a downward slide that ended with her death.

The poor woman was really out of it and believed Jack was so in love that he wanted to marry her. "I am the little orphan waif indulging in free love with the leader of the free world," she bragged. Pathetic or not, Marilyn had the audacity to call me up at the White House and announce that she and Jack were in love and were going to get married, and would I kindly drop out of the picture?

I said, "Marilyn, I'd be glad to. It would be a big relief to me. I'm fed up doing everything required of the first lady. But then you'll have to come live at the White House and take care of all the business of running it." She sputtered a bit and hung up. I received no more phone calls from Marilyn.

A few weeks before her next rendezvous with Jack, she appeared, obviously high (or intoxicated) and unkempt, at the Golden Globe Awards ceremony. Without considering whether another public appearance would bring out similar behavior, Peter invited this very sick lady to attend a celebration of Jack's forty-fifth birthday on May 19, 1962 in Madison Square Garden, and to sing "happy birthday, Mr. President."

There is much speculation about why I didn't attend Jack's birthday party. The official reason was that I was riding in the Loudon County horse show. I did ride there, but it was a competition I could easily have scratched from my schedule. But does anyone believe I would attend a public celebration where my husband's mistress was going to sing "Happy Birthday" to him in front of millions of Americans? That masochistic I'm not.

I've been told that Marilyn wore a fur over a dress so tight it was hard for her to walk across the stage. Wiggling into the spotlight, she cast off her fur and revealed a flesh-colored dress covered with rhinestones. She appeared practically nude. Obviously stoned, she shut her eyes, ran her tongue over her lips, and threw her hands up and down her thighs and stomach, stopping at her breasts. Dorothy Kilgallen wrote in her Broadway column that Marilyn made love to the president in full view of forty million Americans. My husband, the joker, quipped that he could now leave politics after having had "Happy Birthday" sung to him in so sweet and wholesome a manner.

But Marilyn's "sweet, wholesome" rendition proved to be her swan song with Jack. Distressed that everyone was talking about Mr. President and the Movie Star, he instructed his staff to deny the story, and he never saw Marilyn again.

In a panic, Marilyn repeatedly phoned the White House to try to get through to Jack. She kept calling frantically, hour after hour, on the private line to the Oval Office he had installed for her. When he didn't respond, she threatened to go to the newspapers and reveal how Jack had mistreated her. She then embarrassed him by telling all their friends that he made love like a teenager—"a minute-on and a minute-off kind of lover." Annoyed by her persistence, Jack had their private line disconnected and sent Bobby to try to control her. Peter Lawford met Bobby at the airport and drove him to Marilyn's house in Brentwood, where Peter left them alone to talk.

Within minutes, he heard shouting, with Bobby yelling that he was going back to Peter's house and Marilyn screaming that Bobby had said he would spend the afternoon alone with her. I was heartbroken when Peter told me the story. Marilyn became more and more agitated, and said she would definitely call the newspapers the next day and tell everyone how she had been treated by the Kennedy brothers. Bobby, enraged, told her to stop bothering him and Jack— neither wanted any more letters or phone calls from her, or anything else to do with her. Then, according to Peter, Marilyn cursed Bobby and banged at his chest with her fists. Then she picked up a small kitchen knife and leapt at him. Peter seized her hand and, knocking her to the floor, yanked away the knife. The men then called Dr. Ralph Greenson, Marilyn's psychoanalyst, who came within the hour, gave her a shot to calm her down, and stayed with her all night.

For Jack, that would have been the end of the Marilyn story, except that on August 4, 1962, Peter Lawford called in hysterics to inform us that she had been found dead of an overdose of the sleeping pills Nembutal and chloral hydrate. He said he had been worried that she had not shown up at his house for dinner, and went to her home to investigate. There, the housekeeper told him that she had found Marilyn dead in her bed, face down and naked, with one hand on the telephone. (Was the failed call a desperate cry for help, when it was already too late?) Curled up in her fingers was a wadded piece of paper. Scribbled on it was the private telephone number set up for her in the Oval Office.

Lawford persuaded his friend Fred Otash, a private detective, to go through Marilyn's home and carefully remove any evidence that might implicate Jack or Bobby. Otash apparently did his job well: All validation of their relationship with her, along with the crumpled piece of paper, disappeared forever.

After a "psychological autopsy" by the coroner, Marilyn's death was declared "a probable suicide." She was thirty-six years old. Was it a suicide? I don't know. Nor do I dare to think about it.

I was so upset by the way Marilyn was exploited by men that I refused to see Arthur Miller's play, *After the Fall*, when it opened in New York in 1964. In it, he portrayed Marilyn as a self-destructive slut who had brought about her own downfall. But the poor woman had been treated abominably by many men, including Jack and Bobby. Marilyn had valued loyalty above everything else. The last thing she needed was to be betrayed by Miller, the husband she adored.

As far as the relationship this pathetic woman had with Jack and Bobby is concerned, it is one of the few things about them I cannot find a place in my heart to forgive. She was a desperately ill woman who needed to be treated with love and compassion. If they couldn't bring themselves to do so, they should never have taken her on in the first place. I'm afraid that, with all their wonderful qualities and gifts, they never learned to treat women as human beings, but blindly followed the example of Joe, Sr., who regarded all women as objects to be used for his pleasure.

Both Jack and Bobby, however, showed in other aspects of their lives that they could learn and grow. Their affairs with Marilyn took place before the days of feminism. Naive though I might be, I like to believe that if they had lived, they would have learned to correct this abominable blind spot.

Chapter 10

R O S E M A R Y

The most tragic of the Kennedy sisters was the oldest girl, Rosemary, who was born with a mild form of mental retardation. She was a shy child, but nevertheless always seemed happy. While she couldn't keep up with her brothers and sisters at athletics or schoolwork, it never sounded to me as if she was *so* retarded before her surgery. She loved opera and pretty clothes, and was normal enough to be presented to the queen at Buckingham Palace. While the authorized history of the family tells us that Rosemary had the body of a grown woman and the mind of a four-year-old child, the diary she wrote before her lobotomy tells a different story. Here is a sample entry:

Jack and Kick and I went to lunch in the White House ballroom. James Roosevelt came to see us and introduced us to his father, President Roosevelt. The President put his arm around us and said, "I've been waiting for you to come visit me. Which one of you is the oldest? You are all so big I can't tell."

She doesn't sound *that* retarded to me. Does she to you?

Named after her mother, Rosemary was the prettiest of the Kennedy sisters, with a fresh freckled face and an open, direct demeanor. From her earliest days, unfortunately, she developed slowly: She walked late, talked late, and was delayed in all the customary benchmarks of childhood. Mothers intuitively sense these things about their children. I knew exactly how well Caroline and John would eventually do in school, even when they were still in their cribs. (Secret: I always thought Caroline was the smarter of the two. And I was the only one in the United States who wasn't shocked at *The Daily News*'s headline, "The Hunk Flunks," when John failed his bar exam for the third time.)

Although Rosemary passed for normal for a while everywhere else, Rose Kennedy knew quite early that all was not right with her oldest daughter. In those days, mental retardation was considered shameful, and knowledge of such a condition was confined to the afflicted family. This is what Jack and his siblings were brought up to believe. They were informed that anyone who questioned them about her differences was to be told simply that she was a shy and quiet child.

Rose and Joe, Sr. taught their children to be ashamed of their sister. They did not make it clear that there are different ways of being, and people should be valued for who they are. If I had such a child—and I brought Caroline up to think this way, too, which is why she is always so kind and gentle to her aunt—I'd like to think I would have been able to find her lovable qualities and cherish her for them. But thank God it hasn't been necessary for me to test this out.

To try to bring the girl "up to par," Rose, to the detriment of Jack, spent countless hours and days with Rosemary, hitting many a ball to her on the tennis court and trying to teach her to write, spell, and count better. Rose had extremely limited success.

When a procession of tutors and teachers didn't improve the situation much, Rose sent her fifteen-year-old daughter to Elmhurst, the Sacred Heart Convent in Providence, Rhode Island. There was no program for retarded children at the convent, but because the

Kennedys made huge contributions to the school, Rosemary was taught in a schoolroom of her own by two nuns and a special teacher who worked with her all day long. Rosemary wore the same uniform as the other girls and, to the casual observer, looked the same, but she was not the same. She could read and write at only the fourth-grade level, and hard as she tried, she was never able to get beyond that.

She loved her father passionately, tried desperately to win his love, and was most unhappy when she couldn't do schoolwork that pleased him. "I would do anything I could to make you happy," she once wrote him. Whether he couldn't bear the thought of retardation in his family of "winners" or simply wasn't interested in a slow learner, Rosemary never succeeded in gaining his attention, let alone his love.

Watching Rosemary try unsuccessfully to keep up with her younger sisters was excruciatingly painful for Rose, who felt that a mother suffers more for her "special" child than the child does herself. Rosemary desperately craved praise, and Rose sought out the minutest details of Rosemary's life to provide it. "Rosemary," she said, "you have the most beautiful teeth in the family." And, "Oh, what a lovely hair ribbon you're wearing today! Did you pick it out yourself?"

One has to feel sorry for Rosemary, an intellectually challenged child in a brilliant family—she didn't fit in. As a child, she had no friends of her own and usually tagged along with her younger sisters. The girls, who probably resented having to take care of Rosemary, were always way ahead of her on their bicycles, waving at her to catch up, while her brothers shouted at her from their boat while she stood forlornly on the shore.

Picturing her at the dinner table is particularly poignant. Joe, Sr., at the head of the table, would ask Joe, Jr., Jack, and Kathleen questions about various civic events. Try as Rosemary might, she just couldn't grasp the meaning of the questions, let alone the answers. And even if she did figure things out on occasion, the family by then had already moved on to another topic. Tiring of watching, and of unsuccessfully taking part in family activities, she would sometimes break out in an inexplicable rage, the fury pouring out of her like steam from a teapot.

Though Rose somehow got Rosemary through her presentation to the court at Buckingham Palace, the occasion wasn't entirely without mishap. The deep curtsey required for the occasion is different from other curtsies, and many girls making their debut in court traveled to the Vacani School of Dancing near Harrods to learn it. The debutantes practiced for months. Rosemary practiced even more. She first stood holding the barre, as in ballet class, then bent deeply to the floor with a crooked left knee, her left foot behind her, and a perfectly straight back. She rehearsed with a curtain, to simulate a train, gave her gown a kick so as not to get caught in it, and, standing tall, walked gracefully to where her mother was impersonating the queen. When Rose judged her ready to curtsey before the real queen, Rosemary was bidden to wear a fixed smile that was *de rigueur* for the occasion. But no matter how many hours Rosemary practiced, Rose was terrified that she wouldn't get it right and made Rosemary spend so much time at it that her neck went into spasms if she turned her head a fraction of an inch to the left or the right.

The entrance of the king and queen into the giant ballroom signaled the beginning of the two-hour ceremony. The debutantes walked forward two by two to take their bows before the monarchs. Kathleen and Rosemary marched side by side on the red carpet until they approached the thrones. Smiling like carved Halloween pumpkins, they stopped and, kicking their gowns aside, curtsied to the still smiling queen. (Her cheeks must have ached from all that smiling. I know mine often did. A gentle, low-level smile is OK for a while, but it's the really broad fixed smile that exhausts you.) Then the girls, still facing the queen, were to glide off to the right and slip silently out a side door. Just as Rose was about to breathe a sigh of relief, Rosemary tripped and almost fell. She had messed up the most important moment in a girl's social life. Rose gasped, thinking—in spite of herself—*Can't that girl ever do anything right?*

I can feel for Rose. If Caroline had fallen on her face when presented to the queen at the age of eight, I would have died right there on the spot. I was so proud of her when she carried it off flawlessly! But in any case, the pasteboard monarchs pretended not to have seen Rosemary's miscue and kept right on smiling as if nothing had happened. Rosemary recovered and followed Kathleen out the door. Rose never talked about the ceremony and reacted as if it were an absolute triumph for both her daughters. And Rosemary? Because she didn't have the social graces of the rest of the family, and because nobody ever mentioned it, she probably hoped no one was aware of her blunder.

The older she got, the worse things became. A guest said that it was sometimes embarrassing to be around Rosemary. She would behave strangely at the dinner table even though the family pretended not to notice. Or she might suddenly appear in her nightgown when a party was going on in the living room. Worst of all, she could no longer imagine that she was part of the lives of her brothers and sisters. Even Jack did not seem to have time for her anymore. So Rose began to send her away to a special camp in New Hampshire for the summer. Not fitting in with the other campers any better than she did with her siblings, she tried hard to please, to the point where she didn't complain that her feet hurt until a counselor noticed they were covered with blood.

As she got older, she became more and more aggressive and developed violent mood swings. At the Sacred Heart Convent, she began to sneak out at night and wander about the streets. Heaven only knows what she did in her wanderings. Her parents were worried that she would get pregnant or hurt in her nightly walkabouts. I believe Joe was terrified that news of her abnormality or, heaven forbid, of an illegitimate child would creep out, become public knowledge, and interfere with his all-consuming desire to see one of his sons in the White House.

That was the era when Dr. Walter Freeman and his partner, Dr. James Watts, were experimenting with a new treatment called "prefrontal lobotomy." The doctors persuaded Joe that the operation would reduce Rosemary's violent mood swings and ease her rages. I

don't imagine he needed much persuasion. Without consulting his wife, he gave permission for the so-called surgeons (Dr. Freeman had no formal surgical training) to proceed with the operation. Nor did he tell Rose about it—for twenty years.

Watts drilled two holes on each side of Rosemary's head and, with a large hyperemic needle, inserted about two and a half inches of tubing into her brain. He then took a spatula that resembled a blunt butter knife and pounded it into the cavity he had carved out, then twisted the spatula until he destroyed the white matter of her frontal lobe. He repeated the procedure with three other cuts.

The surgery had catastrophic results. Rosemary became almost totally incapacitated and regressed to an infantile state. Left incontinent, she had only the ability to mumble a few words and sat for hours doing nothing but looking at the walls. Only her flashes of rage continued as before. From a beautiful, mildly retarded young woman with a sweet, ingratiating personality able to function in her own slow way, she became a vegetable who required full-time care in an institution.

The family paid her bills, but otherwise abandoned her, except for Eunice, who founded the Special Olympics in honor of her sister. Rose and her other children repressed the horror of what Joe had done to his daughter and behaved as if Rosemary no longer existed. When Rose wrote letters to her children, she addressed them as "my dear children" or "my darlings," mentioning each child in turn by name: Joe, Jr., Jack, Kathleen, Eunice, Pat, Jean, Bobby, and Ted. There was no reference to Rosemary.

When Rose first visited Rosemary after the surgery, unaware that it had happened, she was so upset by what she saw that she didn't come to see her again for twenty years. When Rose finally forced herself again to drop in on Rosemary, Rosemary turned her back on Rose and refused to have anything to do with her. Her caretaker nun, Sister Margaret Ann, said that Rosemary knew both that she'd had the surgery and that her mother had never showed up for her. Rose left the visit deeply upset. I'm sure it hurt her terribly—I know it would me. Whatever Rosemary's condition, she was still Rose's child. And retarded or not, she was smart enough to put in action the maxim, "Don't get angry, get even."

After Dr. Freeman performed over three thousand "ice pick lobotomies," in which he inserted an ice pick through the patient's eye socket into his or her brain to destroy brain tissue, his theory was discredited. It was too late for Rosemary and many of Dr. Freeman's other victims, who lived out their lives in infantile regressions. Even if Rosemary had been initially as retarded as they say, there were other solutions the family could have found to deal with the problem. Hiring a nurse-companion to be with her around the clock or sending her to a psychiatric hospital skilled in managing such cases would have controlled Rosemary's escapades. Many retarded people live comfortably with their loving families. But Joe, who was unable or unwilling to deal with the embarrassment of having a deviant daughter, was terrified that word of her "sins" would become public knowledge. Chopping up her brains at least kept her out of the public eye.

Although I loved Joe dearly, something in me will never forgive him for what he did to Rosemary. Sometimes, in the dead of the night, I would say to myself, "Love Joe? How can I love a butcher? I detest him for what he did to his child." Then I would wake up in the morning and put the whole thing aside. After all, Joe was the patriarch and Jack loved him dearly. I had to live with Jack.

I don't know how much Jack knew or understood about what had been done to Rosemary. He never mentioned her to me. I only found out the true story when Eunice shocked me with all the details. I was upset at the time, but now I'm glad she told me, for it helps me understand Jack better. A man so sensitive to nuances must have picked up on the brutal punishment visited on his oldest sister for failing to conform to Kennedy standards. Even with all the repression going on in the family, some of that dreadful story must have seeped through the cracks in his brain. Somewhere, it must have registered and done irreversible damage.

I think about that when I remember his inability to be alone, his habits of fidgeting with his socks or his nose and drumming his fingers on his knees, and his restless right hand—that busy fist that seemed to have a life of its own. It's interesting that he was the first president to set up a government program for the prevention and treatment of mental retardation. I always thought he launched the program because of Eunice's special athletics program, but now I wonder if it wasn't also to appease his own guilt.

Whatever happened to all the childhood memories Jack must have had that were so intertwined with Rosemary? It's unlikely that they simply disappeared, but like the rest of his family's recollections (except Eunice's), they were deeply repressed. They simply were not discussed among the parents or their children or, to my knowledge, anywhere else.

Jack was born only fifteen months before Rosemary, and would have had very little mother available even if his sister had been normal. Rose herself admitted that it bothered her that Jack had not gotten the early attention he needed, because she had to devote most of her time and energy to Rosemary. In addition, he was a sickly infant and developed a serious case of scarlet fever at the same time his mother, sequestered in childbirth, lay with Rosemary. He lay there listlessly as his fever climbed to 104 degrees, unable to do anything but clutch his favorite teddy bear. He was sent to an isolation ward in a hospital, where he lay frightened and alone for a month.

Well, not quite alone. Strangely enough, Joe, Sr., terrified that he was going to lose Jack, left work early for the first time in anyone's memory and came and sat alongside his sick son's bed until he recovered. This fatherly action must have been a paradigm for Jack, who later behaved similarly at the bedside of Patrick, his dying baby.

Even at this early age, Jack was able to attract people to him. Utterly captivated by him, the nurses and doctors paid him more attention than the other sick children. I read somewhere that abandoned babies in orphanages able to attract the attention of passersby frequently live longer than similarly deprived infants. I believe that, like those neglected babies, Jack's charm saved his life. Besides learning the value of being charismatic, he discovered that pain, fear, and loneliness eventually pass. The knowledge served him in good stead through all his later illnesses.

Although Jack never talked about what it was like for him to have a mentally retarded sister, I know from Eunice that he was held responsible for Rosemary's well-being all through his growing-up years. I disapprove of making one child responsible for another, in particular a "defective" child. It takes the responsibility away from the parent, where it belongs, and places it on the shoulders of a person emotionally unequipped to handle it. It steals away his or her childhood.

In addition, if something goes wrong with the disabled child, the normal one, even if not guilty of neglect, is set up to carry around a load of guilt all of his life. While sailing, sledding, or even walking, Jack and Joe, Jr. were put in daily charge of Rosemary, but they were hardly more than babies themselves. Later, when they were old enough to go to dances, they were ordered to dance with her and get their friends to fill out her dance card. Jack was told to put his name at the top and then go around the room soliciting friends to fill out the rest of it. One cannot help but wonder how much he could have enjoyed those dances. No wonder he was never a great dancer. Joe, Jr., Eunice, and Jack were ordered to watch out for Rosemary and make sure she was safe and secure at all times.

Jack served as her main protector and watchdog. He made her laugh, took her as crew on his boat and, when they were older, was even sent to her school in Rhode Island by his mother to escort Rosemary to dances there. He was a model brother for a retarded girl, though it was work he was not psychologically prepared to take on. Just think of a little boy of two or three having to take care of an older retarded sister! Then again, it may well have trained him to take on and succeed at other impossible jobs—the presidency, for instance.

So why didn't he ever talk to me about Rosemary? I believe that underneath his brotherly concern, he resented being forced to take on a job that should not have been his. Full of guilt, he not only had been given so much more than his sister, but was unable to stop his father from slaughtering her.

But the more I think of how close Jack and Rosemary were, the more I believe he simply couldn't bear the pain of remembering her.

Chapter 11
E T H E L

I have given Bobby's wife, Ethel, a chapter all her own because my
relationship with her was so different from any other relationships
I had with the other Kennedys. She brought out the worst aspects
of my character. I am ashamed when I think about it now, and I wish
it had been otherwise.

Heaven help me, but I never liked Ethel. Nobody knows this,
except maybe Ethel. I found her jealous, competitive, and aggressive.
She appeared cheerful and likeable, but underneath was a seething
kettle of rage that often pierced her veneer like a dart tearing open a
balloon. In front of the public, we were always the dearest of friends.
But in private, despite her moneyed background, she seemed to me
crude, unsubtle, and uncultured—she couldn't tell a Louis Quinze
from a garbage can. A friend spoke of Ethel and her whole family
as "culturally deprived." She was right on target. Ethel's idea of a
great party was to push a person wearing evening clothes into the
swimming pool. I even heard she shoved in a paraplegic friend in a
wheelchair. I suggested that when Ethel give her next formal dinner,
she send out invitations that read "Black tie and flippers." She wasn't
amused.

Jack first brought me to meet his brother Bobby and his wife

Ethel at a St. Patrick's Day party they were giving at their home. Strangely enough, the guests were all instructed to wear black rather than green. I wore a stunning black gown embroidered with silver threads, with a pearl necklace and matching earrings, topped off by a black fur coat. I thought I looked perfect for the occasion, and when he saw me, Jack's shining eyes confirmed my opinion. To my surprise, and everyone else's, Dame Ethel slunk in wearing a green gown, which shimmered under the lights. It was not just one shade of green, but numerous green and silver hues sewed one on top of the other. I must admit it was gorgeous.

I stood in a corner with a wry smile on my face. Now I understood her very well.

After a while, Jack's friend Lem Billings came over to me and said, "Ethel is an interesting woman, don't you think?" When I looked at him skeptically, he said, "When you get to know her, you will like her." I regarded him with a simple smile. Smart fellow that he is, he asked, "Does her behavior tonight upset you?"

"Not at all," I answered. "She's the hostess, and she has every right to dress as she pleases. Personally, of course, I would never do such a thing."

I really am a shy person. Because I didn't know many people at the party, I stood in front of the fireplace and waited for people I knew to approach me. But I heard Ethel loudly whisper to Bobby, "That Bouvier dame is trying to steal all the attention away from me! I know what you're thinking, Bobby—that it's just my imagination. But, believe me, it isn't!"

I ignored her remark, which I could easily overhear, and kept on smiling. Then, a long time before any of the other guests departed, I walked over to Ethel and said, "I'm sorry, Ethel, but I have to leave now."

"What?! Leave before dinner? You can't do that. We have a spectacular meal prepared."

"I'm afraid I have to, Ethel. I have a terrible headache." Jack escorted me to the door, where I had a limo waiting.

"Well, I never . . ." said Ethel.

The next day, I felt bad about my early departure. I wrote her a note thanking her for inviting me to her lovely party and emphasizing how beautiful she looked in all her greenery. Then I invited her to lunch at the Watergate Restaurant and enclosed a green pin in the shape of a shamrock.

The reason I had left the party so early, I told her at lunch, was that I had terrible premenstrual cramps, and I was standing in front of the fireplace only because I was freezing. She laughed. The reason it was so cold, she said, was that Rose Kennedy had called her a spendthrift and said she had to cut down on expenses. She did so by turning down the heat. We laughed heartily together. Apparently, we were going to have something in common after all.

On leaving lunch, I said, "Please, Ethel, can my cramps remain our little secret?"

"Absolutely, Jackie," she said. "I won't tell a soul. I promise." The next week, it was all over Washington society that Jackie Kennedy suffered from premenstrual cramps.

I am a quiet person, and want the people around me to be tranquil and calm. Ethel was neither. She was loud from the day she was born. Although she was a tiny, scrawny newborn infant, I am told she had a cry that pierced the very walls of Chicago's Lying-In Hospital. She hasn't changed much since.

The best description of her that I know of appeared in her graduation yearbook from Manhattanville College in 1948 (where she had to work hard to get mediocre grades). "An excited hoarse voice, a shriek, a peal of screaming laughter, a tousled brown head— that's our Ethel!" Well, she's never been *my* Ethel, no matter how much the Kennedys tried to push us together.

When her son David finally got up enough courage to ask her to talk about his father's death, she said, "It's not a subject I wish to discuss!" David never spoke of it to her again. A few months later, he died of a drug overdose. I still feel sad about his death and wish he had come to me with his request.

It is evident that Ethel was jealous of me, and it's equally evident why. Wherever we went and whatever we did, people made far more of a fuss over me than the "other Mrs. Kennedy." I know it upset her so much that she would often stomp out of the room when I was being feted.

After Jack was killed, Bobby became closer to me than anyone else in the world. For Bobby, I would have put my hand in the fire. In many ways, having him at my side was like having Jack back. I felt so close to him that there is no doubt in my mind I would have married him, were he to have left Ethel. But besides being a devout Catholic, Bobby was a loyal husband and father. At the time, it was hard for me to understand why a sensitive, intelligent man like Bobby was devoted to Ethel and refused to leave her when he could have had me.

Sometimes I have to feel sorry for Ethel. She was brought up exactly the way she raised her own children—a poor little rich girl, undisciplined, allowed to run wild. The Skakel household was large, boisterous, and disruptive, with little parental control. The family was known to their neighbors in Greenwich, who would have nothing to do with them, as "rowdy Irish micks," which I must say was unfair to many well-behaved Irish people I know.

Ethel's mother's world revolved around many outside social activities and centered on keeping her husband happy. As a result, she had little time for her children. Ethel was brought up by maids, with parents who rarely were home and who sent their kids off to boarding school and summer camp as soon as they could get them accepted. I always say that if maids are going to raise the children, the maids should have had them in the first place. When told her parents were going away again, Ethel once threw a terrible tantrum. Her mother advised the maid, "Just keep her busy and she'll forget we're away." No wonder she's run away from problems all her life.

A friend told me that, as a child, Ethel was hyperkinetic and always seemed lost. She had to struggle to find her own identity, which she eventually did (to the degree she did at all) through athletics and horseback riding. Ethel was a hooligan at school and misbehaved outrageously whenever she felt like it. She was permitted to remain in the convent only because her parents plied the nuns with money. Ethel herself told me, guffawing as she spoke, that she behaved so badly that the mother superior called her "a detriment to civilization."

It's true that I was no angel in school, either. I once dumped a pie in a teacher's lap. But what I did was funny, not dangerous. Ethel's brothers were known as hoodlums and punks. Their idea of fun was to shoot up mailboxes and streetlights. Ethel was very much like them—she was irresponsible, defiant, and arrogant. As a teenager, she drove recklessly and at high speeds, smashing up one car after another. She told me that she and her brothers once demolished their mother's brand new car before she had ever been in it. Ethel howled as she told me about it, as if it were a riot. She often was stopped by the police. When I think of some of her children and how they act like little psychopaths, it sounds like déjà vu. But how could Ethel have learned to be a mother when she was never parented herself? With all my complaints about my own mother, at least she disciplined me so I knew how to behave, and as a result was able to teach my own wonderful children to do the same.

To add to her other quirks, Ethel had a reputation for not paying her bills. After Bobby died, Ethel ran into money problems. The Kennedys were on her neck about her extravagances, especially Rose, who was furious with her daughter-in-law for squandering so much Kennedy money.

In Rose's house, if the Kennedys ate steak, the servants ate hamburger; if the Kennedys ate hamburgers, the help ate frankfurters. And believe it or not, the maids and domestics were not allowed any dessert. How stingy can you get? No wonder Jack was not more generous to me. Nobody ever taught him how to be. By contrast, Ethel was far nicer—her servants ate whatever the family did. When they ate steak, so did the help.

In any event, Ethel "solved" her money problems by not paying her bills. Ethel had a little trick she used when she gave an elegant party at home and needed extra furniture. She ordered some lovely antique chairs on approval, kept them until the party was over, and then returned them, often full of food and wine stains. Afraid of arousing the wrath of a Kennedy, the owner let it pass.

Ethel was equally skilled at acquiring sports equipment, such as tennis racquets and skis, for free. She felt that just being able to use her name as an endorsement was payment enough for the merchants.

An incident at Saks West-End, a trendy boutique in Chevy Chase, Maryland, was typical. Ethel, who had an important event to attend, selected an Oleg Cassini $750 black organza dress with a white collar, and instructed the assistant manager, a woman by the name of Jane Alexander, to put it on her account. A week later, while reading a newspaper, Ms. Alexander came across a photo of Ethel wearing the dress. Shortly after, Ethel's maid came to the store with the Cassini, saying Mrs. Kennedy had not worn it and wished to return it. The dress, dirty and food-stained, looked like a limp rag. Ms. Alexander told the maid that Mrs. Kennedy was photographed wearing the designer dress, and the store could not accept its return.

After a few harsh words, the maid took it home. Soon, another maid arrived with the dress on a hanger in a plastic dry cleaner's bag. The dress was still limp because the dry cleaner had not sized it. Ms. Alexander wrote Ethel a note, saying that they were not in the used clothing business, and that if Ethel didn't want the dress, she should sell it to a used clothing store. Needless to say, Ethel never paid her bill to the boutique. The enraged owner decided not to pursue the matter because he felt it wasn't worth more aggravation from Ethel.

There is a rather remarkable postscript to this story. The next year, Ethel had the gall to return to the boutique to buy another dress. Told that the owners had decided she could no longer charge on a personal account anything she selected for purchase, Ethel was furious, and behaved as if she had been abused. "I'll never buy anything here again!" she shrieked.

I must confess that I often sent my used (and sometimes not-so-used) clothing to Encore, a resale shop on Madison Avenue. People have criticized me for this, thinking I should have given them to charity, but in my own mind, I never had enough money, and the clothing was never sent to the shop in disrepair. Taking well cared-for clothes to stores like Encore for resale is quite a different matter than trying to return them as new, but actually in sub-standard, unsalable condition.

As the years went by after Bobby's death, Ethel seemed to deteriorate emotionally. In addition to her bill-paying skirmishes and her miserable rapport with some of her children, her behavior was often outrageous. I half-suspected she was a bit psychopathic, but as the stories about her multiplied, I really began to fear for her sanity. Increasingly, she was abusive verbally and even physically with her servants, many of whom quit after one day's work. Employment agencies received so many complaints about her mistreatment of the servants that some refused to deal with her, saying she was abrasive, tyrannical, and sharp-tongued.

The constant target of criticism and humiliating comments, many of the people she hired left in tears. One poor soul started to throw away a scrap of paper Bobby had written on. "You stupid nigger!" screamed Ethel, who was supposed to be carrying on Bobby's fight for civil rights. "Do you know what you have done? You have destroyed history! Get out of my house. You're fired!"

Ethel's abuse did not stop with servants. At one event, she came up to a woman and informed her that nametags should be worn directly over the collarbone. It seemed the woman was wearing her tag an inch too low. Ethel ripped it off her blouse, then slammed it back in place with an open palm. "There! That's where a name tag should be!" she shouted. "Don't you know how it's supposed to be worn?" The woman fell back against the wall in pain, and later said that Ethel had almost broken her collarbone.

Our relationship deteriorated to such a point that, on at least one public occasion, we didn't even say hello to one another. Without our husbands to hold us together as family, we had little in common. We shared no interests. I didn't enjoy her company.

All I had to do was give a party, and you can be sure Ethel would throw one the next week, flashier and gaudier than mine.

That's OK. People I cared about knew which sister-in-law had better taste. But in many ways, she and I are alike. We were each called spoiled children because we were both brought up in affluent families, although Ethel had more money available to her than I did. We both had a good sense of humor, except concerning each other, and I never pushed well-dressed people into pools. We both loved couture clothes, but I've always preferred simple styles and wouldn't dream of wearing jazzy vinyl dresses reaching above my knees. We were both excellent horsewomen who had loved horses since we were little and won many awards for excellence. She's more at ease with people and more natural. She's more direct and, perhaps, more honest. She's a much better Catholic.

One thing I always envied about Ethel was that she could always eat whatever she wanted and not gain an ounce, while I had to subsist on lettuce leaves. So it gives me pleasure to know that she has gotten matronly, even fat, over the years, while I weigh exactly what I did at my wedding—120 pounds. Well, maybe 125.

But there is only one thing I was really jealous of Ethel about. She was a fertile baby-making machine. I used to say, "Wind her up and she gets pregnant." There was a time when I would have given anything to be in Ethel's shoes, but on comparing her children with mine now, I wouldn't trade places with her for all the antiques in China.

We were most alike in that we both loved our husbands dearly and campaigned for them as well as we could, and we were loyal, kind, supportive helpmates all their lives and ever after. I loved Bobby, too, and on my better days, I'm grateful to Ethel for having been a loving, devoted wife.

Most cruelly of all, we both were widowed in our youth and, despite the other men in my life, mourned our husbands forever.

Although we are alike in many ways, we were very different wives to Jack and Bobby. I was always far more cultured than Ethel. My upbringing was much better than hers. (If I never appreciated my mother before, I certainly do when I look at Ethel.) She is rowdy and raucous; I am soft-spoken and gentle. She is as aggressive as any man. I'm not, although I have my subtle ways of getting even. She loves to beat men on the tennis court. In fact, she was so vicious to poor Paul Newman, screaming, "You play as bad as all the other kikes!," that he cried. I always tended to withdraw from the limelight, while Ethel jumped in with both feet.

Only two things in life mattered to her: Bobby and Jesus Christ, in that order. By contrast, I have always had many interests. And introspective she isn't. When I suggested that psychoanalysis could teach her to look inside herself, she vehemently objected, saying that she and Bobby wanted no part of "Jewish" psychiatry.

Ethel had a tin ear for languages, while I am known worldwide for my expertise in French and Spanish. Her preferred entertainment was cowboy movies, with *Vanity Fair* magazine a close second, while I enjoy films shown in art houses and books, books, books. Everything in Ethel's world is either "sensational!" or "terrific!" "Hey, kid!" and "Hiya, babe!" are her usual greetings. I never spoke that way. I am a poet who loves beautiful language.

In the matter of child-rearing, Ethel obviously preferred quantity to quality. I have greater depth. I am more intelligent. I am a better mother.

But it may be that I am unequipped to appreciate Ethel's good qualities, and I wish I had been a big enough person to have made room for Ethel in my life. If I had it to do all over again, I would try to appreciate her good points and be glad she made Bobby happy. But as a wise old woman once said to me, "We grow too soon old and too late smart."

Chapter 12
JACK'S OTHER WOMEN (PART 2)

Much as I was offended and hurt by the women with whom Jack had intimate relations, one affair was so painful it was all I could do not to act in a way that would have demolished us both. Over and over again, I fantasized about exposing and punishing Jack by divorcing him in a public and detailed fashion. If it weren't for our beloved children, I might well have done so, and maybe, somehow, that would have spared the nation the shock of November 22, 1963. Or maybe it would have been even worse for the country, to watch a maligned first lady evict her husband from the White House. I've always wanted to be a person of historical significance, but that wasn't exactly the way I hoped to achieve it.

It was a standing joke among knowledgeable women in Washington that half the females in town had either had sex with Jack or been invited to. His womanizing was humiliating, but usually I wasn't threatened by it, because I knew that, in his own way, I was the one he loved. But the relationship I'm speaking of wasn't of the playful pool-party type, indulged in purely for the fun of it. This one was different. It was a real love affair that lasted for many years, and the woman, a so-called friend of mine (we used to take walks together along the Chesapeake and Ohio towpath) was a respectable, intelligent, sophisticated woman of my own set who would have been more at home as first lady than I was.

Her name was Mary Meyer, a member of the politically prominent Pinchot family, East-Coast aristocracy with a huge estate. Like me, she was a Vassar girl and an artist. In fact, she was like me in so many ways, I often wondered why Jack needed her at all.

There was, however, one big difference. She was, literally speaking, a golden girl. She wore wheat-colored clothing that accentuated her golden hair.

Jack had first come to know Mary when they were teenagers in boarding school. They had an affair then, but Mary soon married Cord Meyer, a gifted man, both in a literary and political sense. The couple expected Cord to rise to the top of United States politics, but his personality deficiencies stood in the way. He was a terrible disappointment both to himself and to Mary. They had a miserable marriage, and ten years later, when he was a broken-down, abusive drunk, Mary divorced him. In the years after her divorce, Mary reinvented herself as a wild woman who exuded an air of danger and mystery. She didn't avoid peril; she actively sought it out. Men were shocked, excited, and fascinated by the new Mary. To paraphrase the illustrious Dorothy Parker, Mary knew eight languages and couldn't say "no" in any of them.

At a party Jack and I gave at the White House, the beautiful, fine-boned, still golden-haired Mary (perhaps by now with a little help) arrived with the same penetrating blue-green eyes that changed color to match whatever she was wearing. She tried out her new persona on the great actor Walter Pidgeon. He was captivated. Unfortunately, Pidgeon wasn't the only man enchanted by her. Jack couldn't take his eyes off Mary the entire evening, humiliating me and causing much gossip among the Washington hens who apparently had nothing more exciting to do than cackle about Jack's infidelities.

It didn't take Jack long to invite Mary to the White House. Knowing how Jack delighted in a chase, she refused his proposition and hurriedly left the scene. This, of course, heated Jack's fires even more, and he went after her with greater enthusiasm. To no one's surprise, she eventually succumbed. It was the rare woman propositioned by Jack who did not submit sooner or later. And Mary, who was far from being that rare woman, delighted in telling all our friends of Jack's sexual advances, mortifying me even further. In my opinion, she didn't want Jack nearly so much as she did the joy of bragging to all our friends of her conquest. After all, an ambitious social climber can't do much better than seducing the president of the United States!

Mary, a free thinker, was curious to test the boundaries of her new life. So was Jack. To him, Mary's propensity for danger was a great attraction. What happened between the pair is so unthinkable that I find it difficult to believe. As late as 1962, she had meetings with Timothy Leary, the high priest of the hallucinogenic world, to learn how to conduct LSD sessions. She told him about her crackpot scheme to use LSD to influence men in power to end wars, and that one of her subjects would be a man very high in government.

According to trustworthy reports, Mary introduced Jack to LSD, and they smoked marijuana together. Incredibly, he used the hallucinogen at a time when the world was on the brink of annihilation, and the president of this country needed every bit of rational thinking he could muster. Nevertheless, insane as it was, the relationship between Jack and his "dealer," Mary, continued until the mentally ill Phil Graham, publisher of *The Washington Post*, staggered up to the lectern at an Associated Press news convention in Phoenix, Arizona on January 12, 1963 and revealed the name of the president's new favorite. The audience sat transfixed until Graham started to take off his clothes and an official's wife dragged him off the lectern.

But it was too late. Someone in the know had dared to speak of the liaison between Jack and Mary in the presence of renowned newspaper editors and publishers. Even Jack perceived a catastrophe in the making. Realizing the threat Graham posed to his presidency, Jack sent to Phoenix a government jet carrying Graham's doctors, who forcibly tranquilized him and took him to Chestnut Lodge, a

private psychiatric hospital outside Washington. My dear husband was lucky the loyal newspapermen did not give away his secret. Their reticence, however, did not stop the affair from becoming the talk of Washington and breaking my heart.

This was a terrible period for me. Pregnant with John, I spent most of the time in bed, depressed and in tears. A month later, I had recovered enough to issue invitations to a small dinner dance at the White House. To my horror, Mary's name appeared on the guest list. It could only have been put there by Jack. To invite her to social events at the White House when their affair was supposedly unknown was bad enough, but to shove her in front of me after Graham's disclosure was more than I could bear. I struck her name from the list. It finally dawned on Jack that their affair was too much for me to handle in my condition, and he promised to end the relationship. In forcing him to end their liaison, I had done all I could, short of leaving him, to make my own life tolerable.

What is most painful to me is that Mary apparently filled a place in Jack's life that I was unable to. According to one of his biographers, Mary was supportive of Jack and a source of comfort to him. They enjoyed life together. She understood him, and they trusted each other. They laughed together about the pompous asses he had to put up with. This is not so different from Jack and me, and I have always considered myself as supportive of him in all the important issues as any wife could be. Why did he need her in his life? Maybe I was too critical of him. Once, when he didn't want to get up for Sunday Mass, I said, "Get up and get dressed, you son of a bitch! You got yourself into this and now you have to carry it through."

In the midst of his affair with Mary, Jack was going through a moral dilemma of another sort, the outcome of which would have a great influence on the future of all humanity. It is said that when a need arises, a great teacher will be found. So it was with Jack. During the previous two years, he had become close to Harold Macmillan, the prime minister of Great Britain, a wise, older man who served as an example and guide.

"I feel at home with Macmillan," Jack told me. "I'm able to share my loneliness with him. The other diplomats are all foreigners to me."

In 1962, Jack's advisors were pushing him to drop the idea of a nuclear test ban treaty with Soviet leader Khrushchev, for they believed it would fail and harm the president politically. Jack seemed on the brink of following their advice. Macmillan wrote his young friend a warm, detailed letter, in which he urged Jack to reconsider his decision. Macmillan believed the test ban treaty was the most important step their governments could take toward world peace. It was not just the simple signing of a treaty that Macmillan was urging, but also that Jack become a different kind of person morally— someone who would consider the ethical nature of his decisions more than the practical effect they might have on his political career.

Jack's ethical sense in areas outside sexuality was always evident to those who knew him well. As early as 1954, when Jack, as a senator, was attacked by Boston newspapers for his unpopular support of the Saint Lawrence Seaway, he began to study portraits of political figures he felt had shown the kind of courage he did in resisting pressure and standing up for what he believed in. This was the beginning of his work on the Pulitzer Prize-winning *Profiles in Courage*. His idealism also was evident politically in the Senate in 1956, when he first supported a ban on the testing of nuclear weapons. Believing such a ban would prevent other countries from developing nuclear weapons, he took a bold stand on the issue in the 1960 presidential campaign and again risked losing the election.

Once elected, he pledged not to resume testing in the air and to pursue all possible diplomatic efforts for a test ban treaty before resuming underground testing. He envisioned the test ban as a first step to total nuclear disarmament. In his September 25, 1961 address to the United Nations, he challenged the Soviet Union "not to an arms race, but to a peace race."

Another instance of Jack's innate ethical sense occurred when he refused as a freshman congressman to sign a request for a presidential pardon for Mayor James M. Curley. Curley was then doing time in a

federal penitentiary for construction contract fraud committed during World War II. Incredibly, Curley was so popular in Boston that he was permitted to continue as mayor even while in prison. In search of a pardon, he had appeared in court in a wheelchair, pleading that he was suffering from debilitating ailments. His pardon request was backed by all the Massachusetts Democrats in Congress, except Jack, who refused to believe that Curley was as sick as he claimed. Jack's intuition later proved to be correct—after Curley was released, other congressmen having succeeded in attaining a pardon, he returned immediately to his City Hall office, where he claimed to celebrants that he felt better than he had for ten years.

Jack met with Soviet Premier Khrushchev in Vienna in June 1961, just five weeks after America's humiliating defeat at the Bay of Pigs. Khrushchev took a hard line at the summit. He announced his intention of cutting off Western access to Berlin and threatened war if the United States or its allies tried to stop him. Political and military advisors feared secret underground testing by the Soviet Union and gains in their nuclear technology and pressured Jack to resume testing. The public, in a July 1961 Gallup poll, approved testing by a margin of two to one.

In August 1961, the Soviet Union announced its intention to resume atmospheric testing, and over the next three months, it conducted thirty-one nuclear tests. It exploded the largest nuclear bomb in history—fifty-eight megatons, four thousand times more powerful than the bomb dropped on Hiroshima. Discouraged, Jack tried urgent diplomatic means to persuade Khrushchev before yielding to calls for renewed testing by the United States.

But all was not yet lost. Following the peaceful resolution of the Cuban Missile Crisis in October 1962, Khrushchev and Jack again sought to reduce tensions between the two nations. Both men were aware that they had come perilously close to nuclear war over Cuba. Khrushchev stated it well when he said, "The two most powerful nations had squared off against each other, each with its finger on the button." Jack agreed in equally graphic terms: "It is insane that two men, sitting on opposite sides of the world, should be able to decide to bring an end to civilization."

Establishing a private telephone hotline, Khrushchev and Kennedy reopened their dialogue on banning nuclear testing. And in his commencement address at American University on June 10, 1963, Jack announced a new round of arms negotiations with the Russians and valiantly called for an end to the Cold War. "If we cannot end our differences," he said, "at least we can help make the world a safe place for diversity."

Still, when Prime Minister Macmillan urged Jack to disregard the words of his advisers and push for a ban, Jack knew that he would be taking two great chances if he followed Macmillan's advice: First, Khrushchev might not sign the treaty and thus humiliate Jack; and second, even if he did, the U.S. Senate might never ratify it, which would probably endanger his chances for re-election.

Jack went through a week in which he searched his soul, and then, with a little urging from me, he decided to follow the prime minister's advice. He suggested that both the U.S. and the U.K. send special envoys to Moscow communicate their mutual decision. In his inaugural address, Jack had promised the country a new beginning. With his words to Macmillan, he stood ready to discard the potential consequences to his political future. Jack had made a great developmental leap from a candidate determined to win the presidency at any cost to a statesman who risked his own re-election in order to fulfill his ideals. The feeling spread throughout the United States that Jack was about to change the course of East-West history and become the great president he had it in him to be.

A message soon arrived from Khrushchev accepting Jack's and Macmillan's proposal. The speech Jack was about to make to the U.S. Conference of Mayors, where he was to lay a wreath at the Pearl Harbor Memorial, was altered accordingly. Rather than merely announce an offer to dispatch diplomats to Moscow for discussions with high-level Soviet officials about a possible nuclear test ban, he'd announce the Soviet Union's acceptance of the offer. Jack's incredible

moral growth made me dare to hope once again. If he could develop a moral political sense, who was to say that his new ethical sensibility might not lead to changes in our marriage?

On August 6, 1963, thanks largely to Jack, the United States, the United Kingdom, and the Soviet Union signed the Partial Test Ban Treaty. Coming after eight years of troubled negotiations, the agreement prohibited nuclear weapons tests or explosions underwater, in the atmosphere, or in outer space. Underground nuclear tests were allowed only if no radioactive debris fell outside the boundaries of the nation conducting the test. And the treaty obligated all three nations to work toward complete disarmament and an end to the armaments race and the contamination of the environment by radioactive substances. The treaty was signed three and a half months before Jack was assassinated. None of his other White House accomplishments gave him greater pleasure.

In a July 26 radio and television address to the people of the United States, Jack had said, "Let us, if we can, step back from the shadows of war and seek out the way of peace. And if that journey is a thousand miles, or even more, let history record that we, in this land, at this time, took the first step." Jack was instrumental in taking that "first step."

Jack's legacy continues long after his death. As I near the end of my life, I am thrilled to learn that a comprehensive nuclear test ban treaty is under consideration by the United Nations General Assembly. Seventy-one nations, including those who possess nuclear weapons, are expressing interest in signing the treaty, which prohibits all nuclear test explosions. Because of this treaty alone, I am gratified that the Kennedys occupied the White House. The treaty, the culmination of Jack's contributions to humanity, makes clear beyond all doubt that John Fitzgerald Kennedy was a great leader and statesman. He was just beginning to ascend the ladder to greatness. Who knows what monumental world improvements were also killed by the assassin's bullets?

Jack was also ahead of his time on the issue of women's rights in the workplace. His administration heralded the government's entrance into the battle against sex discrimination. The Equal Pay Act was signed into law in 1963 and marked the first attempt of the United States government to safeguard women's employment rights. I am especially proud of Jack for that and believe his love and admiration for me contributed to his interest in fighting for women's equality. For the son of Joe Kennedy, who treated his wife like chattel, this was no small achievement.

But as much as I praise Jack's accomplishments, the same admiration does not carry over to his immoral personal relations with women and his failure to discontinue them at key moments in history. At the time Jack was going through these tremendous changes, his friend and mentor Macmillan was fighting for his political life. His minister of war, John Profumo, had resigned after confessing to an affair with Christine Keeler, a call girl kept by London osteopath Stephen Ward. Keeler was also the lover of Captain Yevgeni Ivanov, assistant naval attaché at the Soviet embassy in London. Even worse, Ivanov reportedly used Keeler to extract atomic secrets from Profumo. Because Macmillan had always supported Profumo, there were underground whispers that the Conservative party would call for Macmillan's resignation. The general impression was that, sooner or later, he would have to go. Because of the scandal, the British government came close to falling.

There was no U.S. connection until the FBI and Scotland Yard discovered that Dr. Ward and Jack had shared the affections of call girl Susie Chang, who had been seen a number of times accompanied by the president, once at the posh restaurant 21, where Jack and I had often enjoyed dining. The FBI continued to investigate Jack's possible part in the Profumo scandal and, at the time of his assassination, was still working on it.

For three months, Jack honored his promise to me to stay away from Mary Meyer, but apparently fearing that the results of the FBI investigation would become public knowledge, at a time when Macmillan's support of him was weakening, the situation became too

much for him, and he invited Mary to a party at the White House.

President Lyndon Johnson once said there are two things that make politicians most stupid. One of them is sex. For a brilliant man, Jack was incredibly stupid, if not downright foolhardy, about his lovers. He was expecting news of a top-secret prisoner exchange at the Glienicke Bridge, the link between East and West Berlin, at which an East German spy held by the United States would be swapped for U-2 pilot Gary Powers, who had been shot down by the Soviets. At that very same time, my friend Betty Spalding encountered Jack and Mary leaving my party and heading toward the schoolroom on the third floor where I had arranged for Caroline to take kindergarten classes. Betty made sure to inform me and all of Washington. Mary and Jack apparently didn't give a damn who saw them and continued on their way. The encounter, followed by a quick act of schoolroom sex, was Mary's way of holding on to Jack by showing just how far she would go to keep him. I had trusted him when he said he was breaking off the affair, and he broke his promise to me.

But his most destructive and dangerous dalliance, an affair so potentially disastrous that even Bobby Kennedy probably could not have kept it secret any longer, was still going on right up to the time Jack was assassinated. One of his pool-party buddies, Ellen Rometsch, was a professional prostitute who operated a hostess service called the Quorum Club, whose founder and director was Bobby Baker, secretary of the Senate Democrats, who later went to jail for income tax evasion, theft, and conspiracy to defraud the government. Rometsch quietly accepted Jack's money and kept silent about their activities. She was born in Kleinitz, Germany, in a village that became part of East Germany after the war. As a child, Rometsch was a member of a Communist youth group and, as an adult, joined another Communist group. A beautiful, sultry twenty-seven-year-old woman who resembled Elizabeth Taylor, Ellen was believed by many to be a Communist spy. Baker relayed to his friends Jack's assertion that Rometsch was the most exciting woman he had ever been with. Baker told his friends that one of his "girls" said she and another prostitute had engaged in group sex with Jack, in which one played the role of a doctor, the other woman the nurse, and Jack the patient.

I understood from what depths in his life this "game" emanated. As a sick little boy, Jack had spent years in hospitals, where his main companions were doctors and nurses. Surely this sick little boy lying on his back for so many months could be forgiven for having erotic fantasies about the people to whom he was closest.

But what I can never pardon is his adult relationship with Rometsch. Apparently, the FBI couldn't either, opening up an investigation concerning Rometsch as a possible spy. Jack became so frightened his relationship with Ellen would be exposed that he was willing to give up the services of "the most exciting woman he had ever been with." On August 3, 1963, he and Bobby hastily had her deported to Germany. It was widely rumored that Jack kept sending her suitcases filled with cash to prevent her from returning to the United States and to keep her mouth shut about their relationship.

Then something happened that shocked even Bobby and Jack—the political demolishment of Bobby Baker. In September, the media began publishing stories of Baker's unsavory ties to a vending machine company. Baker and his investors, it seems, had been awarded numerous contracts while the company was still unorganized, and also had received instant credit from a bank controlled by a United States senator. The story spread like wildfire among the press, and reporters began a serious investigation into the private lives of many senators, including those who had received thousands of dollars in campaign contributions though Baker. Baker's private life was thrown open to the public, including his ownership of the Quorum Club. It took no time at all for the media to learn all about Ellen Rometsch.

On October 26, investigative reporter Clark Mollenhoff revealed in *The Des Moines Register* that the Senate Rules Committee was planning to hear testimony about Ellen Rometsch and her hasty departure from the country. According to Mollenhoff, the Committee was examining one report in which she told an FBI informant she was sent to this country to get information. The committee would also look into Rometsch's relationship with various senators and "high executive branch officials." Mollenhoff added that her behavior concerned the FBI investigators because of the possibility that she was a spy and the elevated position of her male companions. Bobby knew that the investigations of the Senate committee and the FBI could bring about Jack's downfall as surely as similar recriminations had destroyed Harold Macmillan's government.

The Republicans on the Senate Rules Committee began to demand that Ellen Rometsch be issued a visa to return to the United States, where she would be interrogated by committee members and staff. Bobby, feeling helpless in the situation, reluctantly turned to FBI Director J. Edgar Hoover, whose relationship with Bobby was a plethora of private insults and incompatible quirks. Bobby pleaded his concern about the harm that could come to the United States if irresponsible action was taken on the Ellen Rometsch case.

After letting Bobby suffer a bit by implying that the whole business was starkly distasteful, Hoover assured the attorney general that he would personally see to it that Ellen did not get a visa to re-enter the country. Jack was lucky; Hoover kept his word. Jack, however, remained terrified that he was just one newspaper story away from a fate similar to Macmillan's. Less than three weeks before he was assassinated, Jack invited Ben Bradlee, Washington bureau chief for *Newsweek*, to dinner at the White House, ostensibly to chat about the Rometsch case, but in actuality to brief him about writing a story disputing any relationship between him and Ellen Rometsch.

It fell to Bobby Kennedy to provide the final lie about the Rometsch case after Jack's death. In Bobby's 1964 interview with the Kennedy Library, he said that Clark Mollenhoff had written *incorrectly* that Ellen had been intimate with people at the White House. Bobby indignantly said that she had been tied up with a lot of people in the capital, but not at the White House. His only concern, he added earnestly, was for the reputation of the United States. Bobby added his righteous hope that from then on, less attention would be paid to the matter.

Sometimes I think there was a bit of a silver lining to Jack's assassination, because he left the Oval Office a hero and martyr who would go down in history as a great statesman. I know Jack. If he had lived, the devastation from newspaper revelations almost certainly would have killed his political reputation, and thus irreparably injured him personally.

A year after Jack was killed, I was shocked and horrified to learn Mary Meyer had been shot to death as she walked along the Chesapeake and Ohio Towpath, where she and I had taken many pleasant walks together before the beginning of her affair with Jack. Furious as I was with her, I never would have wished that on her. I grieved for the woman who once was my close friend, and for her sons, who would have to grow up without their mother. Like Jack, Mary's life was cut short before she had fulfilled her potential. She was just coming into her own as an artist and, like Jack, the world will never know what heights she might have reached. Jack would have been upset at the officially unsolved murder, and probably would have fought the release of Raymond Crump, who everybody I know thinks murdered Mary.

The week after she was murdered, a white cross appeared on the towpath precisely where the crime took place. Scrawled on the Key Bridge were the words, "Mauvais Coup, Mary"—French for "Bad luck, Mary."

Chapter 13

C A R O L I N E

My baby daughter was named Caroline Lee Kennedy, after my sister Lee. She was born on November 27, 1957. My usually contained mother said, "I'll never forget Jack's face when the doctor came into the room and told him he had a daughter. 'She's fine and is very pretty,' he added. Jack beamed, and got the sweetest expression on his face I ever saw."

When I awoke from the anesthesia, the first thing I saw was Jack walking toward me with the baby in his arms. He lovingly handed her to me—I, who had lived for years fearful that this moment would never come. It was the happiest day of my life.

I adored Caroline. She and I were best buddies from almost the minute she was born. I reveled in her company and took her with me whenever I could. At the age of twenty-eight, I had finally found a female I could love one hundred percent, and with whom I was completely at ease. I think I turned into another woman when I became a mother. Somehow, successfully producing a child, and such a lovely one, did much to restore the self-esteem my mother had damaged so badly.

Caroline's birth signaled a marital rebirth as well. Earlier in the marriage, I had lived in the shadow of my formidable mother-in-law and my controlling mother, both of whom tried to run my home and my life. Now the tables were turned. As wife and mother, I finally got rid of my bosses and was, for the first time, mistress in my own home.

I love this story about Jack and his old pal, Lem Billings, who was one of the first visitors to the hospital: Jack took Lem to the nursery to show off his new daughter. He put his hand on Lem's shoulder and said, "Now, Lem, tell me the truth. Which one is the prettiest baby in the nursery?" When Lem pointed to the wrong baby, Jack wouldn't talk to him for two days.

Richard Cardinal Cushing, archbishop of Boston, came to Saint Patrick's Cathedral in New York for Caroline's christening. Lee, the godmother, and Bobby, the godfather, were, of course, present. Caroline wore the baptismal gown I'd worn at my own christening twenty-eight years before. A mink-coated Lee held Caroline close to her as the bishop dabbed holy water on her head. Jack and Bobby stood solemnly by. Good baby that she was, Caroline didn't cry. I cried enough for the both of us.

From the beginning, Caroline adored her father. He was the recipient of her first smile. When she was four months old, she was lying on her tummy when he bounded into the nursery to say, "Good morning, Buttons!" She turned over on her side, looked up at him, and gave him a great big smile. Her father was as thrilled as when he was elected president. Because Jack was away so much, it is a little sad that her first spoken word was "goodbye." Her next words were "New Hampshire," "West Virginia," and "Wisconsin." It was clear from early on that she was a member of a political family. I used to joke that it was a good thing so few states had primaries, or Caroline would have had the largest vocabulary of any two year old on record.

Her actions were often quite endearing. When Caroline was a little older, she picked up a copy of *Newsweek*, which featured a picture of her father on the cover. Jack was taking a bath at the time, and Caroline dashed into the bathroom, shouting, "Here's your picture, Daddy!" and tossed the magazine into the tub water. Jack was mad. He wanted to see his picture, and it was so water-soaked he could hardly make it out.

As soon as Caroline could walk, Jack would clap his hands and shout, "Buttons!," and Caroline would drop whatever she was doing and come running. Caroline always remembered the sweet sound of her daddy's clapping hands and his voice calling out, "Buttons!"

Once, when Caroline was very little, I took Jack by the hand, sat him down in his favorite rocking chair, and said, "Caroline has a surprise for you." The tiny girl, whose blond curly hair was secured with two large baby-blue ribbons, began to recite Edna St. Vincent Millay's poem, "First Fig":

My candle burns on both ends;
It will not last the night;
But ah, my foes, and oh, my friends—
It gives a lovely light!

Jack lit up like a Christmas tree and clapped and clapped, saying, "That was wonderful, Buttons! Just wonderful!"

Strange that I had Caroline memorize a poem that disparages caution. If I knew then what I know now, I would have chosen a different poem.

From the start, Caroline was amazingly intelligent. She could read by the time she was three. At dinner each night, she bubbled over with news of her day: what she learned in school, what this friend or that said to her, what was new with the pets she had and didn't have. She knew how to pronounce the names of all the foreign leaders. When a friend admired a gold medal she was wearing, Caroline said, "Haile Selassie gave that to me." She would brook no baby talk. Pierre Salinger pointed to a cow and said, "That's a moo-cow." Caroline corrected him: "No, it isn't. It's a Hereford." She was precocious, but then, what would anyone expect of Jack Kennedy's daughter?

It was Caroline who brought Jack the exciting news that he was president of the United States. He had gone to bed at 4 a.m., not knowing if he had won the election or not. At 9 a.m., when he was again soaking in the bathtub, Caroline came racing in, shouting, "Daddy, Daddy, you won! You won!"

"Really?" he said. "Does that mean I'll be president?"

"Oh, yes, Daddy," she said. "Miss Shaw says I have to call you Mr. President now."

He grabbed Caroline and gave her a big hug. If she got a bit soapy, no one minded.

Everybody loved Caroline. Although Rose loved all her grandchildren, Caroline was clearly her favorite. Rose found her a thoughtful, well-behaved, easily managed child, which is more than I can say about her other grandchildren, including, I am sorry to say, John. Caroline kept in close touch with her grandmother until the end of Rose's life. Caroline even named her first daughter Rose Kennedy Schlossberg, which made her grandmother very happy, although I can't say the same for me. I would have much preferred Jacqueline Kennedy Schlossberg.

Caroline was the darling of the White House media. When Jack met with the most powerful men in the world, Caroline was known to stand behind them and make faces at the press. Great leaders or not, Caroline was not impressed. She slid down the banisters as they were walking soberly to their meetings, careened around the Oval Office, or pulled at Jack's sleeve whenever she wanted attention. She always got it, even if it meant making the mighty government leaders wait their turn.

At one White House meeting, the erudite Senator William Fulbright watched Caroline, who was dressed in pajamas and bathrobe, clomping around the Oval Office in my size ten and a half high heels. "I want my daddy!" she called out. Jack gave her a hug, took her arm, and lovingly guided her out of the room. Senator Fulbright and the members of the press laughed uproariously.

At another press conference, she zoomed between journalists' legs on her tricycle. Nobody protested. Jack, however, never let Caroline interfere with affairs of state. It made me laugh to see him continue to conduct a meeting or write a speech with her climbing all over him. At Christmastime, when Caroline made up a list of presents she wanted, Jack had the White House staff put a switchboard call through to the North Pole.

"Mommy, Mommy!" Caroline shrieked. "Guess what? I just talked to Santa Claus, and gave him a whole long list of presents! Do you think I'll get them all?"

"I'm sure you will," I said with a smile.

I never told Caroline, until the day she got married, that "Santa Claus" was a White House operator.

Jack was brilliant at making up original bedtime stories for the children. I admired how he invented them at the spur of a moment. What a creative man he was! The content of the stories varied from Lobo the shark, who ate up people's socks, to an ogre named Bobo, to Maybelle, an orphan who lived alone in the forest. Maybelle in particular mesmerized Caroline, who stared at her daddy with wide-open eyes as he related the story. I was thrilled that he played such a delightful hands-on role in the lives of his children, but now that I'm older and wiser, I find Maybelle, the lonely orphan, a rather sad story. I think it dramatizes how Jack felt as a little boy, and perhaps even as an adult, and may well be the reason he had to keep himself surrounded by people.

Inside the White House, it was hard to keep up with Caroline. She exhausted the Secret Service agents who tried to follow her, as she ferociously pedaled her tricycle up and down the endless halls. One evening, as several of our distinguished dinner guests stepped off the elevator, they were treated to the sight of a stark-naked Caroline streaking toward them, chased by a humiliated Maude Shaw, her nanny. One guest said, "Caroline practically knocked us over. Then she looked up at us with those melting blue eyes and blasted off again. We couldn't stop laughing, even though Caroline was the president's daughter." They needn't have worried about offending Jack. When he heard about the incident, he was delighted.

The public could not get enough of the beautiful, golden-haired, blue-eyed child. One reporter wrote, "Not since Shirley Temple rode to fame has one child received so much international coverage as the president's daughter."

Allowing photos of her was always a bone of contention between Jack and me. He would have let the press photograph her night and day; he thought she was a great political asset and wanted to show her off. I, on the other hand, was interested primarily in her well-being and wanted her brought up as an unspoiled, normal child. How could that happen if she were always in the public eye? "No pictures of Caroline!" I told Jack. "That's final. I won't have our daughter used like some mascot at a football game, no matter how many votes it costs you!" Do you think he listened? Guess.

In one instance, Jack invited Jacques Lowe, a photographer friend of his, to come to the White House and take pictures of Caroline. Lowe told me later that he said, "I can't do that, Mr. President. Jackie will have me hung and quartered if I do."

"Then don't tell her," Jack replied. Lowe took the photos, and, indeed, I was furious and let Jack have it. He played dumb and said he didn't know anything about it.

Nobody was happier than Caroline when her brother John was born. Because he came into the world around her birthday, Miss Shaw told Caroline he was a birthday present to her. She called him "my baby," and it took a long time to convince her that John did not belong to her. I was lucky if she let me hold him. Sometimes I had to fight with her to get to feed him. Totally smitten, she spent every available minute at his side. After all, none of her little friends had a real live baby to play with! The poor children had to be content with dolls.

She became a little mother to John and loved nothing better than to give him his bottle. As his big sister, she advised him and looked after him. "John," she would say, "be a good boy and eat your cereal." John ate the cereal. But Caroline was only human, and not above occasionally "squealing" on her beloved brother. She confided to her grandmother Rose, "John is a bad boy. He spits in Mommy's Coca-

Cola."

Even as an adult, John has said, "My sister is very smart. When she tells me something, I listen." It's too bad my mother didn't tell me, when Lee was born, that she was my birthday present. It might have saved us a lot of hostility all our lives.

I have to hand it to Caroline. From her earliest days, she was pretty shrewd, and didn't miss a thing. She told a friend, "Mommy and Daddy both like movies, but they don't like the same ones. Daddy likes cowboy pictures. Mommy doesn't like them at all, but only watches them with my daddy because she loves him." She added, "Mommy loves ballet. Daddy claps, too, but I don't think he really likes it. When he thinks no one is looking, he makes funny faces."

Jack didn't baby Caroline. Like the rest of the Kennedys, he encouraged risk-taking. One time, she fell off her horse, Macaroni. "Get up, Caroline!" he yelled. "Climb back up on that horse right away!" She did. Jack was right about how to conquer fear. It's common knowledge that, if you fall off a horse, you have to climb right back on again, or you will always be afraid to ride. Still, how many fathers would allow their three year olds to climb back on a horse that had just thrown her? Caroline was lucky to have Jack for a father, even for so short a time. I'm sure his every word is engraved upon her heart.

When Lee and I took a trip to India, Caroline followed every aspect of it in the newspapers. (Maybe something good came out of the press after all.) Miss Shaw told us that when Caroline opened a *Life* magazine story about our visit, she yelled out, "Miss Shaw, come and look! Come and look! Mommy and Aunt Lee are riding on top of an elephant! It's awfully big. I hope they don't fall off." I guess if we had, we would have had to climb right back on again, or else lose my daughter's respect.

When Jack and I were away, the TV was Caroline's best friend. When the first of the four Kennedy/Nixon debates was televised by CBS, Caroline was tuned in to the TV. "Look, it's Daddy! It's Daddy!" she screamed to anyone who would listen. Jack had been away a great deal campaigning for the presidency. Caroline had been with him very little for two whole months, and was thrilled to see him, even in black and white. She ran up to the TV, threw her arms around it as far as she could reach, and kissed her televised father. The rest of the country, charmed by Jack's appearance and personality, was similarly enthralled. That's when I knew for sure he would be elected.

Kennedy campaign strategists gradually insisted that I combat Pat Nixon's Republican cloth-coat image. That was great fun, and the part of the campaign I enjoyed the most. Poor Pat didn't have a chance. I even yielded to Jack's pressure and allowed photographs of Caroline to be used for political advantage. She was pictured in magazine after magazine, looking lovingly at me and, more often, at Jack, hugging her stuffed animals or gazing wide-eyed into the camera. Jacques Lowe, the photographer, said, "Caroline is incredibly photogenic! If she weren't a Kennedy, she could be a model." That was one of the few times I thanked heaven she was a Kennedy.

Caroline was a happy, sparkling little girl. To see her was to love her. After Jack's murder, however, she became a different child—withdrawn and puzzled. It broke my heart to see the change. Although I tried hard to be there for her, it wasn't enough. I was having coffee with Rose in the Oval Room a few days after the catastrophe occurred when Caroline raced in and asked, "Mommy, did people love my daddy?"

"Oh, yes," I answered, "they loved him very much."

"No, Mommy, you're wrong," she said. "If they loved him, then why did they do such a terrible thing to him?"

Rose pretended she had something in her eye. I didn't know what to say, either. In fact, I was up many a night trying to think of an answer to Caroline's question.

She continued, "Do people love you, Mommy?"

"I suppose so. At least some people do," I said, turning my head so she wouldn't see my tears. Then I realized what her question was really about: She was afraid I would be shot down like Jack. I said, "I guess I shouldn't have told you that everybody loved Daddy. Some people didn't. A great many more loved him than me, but some love me, too."

Caroline looked even more bewildered. Grabbing for a straw, I said, "Not everybody loved Jesus, either, Caroline." To my surprise, that seemed to clear up her confusion. A smile came over her face, and she dashed off to join her little friends at John's birthday party in the next room.

Despite her own pain, my six-year-old daughter was my chief comforter. Once, when I couldn't help breaking into sobs in her presence, she turned to me and said, "Please don't cry, Mommy. You'll be all right. I'll take care of you." She reached up with a handkerchief Miss Shaw had given her and wiped away the tears running down my cheeks. Then she grasped my hand like a parent. I gave her a big hug, and said, "Thank you, Caroline, dear. You're my big-girl helper."

Chapter 14

THE PRESIDENT AND HIS SON

Although Jack's murder affected many lives, the biggest loser was little John. Busy as Jack was, he was a wonderful father who always found time for his children. Caroline made Jack beam with pride, but when his eyes gazed upon John, Jack lit up like a full moon. His love for his son was special, absorbing, and sensuous. The boy was pure joy to Jack, as was Jack to John. Jack kept the child with him whenever possible. He took John along on official airplane and helicopter rides whenever he could, taught him to swim in the presidential pool, took baths with him, and played with him between appointments. As was the case with Caroline, heads of state often had to wait until the game John was playing with his father was over. I used to enjoy eavesdropping on the two of them, laughing and having fun together. The memory of them looking adoringly into each other's eyes still fills me with pleasure.

The little boy would come bouncing into the Oval Office, and in a game John loved, Jack would say, "Hello, Sam!"

"No no no!" John would shout. "My name is John!"

"Sam" was an improvement on another nickname Jack had for John. Sometimes Jack called his son "Foo-Foo Head." It never failed to make John scream with laughter.

Yet it took a while for them to become enamored of each other. First, John had to outgrow being a "mama's boy" and realize that daddies were just as important as mommies. John was a late talker, and it wasn't until John began to talk that Jack, like many fathers, fell hopelessly in love with his son. John began to chatter night and day and became the little boy who captured his father's heart.

John wasn't as beautiful as Caroline when he was born on November 25, 1960. In fact, in an unmotherly moment, I, the realist, said that he looked like a "newly hatched robin." A journalist dubbed him Irving, and the nickname stuck with the press corps. It took a while for "Irving" to develop into the gorgeous creature he became later in his life. He had a chipped front tooth and looked like a thousand little boys you might see on the street, but he was friendly, outgoing, bright, uninhibited, and, thank God, unspoiled, so everyone he came in contact with loved him.

From the beginning, Jack disagreed with my appraisal of John's looks. When Jack first saw his son, he gloated, "He's the most beautiful baby I've ever seen." John fooled everybody except Jack and grew increasingly handsome as he got older. His physique ultimately became an exact copy of his father's. It was like looking through the small lens of a telescope. Their bodies were so similar I had to laugh when I saw them walking side by side, and sang a little tune of the times: "I love you a bushel and a peck/a bushel and a peck and a hug around the neck." The resemblance appealed to Jack's vanity.

John had a fresh way of looking at the world which, like nothing else, brought an enamored look to Jack's eyes. One night, when John saw a searchlight sweeping the sky, he called out, "Daddy, Daddy, come look and see. The sky is turning! The sky is turning!" Jack grabbed him and gave him a bear hug.

John wasn't afraid of anybody. Shortly before his father was assassinated, when his nurse took him shopping, a group of people recognized him and clustered around him. He began to shake hands with everyone nearby, saying, "My name is John Fitzgerald

Kennedy, Jr. What's yours?" He acted like a budding Kennedy politician. "What a big boy you are!" one of the onlookers said. "Yeah," he said, extending one of his biceps. "And look at me. I got big muscles, too!"

Next to Jack, John's chief love was anything that flew—airplanes, blimps, rockets, and helicopters. Jack's Army aide, Major General Ted Clifton, said, sadly, "I'm afraid we've lost John to the Air Force." After he was given a small model of the Gemini space capsule—he wasn't yet three years old—he kept taking it apart and putting it together again until he could reassemble it very quickly. When Jack failed to put the nose cone back on properly, John had to show him how to do it.

John's energy put the rest of us to shame. While I was just turning over in bed, he was already banging away on the typewriter of Mrs. Evelyn Lincoln, Jack's secretary, romping with the first dogs—Shannon, Pushinka, Charlie, and Clipper—reading and re-reading his tattered book, *The Lost Kitten*, and trying on the gold-braided hats of any general unlucky enough to be visiting the president at the time. Anyone who wanted a stick of chewing gum had to first consult John, who lavishly handed them out, after making sure one was always saved for Caroline. A neat little boy, he made sure to drop the wrappers in the wastebasket. If he hadn't, Miss Shaw no doubt would have had something to say about it.

Rummaging around in the newspapers, he came across a photograph of himself seeing his father off at the airport. "Why does the picture show me crying?" he demanded. He was told, "Because the president is going away in a helicopter." That made no sense at all to John. "But I like helicopters," he said. Once, he tore into the Cabinet Room and climbed over the high mahogany table, where he was cornered by a journalist who tried to interview him. John was asked, "Do you prefer helicopters or blimps?" "Helicopters!" he shouted in return. The interview made Jack grin.

If someone said, "What a cute boy you are, John!" he would run around the White House shouting, "I'm a cute boy! I'm a cute boy!" He could also give a great imitation of a gorilla scratching himself. Jack thought John was hilarious, and always applauded him loudly, and on more than one occasion was joined in his applause by cabinet members in the middle of a meeting. No wonder John grew up wanting to be an actor!

In the endless waiting for his father, John would look through his favorite magazine, *Aviation Week*, or draw pictures of airplanes on paper tablets provided by Mrs. Lincoln. He also stole chocolates from Mrs. Lincoln's bowl when her back was turned. She pretended not to notice.

Jack loved Caroline very much, too, of course. She had special privileges, such as being permitted to break into Jack's bedroom early in the morning and awaken him, and then share his orange juice. He taught her little poems and glowed when she recited them back to him. He listened attentively to the stories she made up and then added his own embellishments. Father and daughter shared a special, luminous bond. But there was an extra dimension to his love for John.

I loved the way he was with John most of all. There is something precious between a man and his son that is different from any other relationship, even that of father and daughter. In his boy, the father sees himself reborn, with a chance to do it all over again as he wished he had done it the first time round. He sees a kindred male spirit who reflects what he likes best about himself. They are males together, and no woman can possibly understand the pride a man takes in his masculinity. It is a fierce and primitive relationship built on the father's instinctual need to perpetuate the river of life. Having a son enables a man to look into the future and see himself repeated over and over, down through the ages. It guarantees a man a stretch of immortality. When I told Jack I felt he and John were closer to each other than to Caroline and me, he looked at me quizzically and said, "Of course. We're males!"

Jack, who ordinarily was not a toucher and would often retreat a bit if anyone came too close to him, was tactile with both children, but particularly with John. He would run his hands over the silky skin under the little boy's shirt, as if to convince himself the child was really his. He couldn't resist grabbing John whenever he was close and tousling his hair or patting him on the fanny. Sometimes, he would turn him over his knee and give John a mock spanking. It didn't seem to upset John much. In the morning before going down to the Oval Office, Jack made sure the children were there to receive their good-morning kiss, and then the three of them would walk to the Oval Office holding hands. "We are going to work!" John would sing out happily.

Jack, the loving father, was lucky enough to live "above the store." At night, John would come down in his pajamas and robe for a pre-bedtime visit with his father. If Jack went on reading his stack of newspapers, as he sometimes did, John crawled out of sight under the presidential desk. He used to call the carved oaken timbers of the desk "my house."

Jack was the kind of man who, like Bobby, should have had many children. Most men care less about their children than their wives do, but not Jack. He loved John and Caroline with as great a passion as any parent I have ever seen. Jack was a modern president, but he was an old-fashioned father. Like many ordinary parents, Jack carried around all the photos of John and Caroline that could fit in his wallet (he had plenty of room in it because he never carried any money around), and would show them off to anyone he could waylay.

"Aren't they great?" he would ask repeatedly.

"What do you think of John?" he asked one man.

"He's a buster," the man replied. For Jack, it was the only correct answer.

One of my favorite stories about father and son was told to me by Mrs. Lincoln. She said they were all riding in a car together when Jack, in a playful mood, gave John a little nudge. John hit him back. Jack said, "I'm going to tell Miss Shaw on you." John said, "And I'm going to tell Mrs. Lincoln on you!"

Jack's meeting with Soviet Minister of Foreign Affairs Andrei Gromyko didn't impress John. When Mrs. Lincoln told him that he couldn't go into Daddy's office because he was having an important meeting with Mr. Gromyko, John sang out, "G'omyko! G'omyko!" in a voice that must have reached the Washington Monument. When Mrs. Lincoln told him he would have to quiet down, John said, "If you make me be quiet, I won't like you!" She replied, "Then I won't like you, either." This apparently got through to John, and he went back to drawing his airplanes.

Those meetings with Gromyko, conducted in the Oval Office, were held because the Russians had held back two U.S. convoys for fifteen hours on their way to Berlin. As I passed the Oval Office, the door opened briefly to reveal the president deeply involved in conversation with Gromyko, Secretary of State Dean Rusk, National Security Advisor McGeorge Bundy, Ambassador to the Soviet Union Llewellyn Thompson, all-around aide Kenny O'Donnell, and Press Secretary Pierre Salinger. Sitting on top of the table in the middle of this group was little John, who had snuck into the room.

I was delighted when Richard Wilson wrote in his newspaper column that Jack, in both his public and family life, had set a new standard for the nation. I was so pleased with his vision of our family that I wrote him a letter of gratitude. It said, "It is extraordinary to see Jack's family life written about by someone who has never even seen him with his children. I am so happy to have your column to save and treasure for myself, as well as to show the children when they grow up."

Was Jack more at home being president or being a father? I think it was a draw. Six weeks before Jack was murdered, *The New York Times* published an item saying that as the Cabinet walked out of the Oval Office, Jack took a clean white handkerchief out of his pocket and wiped John's nose. E. B. White, editor of *The New Yorker*, composed a darling poem about the incident:

A President's work is never done,

His burdens press from sun to sun:

A Berlin wall, a racial brew,
A tax cut bill, a Madame Nhu.
One crisis ebbs, another flows—
    And here comes John with a runny nose.

A President must rise and dress,
See senators, and meet the press,
Be always bold, be sometimes wary,
Be kind to foreign dignitary.
And while he's fending off our foes,
    Bend down and wipe a little boy's nose.

One of the last events we enjoyed together as a complete family was the Black Watch, a royal highland regiment, which we observed from a White House balcony. The event was presented as a special performance on the South Lawn for seventeen hundred children between the ages of six and thirteen from Washington child-care agencies. Jack, Caroline, John, and I watched the highland dancing and drills until the last note died away. John stood delighted, holding onto Jack's hand, and cried when it was over. Jack patted John's head and said, "That's all right, son. There will be plenty more good things for us to see."

Even sadder was the last time Jack left John, before we traveled to Texas. Loving John as he did, Jack intended to take him with us on the helicopter ride to Andrews Air Force Base, where *Air Force One* was waiting to fly us to Texas. When Jack was ready to leave, he yelled out, "Where's John?"

Miss Shaw replied, "It's raining. I don't know if he should go."

Jack laughed and said, "You're afraid of a little water? Go get him. I'm going to take him with me." The delighted little boy in his London Fog raincoat and sou'wester, which John adored because it looked just like a real Army fatigue hat, excitedly ran to greet his father. Father, mother, and son climbed into the helicopter, which made its way to Andrews. Jack then kissed his son goodbye, told him he would have to leave, and gave him a hug. John began to cry, and said, "I want to come with you." Jack said, "You can't." With a troubled look in his eyes, Jack watched John being pulled down the runway in tears. They never saw each other again.

In what I called an act of God, a series of pictures of Jack and John appeared in *Look* magazine just four days before Jack was killed. It was only because I was cruising in the Greek islands with Lee and Aristotle Onassis, which Jack thought would help me recover from the loss of our newborn son, Patrick, that Jack and the photographer, Stanley Tretick, managed to take the photos and sneak them out to the magazine. I had forbidden the media to publish any photographs of Caroline and John. Jack and Pierre Salinger, like two naughty little schoolboys, waited until I was out of town to have John's pictures taken. Now I'm happy they did.

John was not even three years old at the time, and to that point had been greatly overshadowed in the media by Caroline. Various stolen snapshots appeared here and there in the papers, such as when he was caught greeting the astronauts or peering over the balcony watching his great love, the helicopter, deposit famous visitors on the back lawn. There had even been some newspaper hoopla protesting John's shaggy Prince Charles haircut as un-American, which stimulated the public's appetite for more about the child. People complained that they didn't even know what he looked like, so the editors of *Look* magazine were deliriously happy to publish a photo spread of young John.

Taking photographs of him was not easy—John was a squirming, wriggling little boy. The problem was solved when Jack presented John with a gadget someone had sent to the White House—a toy parrot with a tape recorder hidden inside. Jack previously had recorded a few words in it: "I am Poll Parrot. Would you like to fly with me in my helicopter?" Unfazed by a parrot speaking in his father's voice, John answered, "Yes, I would. Would you like a stick of gum, Poll Parrot?"

The photos turned out to be a magnificent set of Jack and his beloved boy, unlike any I have ever seen of a president and a family member. Tretick took nearly one thousand memorable shots of John, including one of him peeking out from under his father's desk and another of him perched on the presidential rocking chair. They record a presidential father and his son, and are, I believe, of great historical value. I will be eternally grateful to Stanley for the gallery of photographs that not only are great art but also the last pictures depicting the loving, prideful relationship between Jack and his son.

I used to smile when I thought how lucky this adoring father was to be able to work at home, where we, like many working people, were able to live an almost normal family life. Despite Jack's philandering, I remember walking around the Rose Garden thinking, *Please, God, let me stay as happy as this with Jack for the rest of our lives.* I should have known it was too much to ask. I'm so glad Jack and John had each other so passionately, even for that short amount of time.

Chapter 15
THE ASSASSINATION

In the years of Jack's nonstop campaigning, I was lucky if I saw him at all, and on the rare occasions he was able to make it home, he was groggy with fatigue and could only collapse into bed. I missed him, so I dreaded the move to the White House, thinking that Jack's responsibilities as president would keep him away from me even more. I was pleasantly surprised. The children and I saw more of him than ever. He became a man who worked at home, and he lovingly wove us into his days and nights, making for a relatively normal family life. Our time in the White House was the happiest of my life—far happier than the early years of my marriage.

Our happiness was suddenly shattered with the death of Patrick, our baby boy who died in an incubator at Boston Hospital on August 7, 1963, with Jack by his side. When the doctors told him his son was dead, Jack retreated to an adjacent boiler room to weep. Then he came to the room where I had given birth. To comfort me, he put his arms around me and we both cried. "There's only one thing I couldn't stand, Jack," I said, "and that would be losing you."

"I know, I know," he murmured. Jack helped me see how fortunate we were to have Caroline and John, and I felt good knowing how much he loved and appreciated them, and how the tragedy of

Patrick might bring us closer together.

I wanted to stay home with Jack and the children, thinking that would be the best way to soothe the grief stemming from the loss of Patrick. But Jack had another idea. He thought it would help me to go away to another land entirely, a country far from "the scene of the crime." My sister Lee was cruising at the time on the yacht of the Greek millionaire Aristotle Onassis. When Onassis heard the terrible news, he invited me to join them on his yacht. Jack thought accepting was a great idea, so I reluctantly went.

Surprisingly, Jack was right. It worked. I had a marvelous time and was feted everywhere we went. Aristotle couldn't have been nicer to me, showering me with jewelry and gifts worth a fortune. I felt secure with him in a way I hadn't back home. I wrote Jack ten-page letters in which I told him what an exciting time I was having, but I missed him, and was sad he couldn't relax with me in the beautiful Mediterranean. After several months, I came home in far better spirits than when I'd left.

Some people like campaigning; some don't. I was definitely in the latter group. I don't like having strangers breathing down my neck and pumping away at my arm until it's ready to fall off, but Jack loved campaigning, and could have gone on doing it forever. I felt a little guilty that I had gone off to have a good time and left Jack to mourn Patrick alone. So to make up for it, I told him, upon my return, "I will campaign with you anywhere you like."

But perhaps I'm being unfair to myself. It wasn't only guilt that made me decide to campaign with him. I sincerely believed that things had to turn out right for people like Jack, or there was no justice in the world, and I wanted to do all I could to help produce a just result.

By campaigning in Texas, the President hoped to win greater support from the state's Democrats, whose Kennedy-Johnson ticket had barely won in 1960, thanks greatly to then-Senate Majority Leader Lyndon Johnson's capture of his native Texas. There was a bitter, longstanding feud between the conservative wing of the party, headed by Governor John Connally, and the liberal wing, which was led by Senator Ralph Yarborough—a feud that Johnson, as vice president, no longer had the power to heal. Jack felt he had to campaign with Lyndon in order to repair the split and secure Texas's large number of electoral votes in the coming election. Delighted by my willingness to campaign with him, Jack answered my offer with a shouted question: "Does *anywhere* include Texas?" I responded by flicking open my red appointment book and scribbling "Texas" across November 21, 22, and 23. Jack leapt over and gave me a rare hug.

When a journalist got the news and commented, "That girl's got brains!," Jack said wryly, "Do you mean as opposed to the rest of us?" But to me, he said, "See? When you don't stick around all the time, you're much more valuable when you *are* here."

"I'll have to go away more often," I said.

Strange how so many people had premonitions about Jack's death, starting with Jack himself. Incredibly, on the day we arrived in Dallas, he said to me, "Jackie, we are going into nut country. If someone tries to shoot me with a rifle from a window, nobody would be able to stop him, so let's just not worry about it." He once told our journalist friend Joe Alsop he didn't expect to live past forty-five years of age, and that was the reason he believed in living life like there would be no tomorrow. He was remarkably on target. It was less than six months after his forty-sixth birthday that he was struck down by the assassin's bullet.

He was well aware of the potential dangers of being president, and often quoted the former king of Italy who, in 1897, after dodging the dagger of a would-be assassin, said, "These are the risks of the job." Somewhat later, the clairvoyant king was shot to death. When pressed about the possibility of being assassinated, Jack would often say, "If they want to get me, they can get me, even in church."

Then there was his remark on visiting the future site of his grave: "I could rest here forever." Perhaps most revealing of all is a home movie written by a friend of ours—Jack chose to play a character who is assassinated. Jack joked about Eisenhower's belief that anyone

could kill the president who was willing to die for it. I guess he had to take it lightly, or he would have been paralyzed with terror. I was, and had to tuck it away in some remote part of my brain.

Senator William Fulbright, who the year before had been the subject of a vicious attack by the reactionary *Dallas News*, pleaded with Jack to bypass Dallas. "Dallas is a very dangerous place," he said. "Don't go there!" A Dallas woman wrote to Pierre Salinger, "Don't let the president come down here. Something dreadful would happen to him." Adlai Stevenson, who had been assaulted in Dallas on United Nations Day, remarked to presidential assistant Arthur Schlesinger that he seriously questioned whether the president should go there, and advised Schlesinger to convey his doubts to the president. In the campaign of 1960, a mob of Dallas housewives had sprayed Lyndon Johnson and his wife with saliva, and Jack knew that Lady Bird Johnson shook with fright when she thought of returning there. An Austin newspaper editor predicted that Jack would not get through his Dallas stop without something awful happening to him. Even Governor John Connally told Jack that people in Dallas were very emotional and that he should reconsider stopping there. But Jack was stubborn, and on this subject, at least, listened to no one but himself.

The night before we left, I had a terrible nightmare. In it, I stood up to walk and fell onto the floor. I looked down and saw with horror that my right leg had been amputated below the knee. I screamed into the blackness, "Mummy, Mummy! Help! Help!" But nobody was there. I thought, *How can I get to the door? I'll never make it without my leg. Could I walk with a cane? Where are Jack's crutches? Can I find a wheelchair?* I wiggled my toes. They moved. *Funny*, I thought. *I have no toes, but it feels like they're still there.* I started crawling toward the door, but it kept moving farther and farther away, so I swiveled around and crept back.

When I woke up, the nightmare seemed so real I actually looked down to see if my leg was there. Later, I tried to understand what the dream meant, and thought only that without Jack, I wouldn't have a leg to stand on. So many people had warned us against the coming Texas trip that the idea apparently brought terror into my heart. The dream made me think that perhaps my fear was justified, and I begged Jack to call the trip off. But when I told him about the nightmare, he laughed, and said, "Come off it, Jackie! It was only a dream."

When I kept on protesting, he raised his chin and said, forcefully, "I am the president of all the states, Jackie. As such, I am the president of Dallas and *will* go there." Stubborn, heroic, or foolhardy? Perhaps a little of each.

On Friday, November 22, 1963, we went to Dallas. Everybody heard the ominous noise differently. Some thought it was a backfire and laughed. Others believed a giant firecracker or a cherry bomb had exploded. One man said, "My God, they've thrown a torpedo!" Uptown on Main Street, a motorcycle had backfired right beside us. When the shots went off, my first impression was that this was another motorcycle making a ruckus. But a few astute people identified the sound for what it was—rifle fire.

Some thought there were three shots. I and a few others heard only two. Governor Connally suddenly screamed out, "No, no, no! They're going to kill us all!" In a daze, I wondered why he was shrieking.

Secret Service Agent Clint Hill saw Jack lean forward and grab his neck.

Special Agent Roy Kellerman heard the president call out, in his own inimitable style, "My God, I'm hit!"

"My God!" Senator Ralph Yarborough screamed. "The president has been shot!"

Abe Zapruder, who took the famous home movie footage of the assassination, screamed over and over, "They've killed the President! They've killed the President! They've killed the President!"

I turned anxiously to Jack. There was a puzzled look on his face, an expression I had seen many times when he was perplexed about a difficult question asked by a member of the press. In a movement of matchless grace so characteristic of Jack, he raised his right hand

as if to straighten his unruly hair. His hand fell limply to his side. He had been aiming for the crown of his head, but it was no longer there.

Our Lincoln limousine began to slow down. Inside was a scene of incredible horror. The second bullet had pierced the lower part of Jack's brain. I leaned toward him and saw a piece of flesh, notched like a saw, detach itself from his skull. Suddenly, the car was filled with Jack's blood. It poured out all over me, the Connallys, the Secret Service men, and the upholstery. Thick globs of it soaked the clothing Jack had selected with such care only a few hours before and saturated the backseat. The floor was a red river, so viscous one's feet stuck to it. Some of his blood had spurted as far as the sidewalk.

Even the American Beauty roses given me at the airport were covered with blood, so you couldn't tell whether their deep color was the red of his blood or of the roses themselves. Jack's body lurched toward me, as if in his last moments he looked to me for help. But my love could do nothing for him. John Connally, covered with his own blood as well as Jack's, sank into the lap of his wife Nelly and screamed and screamed in agony, until she began to scream, too.

Suddenly aware of the reality, I sprang to my knees and cried out, "My God, what have they done? They've killed Jack. They've killed my husband! Jack, Jack, what have they done to you? Oh, Jack! Oh, Jack, I love you." Without any awareness of what I was doing, I crawled up on the sloping back of the car and began to tumble down to the street. Were it not for Clint Hill's fast thinking, there would have been another casualty to add to Jack's. Sometimes I think that's what I was trying to do. I don't know. I have no independent memory of the moment.

Back in the car, I huddled down on the ruined upholstery, cradling Jack in my arms, his shattered head staining my white gloves crimson. I leaned over him, trying to hold down the top of his head and shield the horror of his wound from everyone's eyes. There was no hair on the back of his head anymore. It had been blown away, along with the bone. On the right side of his face, a space between his eye and his ear had opened up. Some of his brains had fallen out, and

I clutched a large chunk of brain tissue in my hands. Bloody pieces of flesh and bone were flying through the air. I saw pink-rose ridges on the inside of his skull. By now, the car was speeding to Parkland Hospital. A brisk wind caught my pillbox hat and slid it down over my forehead. I violently wrenched it off, tearing out a hunk of my own hair. I didn't even feel the pain.

When we got to Parkland, Jack's pupils were dilated and he didn't seem to be breathing. His brain was utterly destroyed. I was told later that if he weren't the president of the United States, he would have been immediately declared dead on arrival. Nevertheless, I continued to hold him in my arms, hugging his stained but still handsome face and holding it to my breast. I couldn't bear to let him go. In holding him close to me, I could disguise the horrendous sight of his mangled brains, even from myself.

"Please, Mrs. Kennedy," Clint said, "we have to get him to a doctor."

"Why, Clint? You know he's dead. I'm not going to let go of him."

Clint is a sensitive man. He had seen Jack in those awful moments in the back of the car and he suddenly understood why I was holding him so close. Clint ripped off his coat and gently placed it in my lap. I tenderly wrapped the coat around Jack's head. When we arrived at the hospital, they put him on a gurney and wheeled him into the world-within-a-world of Trauma Room Number One at Parkland Hospital.

I sat forlornly on a wooden folding chair by the door of the trauma room, waiting, waiting, waiting . . .

Jack was dead. What was I waiting for? He wasn't going to come back. I had lost my husband, the father of my children, and my president—three terrible losses in one. Nothing else mattered.

The doctors and nurses came out regularly to stare at me. I know they wanted me to leave. But I determined that no matter who ordered it, I was not going to go away without Jack. They were all worried about me. "Would you like a drink of water?" "How about a cup of coffee?" "Can I get you a tranquillizer?" "Would you like to lie down? We'll find you a quiet spot."

I shook my head. "No, thank you. I'm all right."

But I wasn't all right. Three times I almost fainted, and had to hold on to the chair to keep from falling to the floor. But I knew what I wanted—the only thing I wanted on this most horrendous of days. I wanted to be with Jack's body, to touch him, to stroke him, to kiss him, to tell him I loved him. "Just get me in there before they close the coffin," I said to whoever would listen. I wanted to give him something—something of mine that would stay with him forever. But I didn't know what.

A memory of my father's coffin flashed through my mind. I had wanted to give him a possession of mine, too. Dangling from my wrist was the bracelet he had given me for graduation. He was so proud of me, and I treasured that bracelet.

"Yes," I remember thinking, "that is exactly right to keep with Daddy forever." And I clasped his fingers around it.

But what could I leave with Jack? I thought of the St. Christopher's Medal I had given him for a wedding present that he had left in little Patrick's coffin. I had bought him another in gold, fashioned as a bill clip, for our tenth wedding anniversary, and he always kept it in his wallet. But then I thought, no. The medal was his. I wanted to leave something of mine. I looked down at my left hand and saw the simple wedding ring he had bought for me. I loved it, and I knew it was just what I wanted.

To my surprise, I heard an orderly say the word "resuscitation."

"He's still alive?" I gasped. I had been certain he was dead. *Oh, dear God, if only he would live! I would devote my life to him, to his every wish. If only he would live, I would spend my life taking care of him. I would spend every moment by his side. I know it's a thousand-to-one chance he will live, but please, God, one can hope. Can't one?*

I tried to force my way though the doorway, but it was barred by the thick, sturdy arm of Dr. George Burkley, Jack's personal physician. "Sorry, Mrs. Kennedy, but I cannot allow you to go in there."

"Please, Doctor," I said, "I need to go into the room."

"No, no, I can't let you do that," he said. "Only medical personnel are allowed inside."

"Are you afraid it would upset me, Doctor? I've seen my husband murdered. I'm covered with his blood. He died in my arms. Do you really think anything I could see would be worse than that?"

Realizing that nothing could keep me out, he admitted defeat and stepped aside.

Doris Nelson, a hospital nurse, who was also covered with Jack's blood, saw me entering and came rushing up to the door to block it. She said, "She can't go in there, Doctor," and suggested I wait outside. I pushed her away and said, "I'm going in. What's more, I'm going to stay there." She was much larger and stronger than I, but my frenzy to be with Jack gave me strength I didn't know I had. I shoved her again and said, "Get out of my way, nurse! I *will* get in that room! I *will* be there when he dies!" The doctor said, "Let her in, Miss Nelson. It's her right to be there." The nurse reluctantly stepped aside.

More than a dozen doctors and nurses were moving efficiently around the president in Trauma Room Number One, occupied with the elements of emergency medicine, controlling his bleeding, maintaining his blood pressure, and giving Jack a tracheotomy so he could breathe. There was no real blood pressure or pulse. Only an infrequent heartbeat remained.

Kemp Clark, a well-thought-of young neurosurgeon, rushed into the crowded room. Charles Baxter, the doctor in charge of the emergency room, said, "Tell us, Kemp, how bad is the head injury?" Clark hastily examined the president's injuries and blanched as he shouted, "My God, the whole right side of his head is shot off! There is nothing left for us to work with."

Around that time, Jack's heart rate began to drop. I watched it slowly sink from thirty beats a minute to twenty, and then down to ten. Someone opened a chest tray to start a chest massage. "There's nothing to work with," Dr. Baxter said. "We have no reason to resuscitate."

I dropped to the floor by Jack's side and knelt in his blood. Then I closed my eyes in prayer. After a few moments, I stood erect and gently picked up the president's hand. An orderly helped me put cream on Jack's finger to work the ring over his knuckle. Oh, how I wished all the people would go away! I needed so badly to be alone with Jack. But I knew they never would.

It was one o'clock. The doctor reached down and pulled a sheet over Jack's head. He turned to me and said, "Mrs. Kennedy, your husband has suffered a mortal wound."

"I know," I said.

"The president is dead," he added. I lowered my head a bit and touched his cheek with my own. The doctor broke into sobs.

They closed the door while an undertaker, Vernon Oneal, went about his business. He was concerned only that the pale green silk lining of the coffin would become stained with Jack's blood. Two nurses wrapped Jack's body in a second plastic sheet, while Oneal enveloped Jack's destroyed head in eight rubber bags, placing seven protective layers of rubber and two of plastic between Jack's scalp and the satin lining. My beloved husband was lying in his coffin and Oneal was worried about it being stained by his blood!

That wasn't all that troubled me—there was also the sound of raucous laughter floating down the hall and horseplay between two orderlies at opposite ends of the corridor. I was bewildered. How could people laugh and play when Jack lay dead in his coffin? How could anyone go on with anything? For that matter, why didn't all life stop?

I walked beside the stretcher that carried Jack as the aides wheeled him down the hall. Over his chest were some of the roses I had been given at the airport. My hat had also been lying on top of him when he was brought into the emergency room. Jack was a tall man, and I was upset that the sheet was too short for his body, so his feet stuck out. I could see his face. The head wound was covered up, and below the forehead, he looked almost natural, as if nothing were wrong with him. His expression was completely without fear, nor was there any indication of agony. He had a compassionate look on his face, as if he were thinking, "Father, forgive them, for they know not what they do." I looked down at the face I loved and would love all my life, and was ready and poised when the priest entered.

"You can go on the plane now, Mrs. Kennedy," a military aide said, trying to be kind.

"Thank you, no," I said. "Absolutely not. I'm not leaving until I can go with Jack."

I passed some time by reading a copy of Jack's official admission form to Parkland. When asked his "complaint," someone had entered "gunshot wound." Yes, I would say that he indeed had a complaint— that his wonderful life had been abruptly and cruelly brought to an end, that his grieving wife and children would be forever without him, and that his beloved country henceforth would be bereft of his leadership. His "usual occupation" was given as "President of the United States."

Precision was not exactly a trait characterizing Dallas officials that afternoon. There were two errors on the form. His age was listed as forty-four instead of forty-six, and the White House address was given as 600, not 1600, Pennsylvania Avenue. Under other circumstances, I would have found the responses amusing, but now I could only be irritated that the officials knew so little about their president. Was there really anyone in the world past the age of three who didn't know what Jack's actual address was? I have always resented protocol, but especially in the case of the death of the president of the United States, requiring that such a form be filled out was nothing short of ludicrous.

Dr. Burkley entered the room one last time to inspect it. While looking through the trash, he saw bright red petals strewn through it. He recognized them as remnants of the bouquet of flowers the city of Dallas had welcomed me with. The doctor noticed a dying blossom lying on the floor, and another whose stem was sticking out from the lid of the can. He solemnly picked them up and placed them in an envelope. Later, in the hearse, I saw Dr. Burkley burrowing into his clothing and wondered why he was fidgeting. Then he reached into his shirt, took out two blood-covered roses, and handed them to me.

I put them in the pocket of my suit.

The Secret Service men, plus Larry O'Brien, Kenny O'Donnell, and the military aides, prepared to carry the coffin up the steep stairs to the waiting plane.

"It's awfully heavy," Ted Clifton said. "Do you think we can do it?" No one answered. Everyone knew they *had* to do it. Someone whispered, "Good God, don't let go!" In their haste, the body-bearers damaged a corner of Oneal's eight hundred-dollar coffin. A piece of metal from the lower hinge and the entire top of the handle behind Jack's head had been torn off. The slow ascent of the coffin, which weighed nearly half a ton, seemed to take forever. There was scarcely an inch on either side of the steps in which to maneuver. The coffin rose inch by inch, the man in front twisting it at the turn, the men in back doing all they could to keep it level. The smashed handle made the task even more difficult, because the men had nothing to hold on to. At one point, their burden tilted a little. I thought, *Oh, no! Jack is sliding down to the bottom of his coffin. It must be hurting his back!*

The tail end of the plane had been prepared to hold the coffin, and the exhausted men carried it in and laid it against the bulkhead. I sat on the aisle seat closest to Jack's coffin. When the stewards finally locked the back door of the plane, I quietly arose. I wanted to be alone for at least a few minutes. I had refused to leave Jack's coffin even for a moment, but the bedroom was next to the tail. The last time Jack and I had been together in bed had been in that room. A memory of our great happiness there swept over me from the top of my head to the tip of my toes, and I cried. Yes, the bedroom would be the perfect place for me to compose myself.

Because I regarded it as my bedroom, I did not knock, but turned the handle of the doorknob. To my great shock, there was Lyndon Johnson sprawled out on Jack's and my bed. I gasped and tried to rush out of the room, but Lyndon beat me to the door and made a quick exit. With glazed eyes, I stared at him. I couldn't stay in the room. Lyndon had ruined it for me forever.

Once Lyndon decided to return to Washington aboard *Air Force*

One, Jack's plane, there is no way controversy could have been avoided between the Kennedy and the Johnson people. In the previous two hours, our people had gone through horrors most individuals don't experience in a lifetime, while Lyndon himself was in a state of shock. If he had decided to fly to Washington in the back-up plane parked alongside *Air Force One*, much anguish could have been avoided. But he was now the president and was entitled to use the president's airplane. I suppose, too, that he felt the symbolic use of the plane was important in beginning his presidency.

Everyone's nerves were taut, and it wouldn't have taken much for an explosion to occur. To the credit of all of us, we understood that any public sign of a break with the new administration would be harmful to our already traumatized country. Therefore, we kept our feelings to ourselves, expressing them only in the seating arrangements, with the Kennedy people bunched together in one group and the Johnson folks in another.

It was hot and humid in the cabin, but the plane didn't take off because Lyndon was waiting for his friend, Texas judge Sarah Hughes, to come aboard to swear him in. He said Bobby had told him he had to take the oath of office in Texas. Of course, Bobby denied ever having said any such thing.

Secret Service Agent Rufus Youngblood said to Malcolm Kilduff, Jack's assistant press secretary, that we had to take off immediately. Kilduff responded angrily that we couldn't leave until Johnson had taken his oath. Senator Youngblood said that Johnson was not on *Air Force One*, but on the backup plane.

"Well, then," Malcolm said, "somebody better go tell that six-foot-four Texan back there that he isn't Lyndon Johnson! We are staying here until the president has taken his oath!"

Youngblood grew red in the face and said, "I have only one president, and he's lying back there in his coffin."

I knew exactly how he felt, but we have to trust people. I determined to try.

The wait seemed to take forever. The conflict between the two groups had become irreconcilable. The Johnson party refused to leave until Johnson took his oath of office. The Kennedys considered only that Jack was their president, and since he couldn't give orders, they looked to me. I knew only that I was hot and miserable, and desperately wanted the plane to take off, but I didn't want to antagonize Johnson.

I went into the bedroom for a moment of privacy. The Johnsons saw me enter and followed me to give their condolences. Lyndon put his arm around me, but was too overwhelmed to speak and merely shook his head. Lady Bird's face was streaked with tears. "We didn't even want to be vice president," she said. "God help us."

With a sob, I said, "What if I hadn't gone to Texas? What if I hadn't been there by his side?"

Lady Bird sobbed along with me, and said, "I don't know . . . what can I say?" She was right. There was nothing anybody could say that would make any difference.

After a while, Lyndon regained the ability to speak, and said, "What about the swearing in?"

"Lyndon," I began, and then stopped. "I'm so sorry, Mr. President," I said. "I'll never call you Lyndon again."

"No, dear," he said. "Please call me Lyndon all of our lives." Awkwardly, he told me that, at this time, continuity was important, and the country would want me by his side as he was sworn in, though he insisted it was my own choice.

"Yes, Mr. President," I said without missing a beat. "I will certainly stand by your side. Our country demands it." Whatever my private feelings, I had no choice. My action or lack of it would be written in history. I could not shirk my duty. There was a long, grief-stricken silence. The men in the cramped tail were staggering and leaning into the bulkhead to keep from fainting. Then Johnson broke the stillness to come over and give me a compassionate hug. I folded myself into his rough bulk and silently wept. After that, back outside the bedroom, I sat immobile, my eyes glued to the coffin.

Everyone on the plane wanted me to change my clothing.

General Godfrey McHugh, who was probably repulsed by the caked blood under my bracelet, asked me, "Why don't you change your clothes?" I violently shook my head. The men consulted each other until, finally, Kenny O'Donnell said, "Let her be. She can stay the way she is." When Dr. Burkley knelt by my gruesome-looking skirt and gently said, "Wouldn't you like to change your dress, Mrs. Kennedy?," I shouted, "No! I want them to see what they have done!"

One thought kept going through my mind, driving me crazy. I went over and over the last three minutes in the car in Dallas, thinking, *What else could I have done? Would it have made any difference if I had sat farther to the left? To the right? Surely someone wiser, more loving, less self-absorbed could have saved him.* I felt responsible for his death. I was always telling Jack that he should have more protection, but he wouldn't listen to me. Perhaps another wife would have known how to make him take better care of himself.

Then, to add to my guilt, memories of the spiteful feelings I had for Jack over his philandering came back to haunt me, and I hated myself for them. I would have given anything then to erase the crushing guilt I felt for having maintained such hostile thoughts. The survivor does not escape unscathed.

O'Donnell came back and said, "I'm going to have a swift drink of Scotch. You should have one, too, Jackie." I'd never drunk Scotch in my life, and frankly loathed its aroma, but having heard it was good for victims of shock, I thought it might wipe those omnipresent guilty thoughts from my head. It was as good a time as any to find out. My life was over, I thought, and I would just be spending the rest of it waiting to rejoin Jack, so what was a little drink or two in the big scheme of things? To me, it tasted like tar. But I forced it down, and then took another. I might as well not have bothered. It had no effect on me whatsoever. The Irish Mafia—Jack's longtime Irish friends Powers, O'Donnell, O'Brien, "Mugsy" O'Leary, and Ted Reardon—were guzzling enough liquor to anaesthetize a horse, but it had no impact on any of them, either. We might as well have been drinking tap water.

A memory came back to me of when Jack and I had returned from the funeral of a friend. I said, "Jack, where should we be buried when we die?"

He answered, "Hyannis Port, I guess. That's where the family plot is."

I said, "I don't agree. I think you should be buried in Arlington. After all, you belong to the country now, not just to the Kennedys." He got the strangest look on his face, and passed it off with some joke about the tombs of the pharaohs, as if we were fools to be talking about burial plots at so young an age. Now, I wonder if I wasn't being prescient again.

The next morning, Saturday, November 23, Bobby, Caroline, John, and I quietly entered the East Room of the White House, where Jack's body lay in state for private viewing. I had written a letter to Jack, and had Caroline write one, too. Hers said, "Dear Daddy: We are going to miss you very much. I love you very much, Daddy. Caroline." John also scribbled something on a sheet of paper. The casket, which had been closed to the rest of the world, was then opened for us, and I gasped on seeing the wax-like figure that was supposed to be Jack.

"That's not Jack. It just isn't Jack," I murmured, and I was glad I had insisted that the casket be closed to the public. In it, I placed the letters from me, Caroline, and John. I also inserted a scrimshaw carved from whale ivory he had loved, and a pair of golden cufflinks I had given him. Bobby knelt beside me at the coffin and, next to Jack's body, left a silver rosary—it had been a wedding gift from Ethel and Bobby—and the PT-109 tie clip that Jack had given him. Then the coffin was closed for the last time, and we slowly and reluctantly left the room. That was the last view I had of my beloved husband.

On Sunday, November 24, dressed all in black, my eyes swollen from a full night of crying, I held the hands of Caroline and John as we watched Jack's coffin carried by military pallbearers from the North Portico of the White House to an artillery caisson (a gun carriage without a gun)—the same one that had carried the body of Franklin D. Roosevelt after his death eighteen years earlier. Six magnificent white horses pulled it up Pennsylvania Avenue to the Capitol. Approximately three hundred thousand people lined the Pennsylvania Avenue procession route. The silence of the enormous crowd was broken only by the muffled sound of the drums, with their drumsticks beating slowly and rhythmically on loosened drumheads by the corps of the military drummers following the caisson.

When the caisson arrived, a military officer called out, "Present, arms!" His words resounded loudly through the square. In Union Station Park, an artillery battalion began to fire a twenty-one gun salute, after which the Navy band broke into Jack's song, "Hail to the Chief." I couldn't bear any more, and underneath my black lace mantilla broke into sobs. I was told later that my tears brought the whole nation to its knees.

As the song's last notes faded away, the nine pallbearers representing the United States Army, Navy, Marine Corps, Air Force, and Coast Guard unbuckled Jack's coffin and slowly carried it up the thirty-seven steps of the Capitol. The children and I followed. Within the Rotunda, the pallbearers gently lifted the coffin onto the catafalque. The honor guards took their positions, and the mourners closed around them in a circle. A few brief eulogies were given by Senate Majority Leader Mike Mansfield, Speaker of the House John McCormack, and Chief Justice Earl Warren, but their voices were hard to hear in the vast Rotunda, and nobody seems to remember what they said.

What people do recall are the images of me, the grieving widow, and little Caroline, who was trying hard to make sense of the terrible tragedy that had befallen her beloved daddy. Lyndon Johnson came in and said a prayer, and the Rotunda became absolutely still. The ceremony was over, but no one, it seemed, wanted to leave. Suddenly, I realized that everybody was waiting for a sign from me. I whispered to Bobby, "Can I say goodbye?" He nodded.

I turned to Caroline and said, "We're going to say goodbye to Daddy now, and kiss him and tell him we love him and how much

we'll miss him." I knelt beside the coffin, and Caroline knelt beside me. I brushed my lips against the flag. Caroline did the same. The whole world wept as she slipped her hand underneath the flag to feel closer to her daddy. Even the joint chiefs of staff who stood nearby had tears running down their faces.

By the time the viewing in the Rotunda was over on Monday, November 25, at 9 a.m., a quarter of a million grief-stricken mourners had filed past Jack's casket, and over five thousand people had been turned away. At one time, the line was nine miles long. A group of nuns standing quietly in line since one o'clock in the morning were the last people admitted before the Rotunda was closed.

As we went out into the blinding sunshine, I was shocked to see the immense crowd that had gathered. People were lined up as far as my eyes could see. The streets were filled with an ocean of humanity surging toward the Rotunda in a tide that could not be stemmed. Cars were lined bumper-to-bumper all the way to Baltimore, forty miles away.

The wintry weather was crystal clear and milder than it had been. I overheard a servant whisper, "Thank God for small favors." Six limousines were waiting in the driveway of the White House to take me, Bobby, Teddy, Eunice, Pat Lawford, and other Kennedy family members back to the Capitol Rotunda. When we reached the building, Bobby, Teddy, and I climbed the majestic steps again and knelt by the side of Jack's coffin. Then we left for the trip back to the White House.

The pallbearers removed the flag-draped casket from the Rotunda and placed it on the caisson, which would carry it down Constitution Avenue onto Pennsylvania Avenue and to the White House, and then to St. Matthew's Cathedral on Rhode Island Avenue, N.W. The enormous crowds packing the streets were so silent that I could make out the clop of the horses' hooves, the grinding sound of the caisson's iron tires on the asphalt, and the melancholy tolling of the bell at the adjacent St. John's Episcopal Church. The full military procession, including the Marine band, ironically called the President's Own, and drill units from all four military academies—Army, Navy, Air Force, and Coast Guard—moved so slowly that it took forty-five minutes for it to reach the White House. We then left our limousines and joined the foreign heads of state, reigning monarchs, and dignitaries awaiting us in front of the White House.

A few moments later, with my eyes facing straight ahead and shoulders erect, flanked by Bobby on one side and Ted on the other, I began the seemingly endless trip to St. Matthew's Cathedral. One observer noted that I walked as regally as any of the royalty that followed me. I had to. A commentator said that I had hidden tears and a dignity that few women could have kept up in such an event. She'll never know at what cost.

Lyndon Johnson accompanied us. The Secret Service, aware of the great danger the new president faced from the million people who lined the route, urged him to ride in a bulletproof car, but he gallantly refused, and he and Lady Bird walked right behind us in the procession, followed by a color guard holding the presidential flag aloft. Then marched the presidents of twenty-two countries, ten prime ministers, and many kings, queens, emperors, and princes from all across the globe, dominated by the gigantic figure of General Charles de Gaulle. Next came more than two hundred leaders from one hundred countries, the United Nations, and other international organizations, as well as officials of the Roman Catholic Church.

Richard Cardinal Cushing, who had buried our infant son Patrick, married Jack and me, and christened our two children, was waiting to greet us at the cathedral. He put a comforting arm around my shoulder, kissed Caroline, and patted John on the head.

As the military pallbearers struggled up the steps of St. Matthew's, the largest television audience in history watched the unfolding historical event. In the United States alone, more than ninety-three percent of all sets were tuned to Jack's funeral, with over 175 million people affixed to their TVs. A reporter described New York as "a vast church," in which schools and businesses were closed and four thousand people stood silently in Grand Central Station, watching the

funeral rites on a huge TV screen. A United States satellite circling the planet brought the event into homes in twenty-three countries. For the first time in Soviet history, the nation's citizens were permitted to watch live television from the United States. *National Geographic* magazine expressed my feelings exactly with its headline, "All the World Stops for Kennedy's Funeral." The article said that, across the globe, millions of people paused to honor the dead president. Planes halted on the runways, trains shut down mid-trip, motorists in the midst of traffic, in Times Square as well as in Athens, Greece, came to a standstill, and the Panama Canal was closed. All around the world, flags were lowered to half mast.

St. Matthew's Cathedral was packed with over a thousand people, many of whom hadn't been invited. The casket rested at the foot of the altar, as Cardinal Cushing prayed for Jack and the redemption of all people everywhere. Bobby, Teddy, and I, along with hundreds of others, received Holy Communion from the cardinal, and Bishop Philip Hannan preached an eleven-minute sermon in which he quoted heavily from Jack's speeches.

After the funeral service was over, three-year-old John stood by my side outside the cathedral, clutching the pamphlet a Secret Service man had given him to amuse him during the service. As the coffin was returned to the caisson, I bent down to John, took the pamphlet from his hand, and whispered to him. He cocked his elbow and raised his arm in a salute to his father's coffin. A gasp arose from the crowd, and nearby spectators buckled at the knees. Of all the images of the ghastly assassination, John's gesture came closest to breaking the heart of America.

As the caisson started to roll, the dignitaries stood by, waiting for their cars. The distance to the Arlington National Cemetery was too great to walk. The mournful sound of muffled drums again filled the air, but did not drown out the clacking hooves of Black Jack, the jet-black riderless horse. Strapped to his empty saddle was a sword, with empty boots pointing backwards, signifying that Jack would ride no more. Black Jack gallantly trotted sideways to the cemetery, in the age-old tradition of a fallen leader's funeral procession. Behind the caisson snaked a procession of ten cars. Bobby, the children, Lady Bird Johnson, and I rode in the first car, with President Johnson and the Secret Service following us in the three-mile, one-hour-long cortege.

The matched gray horses worked hard pulling the caisson up the winding road that leads to the one-hundred-year-old Arlington Cemetery. Just fourteen days before, on Veterans' Day, Jack had brought John here to lay a wreath on the Tomb of the Unknown Soldier. Now he was about to rest close to him forever.

As the procession neared the site of the open grave, the Irish Guard, a drill unit Jack had admired on his trip to Ireland, stood at parade rest. As the coffin slowly advanced, a mournful wail of bagpipes was heard. As we approached the gravesite, fifty jet fighter planes, one for each state in the union, flew overhead. One slot in the inverted V formation was left open, in deference to the warrior who would fight no more. The last plane flew over the grave at a terrifyingly low level—it was *Air Force One*, and it dipped its wings in a final gesture of tribute. I closed my eyes in response, and shuddered anew as each of the shots of the twenty-one gun salute was fired over the grave by old Guard riflemen.

Cardinal Cushing gave his final prayer at Jack's gravesite and asked God to grant Jack eternal rest. Then Sergeant Keith Clark stepped forward to play "Taps." His chilled lips had turned blue from standing in the cold for three hours, and he cracked a note. It added to the poignancy of the moment.

Then the flag-folding ceremony began. White-gloved hands removed the flag from the casket and quickly folded it into the traditional triangular bundle. It was passed hand to hand through the honor guards until it reached the superintendent of the cemetery, who solemnly placed it in my arms. I hugged it like it was a baby. The cardinal then sprinkled holy water on the coffin. I touched a torch to the nearby jet of flame provided by the cemetery and lit the John F. Kennedy Eternal Flame. May it burn forever. As our hands locked,

Bobby led me from the cemetery.

Despite my state of near collapse, there was one remaining duty I felt I had to perform for Jack. Foreign dignitaries had traveled to the funeral from more than one hundred countries, in some cases for thousands of miles. They were all waiting at the White House. It would be most ungracious of me not to receive them, so I managed a smile and a thank-you for each one.

Near midnight, Bobby and I were finally alone in the White House. Bobby said, "Shall we go visit him?" I picked up a sprig of lilies from a gold cup in the hallway and took them to the cemetery. It was almost pitch black there, the only light coming from the flickering eternal flame, which looked blue in the darkness. I placed the lilies on the grave. We simultaneously dropped to our knees and prayed silently for Jack's soul. Then we turned and walked together into the blackness.

People say recovery from such a loss gets easier in time. That's not my experience. If anything, it gets worse as the years go by. I miss a presence that filled whatever room he was in. I miss his wry smile, his charm, his wonderful wit, his sweet-smelling skin, his vigor and energy, his piercing intelligence, his take on what was going on in the world. I miss the reason I had for getting up in the morning. Everyone says, "Oh, but you've had many men in your life. Surely that helps fill the gap." Nobody can replace Jack in my life, in the children's, or in the country's. I've tried to cry out my sadness many times, following the Chinese saying, "It is better to cry your heart out once than always sigh." I have the greatest respect for Chinese philosophy and have learned much from it.

In this case, however, the wise men were wrong. I keep sighing.

Chapter 16

B O B B Y

Robert Fitzgerald Kennedy was not only a superb brother to Jack, but the brother I always wanted and never had. I loved him as purely as one human being can love another. He was not only my brother, but my best friend and soul mate. I will never have another like him.

On the first anniversary of Jack's murder, I reached the lowest point of my life. There was a heavy black ball banging around inside my heart that hurt so much I didn't think I could live through it. Nor did I want to. I was raw, drowning in the frightful agony of my life. I had been saving up sleeping pills, which I spread out on my bed. They looked beautiful, in all their pretty red and green jackets. I thought, *They will give me peace. The government will bury me beside Jack and I'll be with him through eternity. Nothing else has any meaning for me. I might as well be dead.* But before I took the pills, I wanted to give it one last chance. I'd call Bobby and see if he could help me. If he couldn't, I'd ask him to adopt my children.

I called him and said, "Bobby, can you come over right away? I'm in a bad way."

"I am, too," he said. "I'll be right over."

He was there in a few minutes. I'll never know how he got to me so fast. I always thought he was an angel. He must have flown.

He rushed up to my bedroom two steps at a time, where I was lying in bed, huddled in blankets. I sobbed as I said, "Bobby, I miss Jack so much." He looked at me, and I looked at him and silently nodded. He lay down beside me and took me in his arms.

Then we began to make love. He looked like Jack, he smelled like Jack, he kissed like Jack, he made love like Jack, his skin felt like Jack's. For one brief, shining moment, I had Jack back again. For that moment, I was deliriously happy. It was like a beautiful dream. For all I know, maybe that's what it was—a beautiful dream.

How could I resist someone who meant so much to me? Why should I resist? My husband was dead, my children needed a father figure who loved them, I felt no loyalty to Ethel, whom I disliked, and I needed Bobby as desperately as one person can ever need another.

At the time, I couldn't understand why Bobby ultimately chose his wife over me. But now that I'm older, I realize that the reason people choose their mates is often a mystery to others. I have learned from my own experience that we frequently choose our marriage partners to fill in our own gaps. Bobby was shy and introverted; Ethel was a more conventional, outgoing type. Ethel filled in Bobby's gaps better than I did. Besides, they shared religious beliefs, and neither would have considered divorce.

Our affair continued for four lovely years, up until the time he ran for president, when we had to cut it off lest he not be nominated. He was my friend, my advisor, surrogate father to Caroline and John, and my emotional support. He saved my life and my sanity.

When I was very young, I was the person my mother wanted me to be. As a teenager, I tried to do what my father told me would please the boys. As a married woman, I had to charm Jack. As first lady, I had to satisfy the country. With Bobby, I found the essence of Jacqueline Bouvier Kennedy, and knew he loved and accepted me, whatever I did or said.

I have only one photograph in my living room; it is of Bobby. It is inscribed, "To Jackie, whom I will love forever." When a friend said,

"Jackie, you better store that photo. If the media ever sees it, it will set off fireworks!," I said, "What do I care what they say? With all I've lost in my life, do you really expect me to give up my beloved's photograph, too?"

In a way, Bobby's assassination was worse for me than Jack's. When Sirhan Sirhan fired the shot that killed Bobby, he didn't just murder a magnificent man. He killed off a whole dynasty.

Bad as it was for me, my children, and, indeed, the whole country, the most tragic aspect of Bobby's murder is what it has done to his sons. I have seen what has become of most of them—drugs, police trouble, criminal records, panhandling, jail. Worst of their misfortunes was David's death by drug overdose, Bobby, Jr.'s arrest for heroin possession, the involvement of Bobby's oldest boy, Joe, in a reckless driving incident that left a girl paralyzed for life, and forced stays for many of the boys in rehab centers.

Maybe I have just been luckier with my children, but I think it's more that I have stood behind them, body and soul, since Jack was killed, even more than when he was alive. I make sure they know I love them and that the memory of their father is indelibly fixed in their minds.

Of course, it is harder for Ethel, with so many children, but she didn't help them deal emotionally with the death of their father. Instead, with her stalwart Catholicism, she kept up the illusion with her kids that nothing had changed, that their father was happy in heaven now with their Uncle Jack, and that they would all be together again someday. At Hickory Hill, there was no room for discussing feelings. With Ethel, as with Old Joe himself, if you were weak, you were on your own.

After Bobby, Jr. was picked up for using drugs, his mother threw him out of the house. When David was sent to a rehab program, she never came to see him. If he had been my child, I would have parked outside his door until I knew for sure that he was well. He overdosed and died not long after.

If Bobby were alive, none of this would ever have happened.

With Ethel, the house was always in an uproar, with the kids running around like crazy. They were much calmer when Bobby was there. Unlike Ethel, he was a good disciplinarian. He didn't shout at his children, and he spoke to them gently, but he made them mind him. When he said to do something, they did it. He never struck his children; Ethel did. He was a perfect father, the world's best, who was emotionally with his children every step of the way, just as he was with me. When he and Ethel came home from a trip, the kids would rush up to him, not her, and tell him all their complaints about what had happened while he was away. Do you blame them? If you had your choice of confiding in one of the two of them, which would you choose? There is a picture of him holding all the kids that makes me cry whenever I see it. He would have been devastated at what has become of his boys.

Bobby's courage is perhaps unprecedented in political history. Jack would have had to write a whole new *Profiles in Courage* chapter to cover Bobby's remarkable deeds. On the campaign trail, he was the one white politician who plunged into black neighborhoods where armed Black Panthers spoke openly of revenge after the assassination of Martin Luther King, Jr. In leading the struggle for long overdue racial justice, he was second only to King himself.

He was a strange combination of character traits. He was both ruthless and vulnerable, hard as nails and shy as a teenager at his first dance. But he was also so real and unguarded, it would not be far-fetched to call him saintly. I have never known a man with as deep and abiding a love for humanity, who was unafraid to put his heart where his mouth was. Some people who love humanity in general are sons of bitches to their own family. Bobby was as much a saint to his children and to me as he was to the rest of the world. He was always there when I needed him. Bobby was the most honest person I ever knew. As diplomat Averell Harriman put it, "It was impossible for him not to tell the truth as he saw it. I think that is why some people thought he was ruthless. At times, the truth is ruthless."

Bobby meant hope to the needy. He meant peace. Bobby meant

an end to the horrible Vietnam War. He was the only politician whom desperate, wretched people could listen to with their hearts and know they could believe in him. People who were hungry, without hope, outcasts—African Americans, Hispanics, the homeless, and the impoverished—fought to get close to him. Bobby knew from deep inside himself that it isn't enough just to go on television and talk. People need to see a person and shake his hand. If only they could touch him, they could believe that help was on the way. Despite his own great grief, he instilled a faith in me that someday we would recover. When he spoke, the hearts of millions of the despondent (including mine) soared with optimism anew. What a president he would have made!

Bobby was a rare, complicated, unfathomable, sensitive, flawed human being. He was a person who drove himself mercilessly. Hence, he drove others just as hard. Sometimes I wonder if the terrible competition he put his children through on the athletic fields, modeled after his experiences as a child, made them feel inadequate. Bobby's father had preached, "We don't want any losers around here. We only want winners in this family. Coming in second or third doesn't count."

Is this what Bobby taught his children, or did Joe's philosophy somehow seep through to their unconscious minds? Bobby allowed no time for "resting up" or celebrating a victory. It was almost as if he knew how short his time on earth would be, and felt he had to make every moment count. Sixteen-hour workdays were not unusual for Bobby. There had been no soft touch to soothe little Bobby's aches and pains. He had been left to master them alone. So that is what he expected others to do, and he was called cruel and cold-blooded for it. To my everlasting gratitude, he made an exception for me in my time of great need.

For instance, when he was planning on running for president, we enjoyed fantasizing about what it would be like if he won. I said, "Won't it be wonderful when we get back in the White House!" Ethel snarled, "What do you mean, *we*?" and got up and left the room. Even worse, Bobby followed her. She was terribly jealous of me during the awful months after Jack was killed, when Bobby and I spent so much time together, especially when Eunice whispered loudly, "Bob's spending an awful lot of time with the widder-woman!" Ethel abruptly left the dinner table.

Ethel was so outgoing, and Jack always had so much fun when she was around. He loved being with her, and listening to and laughing at all her jokes. But when anyone raved about Ethel to me, Jack knew me well enough to shut them up.

Anyway, looking back on it now, I think perhaps I've been too hard on Bobby's children, and should take into account the terrible difficulties they experienced going through adolescence without a loving father to guide them. In more recent years, the reports about them are heartening, and would have delighted Bobby. For example, despite his early difficulties, Joe has been able to put his Kennedy talents to good use. On his father's funeral train, the budding fifteen-year-old politician went up and down the train with out-thrust hand, saying, "I'm Joseph Kennedy. Welcome to my father's funeral train."

Eventually, he became a congressman from Massachusetts. To the great honor of the Kennedy family, Robert F. Kennedy, Jr. became an environmental advocate, and Kerry Kennedy is a human rights activist. I'm proud of them all, and hopeful we will have more good news about all of Bobby's children in the future. I just hope I'm around to see it.

From what he told me about his upbringing, I believe it is a miracle that Bobby turned into the man he was. One would have expected the shy, clumsy "runt of the litter" to remain so all his life—someone who, at best, would grow up and have his father buy him a tavern to run, as his grandfather, Patrick Kennedy, had done at the beginning of his career.

Ten years younger than Joe, Jr., eight years younger than Jack, born after Rosemary, Kathleen, Eunice, and Patricia, and squeezed in before Jean and the baby, Ted, little Bobby was almost totally ignored by his father, who called him "runt" and "sissy." When Bobby was away at boarding school, he had to plead with Joe, Sr. to write him a letter, as he did Joe and Jack. When he thought about Bobby at all, Joe, Sr. thought he would never make it, and humiliated him by seating him with his sisters at the girls' section of the table.

Bobby was an awkward boy who kept tripping over his own feet and crashing into expensive vases and breaking them. His hands kept trembling, and he always looked scared, as if he expected to be knocked down at any moment and was trying to keep from crying. His poor coordination was especially painful in a family full of large, overpowering athletes, both male and female. As the third son and seventh child, Bobby said, "When you are that far down the line, you have to fight to survive."

The Kennedy boys were once out on a sailboat on Nantucket Sound. Bobby, then four, was unable to swim, in contrast to his robust brothers and sisters, who seemed to be able to do everything better than him. Narrowing his cold blue eyes, he decided that whatever the cost, the image of him as a clumsy, inept boy had to be destroyed. He leapt over the side of the boat, muttering, "Swim or drown." And drown he almost did, until Joe, Jr. dove off the boat and rescued his little brother. But fear of drowning didn't intimidate Bobby. He dove off the boat again and again, rescued each time by big brother Joe, until at last, the brave Bobby learned to swim.

"It either showed a lot of guts or no sense at all," said Jack.

A friend said, "Bobby was born with a terrible set of handicaps, and a great determination to overcome them all." Bobby himself said, "Like Avis rental cars, we have to try harder." Poor little Bobby, outclassed on every account by his better-endowed siblings, had to push himself mercilessly, even at the possible cost of his life, to win his father's approval. As a child, he flung himself into freezing waters when he didn't know how to swim. As a lawyer and attorney general, he took on the most dangerous cases in the United States. He didn't hesitate to challenge the corrupt, powerful union leader Jimmy Hoffa.

Born with the proverbial silver spoon in his mouth, Bobby became a spokesman for the victims of prejudice. At the height of racial violence in the United States, when civil rights activists were being slaughtered, Bobby allowed himself to become the prime target of armed, hate-inflamed racial segregationists. This is especially significant when one considers that Joe, Sr. was a rabid anti-Semite who visited Hitler in 1934 and admired Germany's pride and spirit.

Bobby was like Jack in his intelligence, his absolute devotion to the Kennedys, his drive, and his courage, but he lacked his older brother's ability to turn away hostility with wit and a gracious smile. Still, he was kinder and more thoughtful toward me.

Bobby was a precociously serious child, and as he aged, he became ever more earnest. In that respect, he was much more like his father, who felt compelled to speak his mind, disregarding the feelings of the individual who had caused his wrath. As a result, Bobby, like Joe, Sr., created many enemies in his short life, which may well have contributed to his murder.

Although Bobby was unable to handle hostility with wit, he sometimes could be very funny, exhibiting a sense of humor much like Jack's, which I loved. For example, in his speech after winning election to the U.S. Senate from New York in 1966, Bobby said, "I would like you to know that I have absolutely no desire to be elected president of the United States. Nor has my wife, Ethel Bird." When Jack wanted Bobby to learn Russian and be appointed the ambassador to Russia, Bobby replied, "Sorry, Jack. I couldn't possibly be the Russian ambassador. Languages are not my forte. I spent ten years trying to learn second-year French!"

One of the qualities Joe, Sr. insisted on from his children is that they keep their feelings to themselves. So Bobby worked on forming a leathery shell around the expression of any tender emotions. Except for his anger, he concealed his inner self from everyone except a few intimate friends. I am happy to say he considered me one of them. Bobby was much more comfortable in revealing his emotions to me than was Jack, who rarely talked about his childhood, his feelings about his parents, or the terrible times when he had come close to death.

Bobby told me that the bond between him and Rose rescued him from deep feelings of inferiority. Bobby, the sensitive, tearful child hiding behind a rigid shield, was his mother's favorite, her pet. Bobby was usually the ideal son, always attentive to his mother. He adored Rose. In early adolescence, when other boys were going through a teenage rebellion, Bobby was closer to his mother than ever. As she prepared to go out each evening, he would dash to the door to see her off, telling her how beautiful she looked and that he hoped she would have a wonderful time. Bobby may not have interested his father, but he was the son every mother wants and rarely gets. Similarly, he treated me like a queen, whose every wish was his command.

Rose was training her favorite son to be a priest and enrolled him in a school where there were morning and evening prayers, special religious retreats, and Catholic Masses four times a week. Bobby prayed with all his heart, as he did everything else. Despite his mother's wishes, he decided against becoming a priest. But unlike his brother Jack, whom Rose considered a "poor Catholic," Bobby remained devoutly religious all his life.

Bobby was like his mother in other ways as well. Perhaps that was why he was less afraid of his soft, feminine side than macho Jack, whose character was more like his father's. Perhaps, too, Bobby could be as loving and tender to me as his mother was to him.

Despite their closeness, the relationship between Rose and Bobby was not always so loving. Rose was the disciplinarian in the family. She would use her hand (Teddy said she had a mean right hand and would have made a great featherweight) or whatever implement was available—a coat hanger, a hairbrush, a shoe, or a belt—to drive home her point. She once slapped young Bobby's face so hard, she punctured his eardrum and split his lip. Rose's disciplinary methods, however, did not seem to temper Bobby's feelings for her. His injuries healed and his love remained intact.

Whatever the reason, Bobby was the one Kennedy with the capacity for deep feelings, which is one reason I loved him so much. I could tell him my deepest, most shameful feelings, and know he not only understood, but was willing to share his with me. Three generations of Kennedys living in America had passed him by, and, to the end, he remained an Irishman at heart. Brooding, fierce, passionate, white-hot, and sentimental under his shell, he was more Irish than all the rest of the clan put together. After meeting him, the poet Robert Lowell remarked, "What an unassimilated man!"

Chapter 17

ARISTOTLE ONASSIS

After Jack was assassinated, I tried to go on with my life, but it was impossible. Not a day went by that I wasn't shrouded in grief. Every place I went and everything I did reminded me of Jack. I had to feel sorry for Caroline, who told her teacher, "My mother cries all the time." It was true. I stayed in bed for days on end, gulping down sedatives and antidepressants, all of which were no more help than a glass of water. Never an outgoing person, I became totally antisocial. I invited people to parties where I didn't show up, made engagements I canceled, and writhed in self-pity. My pride had completely evaporated. Once, I made an appointment with a famous designer to decorate my new house, but I just couldn't go through with it. I buried my face in my hands and wept.

After a while, I got out of bed only to see Bobby, and would have fallen apart permanently had he not been by my side. He gave me solace, companionship, affection, and financial advice. He was always there when I needed him and was the one person who came close to replacing Jack. There is no question in my mind that Bobby saved my sanity after Jack was murdered and that I would have gone under forever without him.

When Bobby was shot and killed, I was once more in danger of

losing my mind. Again, I panicked, and in my confusion, his death became mixed with the horrors of Jack's assassination. The second killing brought back in vivid detail every aspect of Jack's death. Time seemed to loop back onto itself, becoming both flowing and solidified. In my mind, June 5, 1968 existed in the same framework as Nov. 22, 1963; I couldn't tell one from the other. I didn't think I could live through Bobby's death. This time there was no Bobby to support me. I had to have a strong man to take care of me, and to help the kids lead normal lives.

I've been asked why I didn't turn to Teddy after Bobby was killed, as I did to Bobby when Jack died. I suspect that, much as I liked Teddy, he was always a little brother to me, as he was to Jack and Bobby. Even his mother didn't take him as seriously as his brothers. Rose said, "He was my baby, and I think every mother will understand that I tried to keep him my baby."

The media were always cooking up one romance or another for me, with everybody from Marlon Brando to Prince Charles. The most preposterous of all was the one they fabricated with Teddy. I never would have had an affair with him. He didn't appeal to me that way. He was neither articulate nor scholarly like Jack, nor tender like Bobby, and I suppose somewhere in myself, although I stood up for him at the time, I never forgave him for leaving Mary Jo Kopechne to drown at Chappaquiddick. Nor did I care for his excessive drinking. At Jack's cortege, I stood behind the black caisson, escorted by Bobby on my right and Teddy on my left. I held Bobby's hand. I did not hold Ted's.

But even more important, Ted's wife, Joan, and I were good friends. It was to me she turned when she had a problem like her alcoholism or felt distressed about Teddy's womanizing. Ted was not a good husband to Joan. According to Myra MacPherson in *The Washington Post*, "He did not talk to his wife, did not touch her arm or laugh with her. . . . Even some staff members worried at how distant they seemed as a couple." As it was for some of the other Kennedy men, sex was Ted's ambrosia, but unfortunately, it was not sex with his own wife.

I liked Teddy, and found him to be a good friend. But I enjoyed teasing him and admit I got a kick out of making him uncomfortable. He was nice about taking care of my financial interests when I decided to marry Aristotle Onassis, and he was a good uncle to my children. Early in my marriage to Jack, I even inserted a clause in my will that, in the event of Jack's and my death, Caroline should be raised by Ted and Joan, because Caroline has always loved him. I also think Ted is a magnificent senator, perhaps the best the United States has ever had, and in that respect is carrying on the Kennedy heritage. I am proud of him for that. But Teddy was not the strong man I desperately needed at that time of my life.

When Bobby was assassinated, I became paranoid, and screamed, "I hate America! I despise this country and won't have my children living here anymore. If they're killing Kennedys, then Caroline and John will be the next ones on the list. We're sitting ducks, waiting to be the target of another Oswald. It's crazy to stay here. I want out!" I was going over the edge again, and needed a man powerful enough to pull me back.

Who better than Aristotle Onassis to protect me from disintegrating—Aristotle Onassis, one of the wealthiest men of all time, who owned a huge yacht and a private island where my children and I could escape from the crazies of the world? I had seen Ari off and on during the years after Jack's death. In fact, ever since Patrick died, he'd been a source of great comfort to me. My only thought was, *He will be my safe harbor.*

Ari was absolutely the man I needed at this lowest point of my life. He had survived the death of his mother when he was only six years old, and was raised by his grandmother, who taught him that "men have to construct their own destiny." Like Jack and his father Joe, Ari was master of his own fate. I knew he would take care of me and my children. In many other ways, Ari reminded me of Joe. Both were resourceful, confident, self-made men who knew how to live their lives to the fullest.

Ari was there when I needed him. He flew to New York and attended Bobby's funeral at St. Patrick's Cathedral, giving me the support I needed to get through the service without breaking down emotionally. The swiftness with which he rushed to my side in my time of need—as he always had, really, over the previous five years— told me I had found the love I needed to carry me through. So when Ari offered me the chance to escape what my life had become—when he proposed—I was thrilled to accept. As soon as I decided to marry him, I felt a sense of relief, as if someone had tossed a life jacket into a raging sea which was about to tug me under forever. I knew he would help me stay afloat.

That's why I stood up to all the Kennedys who pleaded with me not to marry Ari, as well as the newspapers who barked one insult after another about me and the millions of disillusioned people who saw pedestals crumbling on hearing the news. Everybody thought I was marrying Ari for his money—that I was simply an expensive courtesan who would sell her favors to the highest bidder. They had no idea how much I emotionally *needed* to marry him. "Let them think I am selling myself for money," I mused. "It's better than if they knew the truth."

The reaction in France hurt me the most. The French had a particularly despicable explanation for the marriage: "Jackie has a bank vault for a heart." Despite myself, I cried when I read it. I had always loved France and the French, and they loved me, but that was the end of our love affair. For years, I fought every nasty word that was said or written about me, but then I learned to say, "The hell with it! They can say what they want. I know who I am." And I knew who Ari was. He was a domineering person, and one of the few men in the world who never would become "Mr. Jackie Kennedy."

It was a surprise to me that, of all the Kennedys, the only one who gave me unconditional support was Rose. She said, "Don't worry, my dear. He is a good man." Here I was, the wife of her dead son and the mother of her grandchildren, and she was encouraging me to do what I thought would make me happy. For the first time in our decades-long relationship, I was filled with love for her. But par for the course, someone had to ruin things by saying, "Of course Rose wants you to marry Onassis. She's tired of paying all your bills." I tried not to listen, but that thought kept sneaking back into my head.

Ari was a sympathetic listener, far more so than Jack. I told him about my bitter disappointment at Jack's philandering, my grief at the loss of our baby Patrick, and the horror of seeing Jack murdered before my eyes just as the marriage was beginning to work. I told him about the White House years, and how humiliating it was to be shackled to the Kennedys for every penny. To Ari alone, I confided my worries about my children—in particular John, who wasn't doing well in school, and was frequently in trouble for punching his classmates. Ari listened compassionately. His heart ached for me, and he understood at a deep level how wounded I was by Jack's womanizing and believed that Jack had never appreciated me. He was especially angry at how begrudging Jack was about money, and hoped he would be able to ease and enrich my life as my new husband. Of course, it didn't hurt that he wanted a trophy wife to demonstrate he was capable of capturing the most famous woman of the century.

Everybody thought Jack had left me well-situated financially. He didn't. Jack left me an income, but not capital. At his death, I received a lump sum of only $25,000, plus all his personal effects and household contents, as well as $43,229.26 from his Navy retirement pay, the Civil Service system, and the salary owed him as president. That all added up to less than $70,000. He had established trust funds for me and the children, but my annual widow's share was limited to only ten percent of the value of the trust. Perhaps that was his way of getting back at me for what he called my extravagances. When I married Ari, I had exactly $5,200 in the bank. It makes me furious to think about it, so I don't.

As a woman used to spending forty thousand dollars in department stores every three months, I wondered how I was going to survive on my new allotments and continue to raise Caroline and John in the style to which they were accustomed. I had offered to let Bobby adopt them, but he refused, saying that children belong with their mother.

There were other contrasts between Jack and Ari, most of which, in the conventional sense, favored Jack. He was a tall, handsome, all-American-type boy, while Ari was a short, aging, barrel-chested foreigner. I was Jack's first and only wife, while Ari was a divorced man and a member of the Greek Orthodox Church. I knew the Vatican would never approve of my marriage to him and that I risked being excommunicated. Personally, that didn't bother me too much, but I was concerned about what it might mean for my children. I knew people would get their kicks from comparing the two men, but Jack was dead and Ari was the husband I needed.

As a good brother-in-law and representative of the Kennedys, Teddy flew over to Skorpios with me to discuss a premarital agreement. "Why is that necessary?" Ari joked. "I don't expect a dowry from Jackie!"

Ari had problems of his own with his two children, Alexander and Christina. They adored their mother, who was divorced from Ari, and hoped to the bitter end that their parents would eventually reconcile. They resented any woman their father was serious about, and me in particular, whom they considered an interloper, a gold-digger, and a money-grabber. Among other indignities they put me through, Alexander was delighted to recycle Truman Capote's description of me as "an American geisha." When Ari told his children of his plan to marry me, Christina threw a tantrum and Alexander walked out of the house and spent the day speeding around Athens. At first, they insisted they would boycott our wedding, but Ari convinced them, probably through a bribe of some kind, to attend. I kept trying to woo them, but without success.

As a Greek, Ari had to follow the country's law of *nomimi moira*, in which a husband was required to leave at least 12.5 percent of his estate to his wife and at least 37.5 percent to his children, thus making it impossible for family members to be disinherited. Ari loved me and wanted to protect me, Caroline, and John, and to look after us financially, but not at the expense of his own children. I wouldn't have thought well of him if he had slighted them in any way. Under the law as it stood, in the event of Ari's death (and he was no youngster), I would inherit at least sixty-four million dollars from assets worth approximately five hundred million dollars.

Later, Ari asked me to waive my *nomimi moira* rights. In exchange, he said he would give me, outright, three million dollars for myself and one million dollars to each of my children. He also agreed to replace any of Jack's income sources I would lose as a result of my new marriage and, in the event of a divorce or his death, to grant me the freedom to remarry without losing any income. Despite rumors to the contrary, there were no other prenuptial agreements. While Ari and Teddy argued about the terms, I went shopping and returned with a dozen pairs of new shoes and matching purses. Wanting to please Ari, I signed the papers without even reading them. Later, I realized how naive I had been to surrender my marital rights under Greek law.

On October 17, 1968, Mrs. Hugh D. Auchincloss, after much dragging of feet, finally and begrudgingly announced to the press that her daughter, Mrs. John F. Kennedy, after five lonely years of widowhood, was planning to marry Aristotle Onassis the following week. Two hours later, holding a child in each hand and looking straight forward, I walked out of my Fifth Avenue building. Wearing a simple gray jersey dress, I entered a waiting limousine, which spirited us away to the airport. There, I met my mother, stepfather, Jean Kennedy Smith, Patricia Kennedy Lawford, and her daughter. An empty Olympic Airways plane was waiting for us. Ari had bumped ninety passengers to give us privacy during the long flight to Greece.

By announcing the marriage, you'd think I had dropped a bomb on the Lincoln Memorial. A friend who objected to the marriage said, "If you marry Ari, you will fall off your pedestal." I said, "It's better than freezing to death up there." The newspapers shrieked, "Jackie weds blank check," "How could you do that to us?," and "She has killed President Kennedy again." But the hullabaloo didn't reach

us in the tiny whitewashed Chapel of the Holy Virgin, which rested serenely amidst bougainvillea and jasmine on the quiet little island of Skorpios. There, on October 20, 1968, beneath the raindrops—a Greek sign of good luck—the former American queen and the Greek multi-millionaire united in matrimony.

I entered the chapel tightly holding onto Caroline's hand, wearing a beige chiffon and lace dress by Valentino, which reached three inches above my knees, and which I had worn to the wedding of Bunny Mellon's daughter several months before. I couldn't help but compare the dress to the creamy white, taffeta faille gown and faintly yellow lace-point veil I had worn at my wedding to Jack, when I was young and hopeful, and the whole world was stretched before us. For this wedding. I wore an ivory ribbon in my hair, which understand now as a symbol of the little girl inside me. The groom, as was his wont, wore a baggy navy blue double-breasted suit with a white shirt and red tie. The tie was nice.

A heavily bearded Greek Orthodox archimandrite dressed in a gold brocaded vestment and a steeple-shaped hat performed the half-hour ceremony. Hugh D. Auchincloss, my stepfather, gave me away for the second time in fifteen years. I idly wondered how he could give me away when I no longer belonged to him, assuming I ever had. The priest said I should obey and fear my husband, and that Ari should love me as Christ loved his church. It seems to me that a wife should not be afraid of her husband, and that a husband should love his wife as a woman and not as a church. But the chapel where I was getting married was hardly the place to make a fuss.

Ari and I each held a flickering candle symbolic of our short span on earth. Prayers and hymns were chanted first in Greek and then in English. Ari's sister, Artemis, placed a delicate wreath of lemon blossoms and white ribbons on each of our heads and crisscrossed the wreaths three times. Simple gold wedding rings on our fingers were passed back and forth between us three times, representing the Holy Trinity. Then the priest offered us a silver goblet of red wine to kiss before drinking three sips. This was followed by the Dance of Isaiah, in which the priest, Ari, and I joined hands and moved rhythmically around the altar three times, as is customary at a Greek wedding. I couldn't help remembering how the dance floor cleared at my first wedding, and Jack and I waltzed to "I Married an Angel" and "No Other Love."

My poor children seemed bewildered, and kept their heads down throughout the ceremony. I kept looking at them anxiously to see if their spirits had lifted, but they never did. Unlike in America, there was no kiss to symbolize the end of the ceremony, but only the priest's words, "The servant of God, Aristotelis, is betrothed to the servant of God, Jacqueline, in the name of the Father, the Son, and the Holy Ghost." As we emerged from the chapel, we were pelted with sugared almonds and rice, the sugar standing for happiness and the rice representing fertility. Ari was sixty-two years old; I was already thirty-nine, and we had no plans for children. We held a reception aboard Ari's yacht, the *Christina*, and on it spent our first night together as man and wife.

Ari was a short man. I towered over him by at least three inches, and that was when I was wearing flats. He was anything but a stylish dresser. He must have had three or four hundred suits, but he always wore the same blue one in Greece, the same gray one in Paris, and the same brown one in New York. Opera singer and former Onassis mistress Maria Callas loved to joke that all of Ari's clothing was made in London, but, unfortunately, he was in New York at the time.

Ari was also a dangerous man. I always fell for men who seemed menacing to me. While being with such a man always denoted a risk, it made for excitement, as one never knew what to expect. Ari was a "bad boy" who held out the promise of thrills and adventure to everyone around him. Life was never dull with him. He knew how to penetrate my shell and make me feel devilish. I fell completely under his spell, and once I got over the initial shock of his appearance—he looked to me at first like a gnome on Notre Dame Cathedral—I rarely gave it a thought. We Americans are so hung up on the way people look. For me, character and personality are far more important.

In terms of appearance, all I cared about was that the man weigh more than I did and have bigger feet, and Ari met both of those requirements. When everybody was attacking me for marrying Ari, my sister Lee came to my rescue. "If he were a young, blond, blue-eyed WASP," she said, "do you think people would object to him so vehemently?"

Besides, he was magnetic and charming, and while he was no beauty, the longer you knew him, the more handsome and appealing he seemed. Some individuals take poor photographs. Ari was one of them. His photos overemphasized the bags under his eyes and the bulk of his body. In person, his face was much smoother than the photos indicated, and his build was trimmer. He didn't have an ounce of fat on him, and years of swimming in rough waters had given him powerful arms and legs. He had a gentle look in his eyes, and unlike many people of his age, a firm chin. He also had an attractive, ready smile. Women of all ages and persuasions were attracted to his personality. Gina Lollobrigida, one of the world's great authorities on men, said he had more sex appeal than any of the pretty boys in Hollywood. I wholeheartedly agreed.

Like my father, Ari was a womanizer, and he had an endless stream of anecdotes to tell me about his conquests. And as with my father, I loved listening to them. It took me back to being Daddy's darling little confidante. One of my favorite Ari stories centered on his fling with Evita Perón, the wife of the president of Argentina. When they finished making love, Evita made Ari an omelet. As a reward, he wrote out a check for ten thousand dollars for one of her favorite charities. "They were the most costly eggs I ever ate," he said.

From the moment we first met on Aristotle's ship, we'd been passionately attracted to each other. We always enjoyed each other's company, and at first were very much in love, in a way neither of us had been before. We had a lot of fun together, and he could always make me laugh. He took a lot of pleasure in me and called me his "class A lady," a line he stole from the pack of L&M cigarettes I always carried with me. Another plus: Marrying Ari got me out from under the thumb of the Kennedys. I didn't have to ask them for money anymore and listen to their endless lectures on why I should cut down on my spending. I don't know why they bothered, because I never heeded their advice.

Nor could they understand why I preferred Ari's squiggly little name to the glorious name of his predecessor. Little did they know that I enjoyed seeing everyone, including them, struggle with the little squiggles. Besides giving me credit cards with no monetary limits, Ari had an endearing habit of leaving charming little presents on my silver breakfast tray—gifts like a string of cultured pearls, an antique lace handkerchief, or a ruby-studded bracelet. Occasionally, he left me an original poem (Robert Frost didn't have to worry) or a letter, along with my coffee and a single red rose. He liked being my protector, my big Daddy O.

Ari treated women in an old-fashioned, chivalrous, respectful manner, acting as both boyfriend and father at the same time. How can you beat that combination? Gossip columnist Elsa Maxwell quoted a famous female movie star as saying that the moment she met him, she felt that he understood all her problems, and would help her solve them, and that she wanted him to protect and advise her.

Around men, he was merciless. Around women, he was magnanimous.

In the beginning, Aristotle Onassis wasn't difficult to love. When the marriage was good, it was very good. That leads to another reason I enjoyed Ari, which many people find difficult to believe: Ari warmed me up. Years ago, when I went to see Dr. Henry Lax, a distinguished Hungarian-born internist, whose patients included Merle Oberon, Doris Duke, Zza Zsa Gabor, and Greta Garbo, he was flabbergasted to discover how sexually naive I was. He had to draw me a diagram of the female genitalia to show me where I should be experiencing pleasure. Jack laughed when I showed him the diagram. He had just begun to improve his technique when he was killed. Nevertheless, the doctor helped me feel better when he explained that the sexual problem was not my fault.

Ari was a different story. He may have been an international buccaneer with a sixth-grade education, but he had another skill that in my book is just as important. If Ph.D.s were given for love-making, he would have been awarded many of them.

He awakened me sexually, so I became as passionate as a teenager with her first love. He was so different from Jack it hardly seemed we were performing the same act. I didn't want to get out of bed the first year of our marriage. Ari used to brag to his friends that we made love five times a night, and that I was superior in the sack to any woman he had ever known—and Lord knows there were plenty! Would you believe that former first lady Jackie Kennedy, known far and wide for her reticence and extreme need for privacy, was delighted that her newfound skills were being broadcast to others? I was so proud of myself after all those years of frigidity that I wouldn't have protested too much if he had filmed us in bed and shown the footage on TV. Well, maybe not on TV, exactly. Just to a few close friends.

Actually, Ari should have taken the credit himself. He was a warm and generous lover, and knew exactly what to do to please me. He didn't need any doctor's drawings to show him what I liked, and I never left his bed without being satisfied—I, who hadn't known what an orgasm was before he showed me. We shared a deep, physical love, and our pleasure was unbelievably heightened by the drugs Ari got from his doctors and friends to enhance his sexual prowess and desire. And the drugs definitely worked. Sex with Ari, intensified by drugs, was one of the high points of my life.

Ari liked me to wear see-through blouses, and was excited when I did. I bought dozens and wore them a lot around him. Ari and I also were excited by making love in unusual places. Once, a steward caught us *en flagrante* in a rowboat. I don't remember all the details, because I was at the height of passion, but I seem to recall that we went right on until we finished. For our honeymoon, Ari had all the seats in the first-class section of an Olympic plane ripped out and replaced with a giant bed. No sooner had the plane taken off than we were at it again, and I experienced all the frantic desire stored up during years of deprivation. Here again we were interrupted by a crew member, but we were just short of oblivious to his presence, so I assume he simply closed the curtains and backed out of the room.

After enduring five years of loneliness, I wasn't lonely anymore. Few people knew how much I loved Ari. On the tiny island of Skorpios, I found refuge from a hostile world. Little did I know that my happiness would be short-lived, and that the next seven years would bring a series of deaths and scandals that would rival the Greek tragedies.

I was only with Ari for a month after the wedding before I first flew alone back to New York. During that month, Ari had gradually calmed my fears of a gunman waiting to strike against myself and my children—after all, neither I nor they held political office, as Jack and Bobby had. In fact, with a renewed certainty of their safety, I'd sent Caroline, now eleven, and John, eight, back a couple weeks earlier, so they could resume their New York City private school educations. I would never be away from them for very long.

Ari didn't mind. He was in the midst of negotiating a giant deal with George Papadopoulos, the dictator of Greece, for a four hundred million-dollar government investment in a massive private undertaking. The negotiations soon collapsed, but that didn't stop Ari. He went right on planning his new shipyard, oil refinery, air terminal, aluminum plant, and tourist resorts, all designed to make him the richest man on earth.

I have no doubt Ari was a genius. Keeping ledgers on his businesses was unnecessary to him—he carried all the information in his head. He could tell you the exact location of every one of his ships at any particular moment. He overwhelmed people with his photographic memory, his intelligence, his charisma, and his ability to analyze character at first glance. I thought I had talent as a "shit detector," but next to Ari, I was an amateur. He had an x-ray eye. On first meeting you, he undressed you emotionally and could tell you the contents of your wallet, how much money, if any, you had in the bank, if you were a Republican or Democrat, and if you were a teetotaler or a drinker, and if the latter, what you drank. If you took a walk down a strange street with him, a friend once told me, you probably wouldn't remember, when you got to the next block, what you had seen in the last one. Not Ari. He could tell you exactly what kind of stores lined the street, and all about the passersby—how many were men and how many women, the number of hustlers, old men, old women, housewives, blue-collar workers, etc., etc. Ari didn't miss a thing.

A school dropout, he was at home in at least six languages: Greek, French, English, German, Spanish, and Turkish. He also knew a smattering of at least six or seven other languages. On a trip to Arabia, without taking a single lesson, he picked up enough of the language to be offered a job as an interpreter, in case he was looking for employment. A friend quipped, "Ari is conversant in many languages, but it is money he thinks in." When I asked him why he needed to make more money, he said, "It's not just money that interests me. When you have reached a certain point, that doesn't matter: It is success that counts. Each new triumph thrills me, but like an alcoholic who needs to drink more and more to achieve his high, I have to reach higher and higher to experience a rush of excitement." For a while, I was thrilled along with him, but then I got tired of it.

A few days after I first left for New York, he flew over to spend a weekend with the children and me at our rented country home in Bernardsville, New Jersey, but he hated it there and complained that the mud and horse dung ruined his shoes and pants.

"Why should you care, Ari?" I said. "You're a terrible dresser. A little mud won't make much difference." He ignored my remark and soon flew back to attend to his business, his real heart of hearts. Much of my time was spent flying back and forth to Greece. Caroline, John, and I would join Ari for holidays, as well as their entire summer vacations, before we would all return to New York, where they could resume their schooling. Ari stayed in Greece to take care of his financial empire. I nurtured my children; he nurtured his money.

Throughout our marriage, we continued this pattern of separate lives. Ari tried to make up for his absences with fantastic gifts that would impress an empress. He bought me buckets of jewelry, lavish furs, priceless paintings, and antiques. He let me shop and spend as much as I pleased—I would spend as much as thirty thousand dollars at a clip.

"She has had great misfortune," he said. "If spending makes her happy, let her spend to her heart's content. I want her to do whatever she pleases. If that includes international fashion shows and travel, so be it. I don't question her and she doesn't question me." He was also good to the children, which warmed my heart. He bought John a speedboat and Caroline a sailboat on Skorpios. He also got them Shetland ponies. He went to their school plays in New York, and took John fishing and to ball games. He tried to be a parent to my fatherless children, and I will always be grateful for that.

The long-distance marriage was ideal for me for a while—I am a person who is never happier than when alone. Ari made no demands on me and left me free to spend time by myself or with my children. He made sure I thought of him wherever he was. Even when we were apart, I never knew when or where I would find some delightful, unexpected present. And when we were together, I might discover a tiny, jeweled cigarette lighter next to my breakfast coffee. Who couldn't love so generous and thoughtful a man? It was fun, and nice, too, to have all the money I wanted for the first time in my life.

I repaid Ari in the best way I could. I put together a red leather scrapbook as a gift to him and filled it with English translations of Homer's *Odyssey*. On each page, I pasted a photograph I had taken of Ari, and wrote in my own handwriting how he was like Odysseus. The present moved him very much, and I thought I even saw a tear or two roll down his cheeks. After he died, I reclaimed the book, which I will always treasure. In my living room, it occupies a place of honor.

Some people have intimate friends, some do not. I am not the type who does. I am more comfortable having many acquaintances and social friends like Bunny Mellon, Jayne Wrightsman, and Nancy Tuckerman. I do get crushes on people once in a while, but they rarely

last. I am embarrassed to admit that the only women friends I keep for any length of time are those with whom I can call the shots. If someone puts a single line in print about me, that person is dumped from my list. I wish it were otherwise, but I cannot bear to feel under someone else's control and be forced to follow their wishes and not my own. I would never get what I wanted that way. I think, too, that I am afraid of being envied by women, so I can't let myself get too close. People tend to use those who have money, power, or fame, and I rarely feel I am cared about for myself. I have that problem with men, too, but not as much, maybe because *I* need *them*.

I must add that being a loner has its disadvantages. I became a bit lonely without Ari and started seeing old companions like Franklin D. Roosevelt, Jr., Kevin McCarthy, the actor, and Jack's dear friend, Bill Walton, who would escort me around town. It set off quite a metamorphosis in me. To my surprise, I found that marriage to Ari had loosened me up in places other than the bedroom. I began to have fun socially and enjoyed showing off the buckets of diamonds, rubies, and sapphires showered on me by my generous husband. I stopped wearing the prim white gloves that had characterized the White House days and began to gambol around in tight jeans, braless t-shirts, and flamboyant skirts.

I became the acting-out adolescent I had never been, and hardly recognized myself as Jack's prissy little schoolgirl-wife. I had entered a brave new world in which I traded politics for international society. Ari understood this side of me better than anyone. "The world doesn't understand Jackie," he said, "and holds her up as a model of propriety and all those other boring American virtues. She is full of mischief and needs a small scandal, an indiscretion, some transgression to keep her alive." He recognized the child in me who "accidentally" dumped a chocolate pie in my teacher's lap. Wasn't it this side of Ari, the "bad boy" who understood Jackie the "bad girl," that originally drew me to him as much as anything?

At the same time, I began to get irritated with him. We were quite different. His favorite food was pot roast, and he preferred a simple café to the fancy restaurants I enjoyed. You won't believe this, but when we went to 21, he ordered knockwurst and a bottle of beer. He would go on crockery-smashing sprees at taverns. When I objected to his unruly behavior, he would go without me. He enjoyed nightlife at international clubs; I could barely tolerate them. I couldn't stand his hours of no sleep (he never stopped working), his habit of making business calls until 3 a.m., and the boorish way he slurped his soup, ate with his elbows on the table, and tore off pieces of bread. It disgusted me so much I refused to take my meals with him. He disliked the theater, opera, museums, art galleries, the ballet, and everything else I hold dear. He never read a book and couldn't understand why I spent so much time curled up with one.

He also thought nothing of publicly humiliating me. Once, in front of our guests, he told his chauffeur to take us to Maxim's, because he wanted to see a beautiful girl who had made advances toward him. Another time, at a dinner party we were giving, I corrected a mistake he had made about the capital city of an African country. I knew because I had been there with Jack.

"Don't you dare contradict me in front of others!" he yelled at the top of his lungs. I left the table and went to my room for the rest of the evening, thinking, *Is this the man I've chosen to spend the rest of my life with?*

Then, to add injury to insult, he started to complain about my spending, and cut down my monthly allowance from thirty thousand dollars to twenty thousand dollars. Wasn't he to blame for the problem? First, he encouraged me to buy everything I wanted, telling everybody I deserved it because of all the suffering I'd gone through. And then, after getting me used to it, he tightened the purse strings. I might as well have been back with the Kennedys. His assistant said, "Jackie loves Ari to the degree that he lets her spend money." That's unfair! I had loved him *before* he let me spend money.

To make matters worse, I heard through the grapevine that he had resumed his affair with Maria Callas, the famous opera diva. They had been involved for ten years before Ari dumped her to marry

me. I understand that she loved him very much and was devastated at the break-up.

Our differences began to puncture so many holes in our relationship that it began to feel like Swiss cheese. In 1972, when Ari had the *Christina* take the children with us to Palm Beach for their annual visit with their grandmother, he and I were barely talking to each other. The atmosphere aboard the *Christina* was lethal. He was more and more exasperated by my spending, and hit the roof when he heard that I had taken twenty-three Olympic airplanes and helicopters out of service for my private use. Why have a husband who owns an airline if I couldn't make use of it? He also thought I should have made more of an effort with his own children, and he often screamed at my habitual tardiness. But a terrible tragedy in 1973 was to sound the death knell for our marriage.

Ari's son, Alexander, was an airplane pilot who planned to train another pilot to fly the new Piaggio airplane, which was onboard the *Christina*. The two men took off from Athens, but shortly after they were aloft, the plane banked sharply, turning upside-down and crashing into a mountainside. Alexander's head was reduced to the human equivalent of pulp, and rescuers who hurried to the scene of the accident were able to identify him only by his monogrammed handkerchief. He was rushed to the hospital, operated on for three hours to remove blood clots, and then placed on a life-support system.

Though we hadn't gotten along, I was terribly upset by his accident. It still upsets me to think about it. Ari and I were in the United States at the time, and flew immediately to Alexander's bedside, praying for a miracle to snap him from the jaws of death. It did not happen. Realizing that nothing could save his son, Ari ordered the doctors to turn off the life support and stood by helplessly as Alexander died. Ari was utterly destroyed by the death of his only son and heir. He could not accept it as an accident. He believed he had overstepped himself by marrying me and that the gods were punishing him for his hubris. I tried sincerely to ease his terrible grief. I held him in my arms as he sobbed, and sobbed with him.

Instead of being comforted by me, however, Ari blamed me for his misfortune. He believed I had put a curse on his family. In the time I had known Ari, he had lost his sister-in-law and his son. He also thought I had brought misfortune to the Kennedys with their many tragic deaths, including those of Jack and Bobby. Ari called me the "Black Widow." I know what he meant. Sometimes, I myself felt like Typhoid Mary, who innocently enough brought tragedy wherever she went.

Turning away from me, Ari went to Maria Callas for sympathy. She, of course, was delighted to give it to him. The death of Alexander marked the beginning of the end for Ari, as well as for our marriage. I think he lost interest in living and began to give up. After that, it was downhill all the way for him and for us.

When Ari's former wife, Tina Niarchos, died soon after, he could not bear to attend her funeral. He felt old, defeated, and more and more aware of his own mortality. He began to have a difficult time keeping his eyes open, and he slurred his words so much that it became hard to understand him. He checked into Lenox Hill Hospital in New York, where his illness was diagnosed as myasthenia gravis. His drooping eyelids had to be taped to his eyebrows to keep his eyes open. He hid behind dark sunglasses to disguise his condition. It was painful to watch this formerly vigorous, virile man breaking down and becoming a shadow of his former self. Trying to save our marriage, I planned outings with friends to try to make him feel better, but nothing worked. When a person decides he does not want to live anymore, there is nothing anyone can do about it.

In a final attempt to try to save the marriage, I arranged for a vacation in Acapulco, where Jack and I had honeymooned. I thought the pleasant climate and the beautiful setting would make Ari feel better—that amid the beautiful flower-covered cottage, we might regain some of our early passion. Flying down on his private Lear jet, I asked Ari to build a house in Acapulco, a place I had fond memories of and loved. He was infuriated. Didn't I know that his businesses were going badly, and Olympic Airlines was steadily losing money?

He was not interested in owning such a house, he shrieked, and my request to build it was just another form of bloodletting. I screamed back at him that it was a hateful and mean thing to say, and he was an ingrate. I said I had never wanted his goddamned money and didn't now.

"That's good," he said. "Because you're not going to get any of it."

Then, without another word, he took himself to the rear of the plane, where, for the rest of the trip, he wrote a new will. As I found out later, he designated Christina as his major beneficiary and included a clause to establish a foundation in memory of his son. He took care of me (if you can call it that) by limiting my share of his assets to $150,000 a year for as long as I lived, and $150,000 a year to my children for the rest of their lives. Though I had earlier waived my rights to *nomimi moira*, I was sure that, were I to challenge his will, I would still receive the legal minimum—12.5 percent of the estate. I wasn't too worried, because I felt the children and I were legally protected. At least I hoped so.

In Acapulco, we didn't say two words to each other, but rather ate, slept, and swam separately. I couldn't wait for our "second honeymoon" to end, and we left after only a few days. Ari's health deteriorated drastically after that, and we no longer bothered to keep up the pretense of a marriage. We now lived completely different lives. We were seen together rarely, and then only in the company of others. I continued to live in my Fifth Avenue apartment, with its comfortable, deep-seated settee and arm chairs, paneled walls, eighteenth-century tables, and bookshelves filled with books on history and art, my children's handiwork, and souvenirs from all over the world. When in New York, Ari stayed at the Hotel Pierre.

Then, unbeknownst to me, Ari contacted lawyer Roy Cohn to ask him to file for a divorce. He also hired a private detective to follow me around, hoping to gain evidence of my infidelity, which could be used against me if I fought the divorce. He figured that if I were sleeping around, it would cost him a lot less money. But I had anticipated such an action and didn't fall for it. If I *were* sleeping with anyone—

and I'm not talking—I would make good and sure to keep it private. After all my years at the White House, I had gotten pretty good at keeping secret what I didn't want known. As far as the detective's discoveries were concerned, my extramarital adventures were limited to luncheons, dinners, and innocent nights on the town.

Ari now believed I was attempting to exploit him for everything he was worth. I felt bewildered and betrayed by his behavior, and loathed him for withdrawing what he had so generously given me. I hated having to plead with him for every little thing I wanted—he had become as bad as the Kennedys—and refused to cut back one penny on the lifestyle he had instigated. We quarreled bitterly on the rare occasions we were together, even in the presence of mutual friends. I no longer valued the presents he had given me. He had once gifted me rubies as large as pigeon eggs. I now considered them vulgar and kept them locked in a safe. The next time I asked him for money, he said I should sell the jewelry, because it was only taking up valuable space. I refused to put up with his sarcasm and kept as far away from him as possible. He soon put divorce proceedings in motion. He flew back to Athens to transfer Olympic Airways to the Greek government, to make sure I wouldn't inherit it.

In February 1975, I received a phone call that Ari had collapsed with agonizing pains in his chest. His liver and lungs were now contaminated with his disease. Frightened for his life, and in spite of our disagreements, I contacted a top New York cardiologist, Dr. Isidor Rosenfeld, and flew him to Athens. The doctor examined Ari and insisted that he be flown to the American Hospital at Neuilly-sur-Seine, France, where the finest care was available. Ari dragged his heels, saying he knew if he went into the American Hospital, he would never come out alive. His long-time physician in Paris, Dr. Jean Caroli, Christina, his sister Artemis, and I all insisted he go into the hospital. Finally, he agreed, talking of death and dying the entire flight to Paris, and saying he felt close to Alexander. Hearing him talk that way, I felt a terrible foreboding in my heart. Much as we fought, I still felt a certain fondness for him, and didn't want him to die.

Typical of Ari, he wouldn't go into the hospital on arriving, and insisted on spending the first night at his Avenue Foch apartment. I wouldn't have been surprised if he went there to see Maria Callas. The next morning, underweight by forty pounds, looking shriveled and cadaverous, he refused to be carried on a stretcher and walked into the hospital under his own steam. Shortly after, his gall bladder was removed. An announcement was made to the public that Ari was progressing nicely, but that was pure baloney. He kept drifting in and out of consciousness for five weeks, and was kept alive on a respirator with dialysis and massive doses of antibiotics.

Christina and Artemis took over, pushing me to the side and allowing me little say in his care. That was all right with me. I'd had my fill of dying husbands, and wanted as little to do with his health management as possible. I did go to see him every day, and still tried to seem a caring wife, but I spent the evenings dining out and socializing with friends. Christina and Ari's sisters paid little attention to me during my visits, and Christina pointedly left the room as soon as I arrived. After Ari died, she told a reporter, "Jackie is a dangerous, deadly woman. She survives, while everybody around her drops. She's destroyed two families—the Kennedys and the Onassises. I hope never to see her again."

I'd never heard anyone say such awful things about anybody. Obviously, she didn't care how terribly she hurt my feelings. Perhaps she thought that rolling in money gave her the right to be vicious. I disliked her as much as she did me, but at least I had the decency to be quiet about it, and would have been glad to try to comfort her if she had let me.

The day after Ari's gall bladder was removed, I phoned Dr. Lax and asked him to come see Ari. He said he had talked to the doctors at the hospital, that they were doing everything possible for the patient, and that there was no point in his coming to France. I think he just couldn't be bothered.

I called him again a few weeks later to say there had been a slight improvement in Ari's condition and ask if he thought it would be all right for me to come to New York for a few days. No, he said—I should stay, because the eyes of the whole world were upon me. Despite his advice, I was tired of the whole situation and wanted to come home for a while. Ari didn't seem upset at my leaving, and Christina certainly wasn't. In fact, she looked overjoyed.

I left Paris on a Friday. On Monday, I called Artemis, who said Ari's condition was unchanged. Because there was nothing I could do about it, I went skiing in New Hampshire. Ari picked just that time to rapidly deteriorate, and they were unable to reach me by phone. Back in New York on Saturday, I received word that Ari had died, with Christina by his side. Despite knowing of his deathly illness, I was stunned. This vital, energetic world entrepreneur, dead? Surely my informant was mistaken and would call back shortly to tell me Ari was only joking. He didn't call back.

The next day, my mother, Caroline, John, Teddy, and I arrived in Paris. Bronchial pneumonia was given as the cause of Ari's death. I visited his body in the small hospital chapel, where it was lying in his open coffin. There was a Greek Orthodox icon on his chest. I was deeply saddened. I immediately called fashion designer Valentino Garavani to meet me in Paris with a black dress suitable for a funeral.

Ari's body was in the main section of the plane carrying him home to Greece. I sat reading a book during the flight, remembering how I had refused to leave the side of Jack's coffin on the plane returning his body to Washington. Wearing my new Valentino under a black leather coat, I was the first person off the Olympic Airways plane when it landed at the military airport of Aktion. I was followed by Teddy, and then Christina Onassis, who had been sobbing loudly for the entire plane ride. I felt bad for her—I know what it's like to lose a father you love. Leading her to the waiting limousine, I put my arm around her and said, gently, "Easy does it. It will all be over soon." She yanked her arm away and gave me a look that could blow up a shipyard.

Teddy, Christina, and I sat in the back of the first limo. As the procession began to move, Teddy, who was there to protect my financial interests, said to Christina, "Now, let's look out for Jackie."

Christina burst into sobs again and yelled to the driver, "Stop the car immediately!" She unlocked the door and jumped out to join her aunts in the next limousine.

Looking back at it now, I am appalled at Teddy's crudeness and unfortunate timing. Christina was deeply mourning her recently departed father and in no shape to discuss money to be inherited by a hated stepmother. I wish I had instructed Teddy to be quiet about it, at least until after the funeral was over, although I doubt Christina would have been happy to discuss the situation at any time.

Six pallbearers carried Ari's coffin up the winding path to the small chapel in Skorpios where he and I had been married six and a half years before. I felt mournful on seeing it, remembering how happy we had been for our first several years together. When he was nice, nobody was as nice as Ari. The funeral procession, led by a priest holding aloft a large cross, made its way past six large wreaths of red, white, and pink flowers, including one from me, which said, "To Ari from Jackie." The service was simple and brief—only a half-hour long, in accordance with Ari's request. I knelt to kiss the coffin during the ceremony, as was expected of me, but did not cry.

Except for old memories, there was nothing left for me to mourn.

Chapter 18

WHERE I SHOULD HAVE
BEEN ALL ALONG

Six months later, once I had gotten Caroline off to college and John to boarding school, I began to grow a little bored. I had been married to a great charismatic president and to one of the richest men on earth, and I was used to meeting the world's most important statesmen, artists, writers, politicians, actors, and musicians. How long could I be expected to be satisfied jogging around the Central Park Reservoir, working out at the Vertical Club, and visiting my psychoanalyst, Dr. George Gross, and Kenneth, the famed hairstylist? I was also lonely. I was used to living a life built around a man, and none of my many dates and escorts filled the void.

I complained about the situation to my friend, etiquette expert and author Tish Baldrige. "Why don't you get a job?" she said.

"What, me work? You've got to be kidding."

She wasn't. For my own mental health, she said, I had to get back into the world. When I asked her what I could do, she said, "You were always interested in writing. Why don't you go into publishing?"

She recommended I call her publisher, Tom Guinzburg at Viking Press, and ask him about it. As it happened, Guinzburg had been a

friend of mine for twenty years. I called him and broached the idea over lunch at Le Périgord Park restaurant. At first, he was dumbfounded, and then blurted out that my name undoubtedly would add prestige to the house, that few people had as much influence or as many connections as I, and that many fine authors would be attracted to Viking by the idea of having me edit their books.

He hired me then and there as a "consulting editor" at a salary of ten thousand dollars a year—the first money I had earned since working as the inquiring camera girl so many years earlier. I must say it felt good, and I valued that money almost as much as all of Ari's millions.

Four times a week, between 9:30 and 10 a.m., I took a taxi to Viking. One cab driver who recognized me said, "Lady, you're *working* when you don't have to?" When I said yes, he commented, "Madam, I think that's great!"

I smiled and said, "So do I."

At first, my co-workers were intimidated by me and kept sneaking peeks when they thought I wasn't looking. But after they saw me making my own instant coffee, placing phone calls myself, doing my own typing, and standing in line with them at the copy machine, they began to get used to me. I had a simple, windowless office like theirs with only a small desk, a typewriter, a few filing cabinets, and a chair. I practically had to go into the hallway to turn around. I tried to dress pretty much as the others did, wearing cashmere sweaters, slacks, and no jewelry, but I overheard one editor say to another, "She may wear the same kind of clothes we do, but she looks better in them!" I had to laugh. It reminded me of Jack telling the crowds waiting for me in Ft. Worth: "Mrs. Kennedy takes a little longer to get dressed than we do, but when she's finished, she looks better than us."

Everybody asked me what I expected to be doing as a consulting editor. I said, "Mostly I'll be learning the business. I'll sit in at editorial conferences and listen to the general discussions until I'm assigned a project of my own, and then I'll *really* get to work. In general, I expect to do what my employer tells me to."

"Isn't that hard to do, after being queen of the universe and having hundreds of servants at your beck and call?"

"No," I said. "It's kind of a relief. I like feeling part of the human race." I told everyone there to call me Jackie. I once called the office boy "Mr. Jones," and he said, 'Way to go, Jackie!'"

Some people didn't take me seriously as an editor, considering me a dilettante. One editor said I was Marie Antoinette playing milkmaid, which I found insulting. I was serious about my work. I had been part of a history that few people were privileged to see first-hand. I knew I could bring a lot to the job that few others could.

After being around a few weeks and getting to know what was available at Viking, I found myself drawn to the Studio Books division. I've always been interested in art and art history, and thought I would enjoy editing large, opulent, beautifully illustrated coffee-table books. One of my favorites was *In the Russian Style*, which I worked on with Diana Vreeland. I wrote the text, selected the illustrations, and personally chose the gowns and accessories for the photographs. It became a lavish book shown at the Metropolitan Museum of Art to coincide with Diana's show on the elaborate clothing worn in the Russian imperial court. The book provided me an all-expense-paid and tax-free trip to Russia. I hadn't had my expenses taken care of so generously since my early days with Ari.

I wanted to go so I could bring back the imperial clothes for Diana's exhibit, but the Russians wouldn't let me. I guess they were afraid I would abscond with the whole collection. But they did let me try on Alexandra's hooded white fur coat, and I *was* tempted to prove their suspicions justified.

After the book was published, a reporter asked me how my children viewed the book.

"Rapidly," I replied.

She asked if I didn't miss the luxurious clothing of the White House years. I said yes, but I wouldn't want to wear them anymore. I found blue jeans and t-shirts much more comfortable. She also asked why I always wore sunglasses. I replied that they were a form

of disguise, yet also a kind of signature accessory. I wore them more as Ari's wife than as Jack's. Everybody knew who I was when I lived in the White House, but now sunglasses keep busybodies from reading the thoughts and feelings expressed in my eyes. They also shut out distractions.

Most important of all, they allow me to scrutinize others without being detected. You might call me a voyeur. Watching people out of my Fifth Avenue window with a telescope gives me a lot of satisfaction. I take pleasure in critiquing all the little figures fifteen floors below.

I've always loved being around books, so in that sense, working at a publishing house was pure pleasure. I like special books that are outside my regular experience and take me into another realm of existence. Reading them expands me and transports me into lives other than my own. I also like books that deal with the times I've lived through. Seeing them through the eyes of the author somehow crystallizes the events for me. I enjoy hearing writers talk about their work and the creative process. I also like that it is not the editor who is promoted, but the author and the book. One day, as I was coming to work, I actually found myself feeling so happy I kept singing Beethoven's "Ode to Joy." I couldn't believe it. I had thought for a long time I would never be happy again.

To celebrate my new status as a working woman, I gave a dinner party for some dear friends. Among them were Barbara Walters, Arthur Schlesinger and his wife, Candace Bergen, Tish Baldrige, George Plimpton and his wife, and Mr. and Mrs. Peter Duchin. They all stood and toasted me on leaving the ranks of the idle unemployed. I beamed—after wiping away the tears. Everybody was amazed at the change in me. George Plimpton said I was much more like the girl he had known in the 1950s—the one full of enthusiasm and fun. I must admit that, although I loved Jack and dearly enjoyed all the acclaim he received, I was always in his shadow. I was famous, yes, but famous as Jack's beautiful, accomplished wife. Now, for the first time, I was being saluted for an accomplishment all my own.

Tish Baldrige was especially delighted that I had taken her advice. "Yes," she told some of the guests, "work has helped Jackie pull herself together and become more independent. She always felt she had to lean on some man to have any status in life, and now she has earned stature of her own. The job has been great therapy for Jackie. She looks absolutely luminescent!"

I had some setbacks and frustrations at Viking, I must admit. When I tried to get the queen of England to write her memoirs, I was rudely rebuffed. I had kindly offered to show her around Washington on her state visit, and in return received a note from one of her many assistants, saying it was totally unacceptable for the queen to accept the escort services of a private individual.

I was treated equally badly by the duchess of Windsor. When I wrote to ask her to write her memoirs for Viking, the duchess responded that she had no intention of discussing her life story with any publisher's assistant. My streak of bad luck continued with Lord Snowden, Princess Margaret's former husband, who Viking didn't consider high-brow enough for me to work with. I even struck out with Frank Sinatra, who was interested in me more for romantic than literary reasons.

On a smaller scale, my secretary didn't like me, and resented being assigned to do any of my work. My co-workers were polite to my face, but as someone who is highly intuitive of what people are really thinking, I knew they didn't regard me as a serious editor. I brought up many ideas at editors' meetings, only to have most of them quashed. For example, I was ridiculed when I suggested a coloring book for children based on architectural ruins like Angkor Wat, which I still think is a great idea. When I suggested that my good friend, Doris Duke, write a book on her historical restoration in Newport, the idea was unanimously ridiculed, with a faint smile on the faces of many of the editors.

I was disillusioned with Tom Guinzburg, too, and began to believe I had chosen the wrong publishing house. So when an event occurred that upset me badly, I was more than ready to leave.

In 1976, Lisa Drew, a Doubleday editor, rejected a novel by Jeffrey Archer called *Shall We Tell the President?*. It concerned the imaginary election of Ted Kennedy to the presidency and a subsequent attempt on his life. Drew felt the novel was in bad taste and refused to have anything to do with it. When Viking, a competitor, bought the book, Drew was horrified and lost no time telling me about it over lunch. I immediately went to Guinzburg, who assured me the book would have nothing to do with me. I forgot all about it until Viking published it the next year to terrible reviews, one of which categorically stated that the book lurked at the bottom of the American cesspool. Not only that, but *The New York Times* blasted the "news" all over the front page that Guinzburg had told me all about the contents of the book and that I had approved it. Needless to say, I had known absolutely nothing. Most painful of all was the reviewer's comment that *Shall We Tell the President?* was sheer trash and anyone who had anything to do with its publication should be "ashamed of herself."

Two hours after I read the review, Tom Guinzburg received my handwritten resignation by special messenger.

When John Sargent, the head of Doubleday, heard the news, he contacted me and offered me a nice deal, which I quickly accepted. I received a raise to twenty thousand dollars a year for working only three days a week—Tuesday, Wednesday, and Thursday. I was upgraded to associate editor and hired as an acquisitions editor, whose job was to attract authors to the publishing house. I was given a cramped, unimposing twentieth-floor office, much like the one I had at Viking. Sargent apologized for its windowless state.

"Don't worry about it, John," I said. "I have plenty of windows at home." I dressed up the office a little with books, paintings, and one or two photos of my children, but wanted no decorations or personal touches at all. I was determined not to be the former first lady, photographs of whom had appeared in every magazine in the world. I wanted to be seen as a professional Doubleday editor.

My second entry into the publishing world turned out to be far more to my liking than the first. What was nicest at Doubleday, in contrast to Viking, was that I was permitted to do practically any book I wanted. And turn them out I did, one after another.

I must say, it didn't work too well at first. I had a lot to learn. I would bring in books about minor figures in the art world, or people in dance or theatrical circles who fascinated me but left my co-editors cold. One editor said on my first attempt, "That one's a sure bestseller! It might even sell seven copies, Jackie if you bought six yourself." But I worked hard at it and eventually was able to distinguish between books I liked and books that would sell. Only a year after I began working at Doubleday, I was thrilled to acquire what would become my first bestseller, *Call the Darkness Light*, by Nancy Zaroulis. The novel dealt with the plight of women mill workers in Lowell, Massachusetts in the 1940s, and reflected my own growing interest in complete equality for women. I like to think I was growing in my character as well as in my career.

But I was not yet ready to cut my ties to the world of fashion and art. At the same time I was working on the Zaroulis book, I was editing a volume of photographs of gorgeous flowers called *Atget's Gardens*, by Eugène Atget. I enjoyed the process because it brought back memories of working with Bunny Mellon on the Rose Garden, which Jack loved.

As a result of my success, I was promoted to senior editor. Best of all, my annual salary was raised to fifty thousand dollars. While I couldn't live on that in the style to which my children and I were accustomed, it made a nice addition to the income I received from Ari's money and the trust funds Jack left me. I edited ten to twelve books a year, which is pretty much the average for senior editors. It's true I worked only three days a week at the office, but I have never been a nine-to-five person and put in many hours at home on my manuscripts. It was not uncommon for me to work all night when the spirit moved me. While my first books for Doubleday were large, heavily illustrated coffee-table volumes about Russian culture and fairy tales, I soon turned to more popular or literary titles.

One of my favorites, which also landed on the bestseller list, was

Moonwalk, by *the* Michael Jackson. When the moonwalk dance step was popularized by Jackson, I got the idea of asking him to write a book with that name. Sometimes being a former first lady has its advantages. Michael was so impressed by my phone call that he agreed to have me fly out to Los Angeles to discuss the matter with him.

I liked him right away, and found him different from the flamboyant entertainer known to the masses. He was open with me and said he wanted to write a book about his life because "people don't understand me, and often write hurtful lies about me. They make my heart bleed and often make me cry." He said he wanted to explain his true self in the book, so people would know who he really was. I thought we were very much alike. For different reasons, we each needed to present a picture of outside perfection that was quite different from what we felt on the inside. People have called the both of us "all cage and no bird," but I have no doubt we both are "more bird" than most people.

I think Michael liked me as much as I liked him, and we drew up a contract calling for an advance of $450,000. We celebrated together, with Michael taking me on a guided tour of Disneyland. The tourists had a field day that afternoon—they were more interested in us than in Disney's attractions. In April, more than three hundred thousand copies of *Moonwalk* reached bookstores. The title reached number one on the bestseller list. I could hardly believe our success, and deep inside myself, I dared to fantasize that we had produced a masterpiece. *Jack would have been proud of me*, I thought. I was proud of me too. I wrote a brief introduction to the book, but I must say I didn't have much to add.

I have been first lady of the greatest country on earth. I have been the pampered darling of the press, beloved by millions of people of all colors and faiths. But I didn't know who I was until I became a book editor. When I was a young wife campaigning with Jack and had no time for myself, I had a dream. I dreamed of a huge fountain pen squirting ink up into the sky. I have become that fountain pen, squirting comments over the manuscripts of world-famous authors. I am Jacqueline Bouvier Kennedy Onassis, editor. In my heart, I always was an editor.

My life at this time was all the more satisfying because I became active in a few carefully chosen causes. I was the chairman of the American Ballet Theatre's annual fund-raising gala, and took part in several distinguished demonstrations against the building of obnoxious skyscrapers, one of which I proved would cast its shadow over a mile of Central Park.

But the New York project I am most proud of was helping save the irreplaceable and elegant Grand Central Station from demolition.

I also played a part in the preservation of Saint Bartholomew's Church and Lever House.

Every time I pass these buildings, a shiver of pleasure runs through me. I think, *I have done for my beloved New York what it has done for me. I have saved it, just as it has saved me.*

Chapter 19

THE TEMPELSMAN ERA

Becoming an editor changed me, perhaps making me into what I was meant to be. Because I now know who I am, I don't have to look for an identity by merging with some famous, powerful, or wealthy man. One would think all the hoopla and front-page news coverage I received (and am still receiving) would have provided enough identity for anyone, but I would look at all those lovely photographs and say, "Who is that woman? She looks familiar, but do I know her?" Now, all I want is a kind, friendly, supportive man who will be my confidante, companion, and lover. If he shares my artistic interests, as neither Jack nor Ari did, so much the better.

I will now introduce Maurice Tempelsman, my latest and (I hope) last lover, a man with all of the above qualities. No one would ever choose Maurice for my companion. In fact, we are so improbable a pairing that I got away with dating him for years without a soul (or journalist) suspecting we were an item. He is my age, and fat, with a belly that hangs over his bathing suit. At five foot eight (only an inch taller than I), he weighs 180 pounds, which he tries to disguise by wearing well-cut, dark, double-breasted suits. He has a moon-shaped face and wide, thin lips that wouldn't launch any ships. His smiling, friendly look is the sort that one generally thinks of as belonging to

a kindly uncle. I've heard some cynical "friends" label Maurice as nothing more than "a poor man's Onassis," because both men are short and heavyset, look older than their years, smoke Dunhill cigars, are financial wizards, collect rare art, and love the sea. The gossips have a point, but they couldn't be more wrong in their evaluation of Maurice. He is the perfect person for me at this time of my life. It just goes to show you that nobody can ever select a mate for anyone else.

After Ari died, there were numerous men in my life, many of them rich, famous, and handsome. The list reads like a virtual *Who's Who in America*. Among others, there were George McGovern, presidential candidate and senator (in case I was looking to replace Jack), the president of Tiffany's, Henry Platt (if I wanted a substitute for Ari's billions), and Frank Sinatra. The list also includes movie stars Warren Beatty, William Holden, and the great Marlon Brando. Also on it were Pete Hamill, the handsome, well-known journalist, and Felix Rohatyn, internationally famous financier.

I was forty-seven at the time of Ari's death, and my appearance hadn't changed much, thanks to healthy eating, daily exercise, and a little nip and tuck here and there. But as impressive as my list of suitors was, there was no one on it who interested me as a long-term partner, although several of the men and I have remained friends for life. Most people would not believe how few of them I slept with, and that the majority of these men served merely as window-dressing and escorts around town.

At this point in my life, I felt I no longer needed to be dependent on older men. Jack was twelve years older than I, and Ari twenty-nine years my senior. I no longer wanted a sugar daddy to tell me what to do, though I can't deny that I have always felt older men to be attractive. I remember telling Jack that, to me, men over sixty often look better than younger men. When he looked at me with surprise, I said, "Well, look at General Maxwell Taylor, for instance. He plays a mean game of tennis and is marvelous-looking and slender, while some of your classmates have let themselves go and look simply awful." Jack shook his heard and said, "Jackie, I think you have a father complex."

Maurice is one month younger than me. Although he was born in Antwerp, Belgium, where he and his Orthodox Jewish family had to flee from the Nazis, he is America's premier diamond connoisseur. Unlike the others on my list of suitors, his name does not appear in *Who's Who in America*. He is the kind of man who does not need the spotlight to feel important. For example, he attended my children's school plays, but always sat a few rows behind me, so journalists could not photograph us together. Maurice is always quiet and unassuming in public. Just being with me is enough to make him happy. He loves me for myself, not who I was.

After living decades with culturally illiterate husbands, it is a joy to have a companion like Maurice, whose knowledge of the arts is equal to, or surpasses, mine. He has an extensive understanding of theater, dance, music, literature, and film. He loves to travel and, like me, loves to go to the opera. He is a connoisseur of good food and wine; quite different from Jack, who loved to gulp down steaks and hamburgers, and Ari, who perpetually gorged on knockwurst and beer. Maurice and I both love nature, and enjoy nothing so much as an afternoon at a bird preserve, or simply walking hand-in-hand through Central Park.

Maurice is a charming and witty conversationalist, at home in society all over the globe. He is not a glamour boy, but he is loving, compassionate, gentle, and supportive of me, and never utters a nasty word. He always has been attractive to women, and at parties, he practically has to push them away. But miracle of miracles, he is not a womanizer! He enjoys what he has, and unless I am mistaken, has no eyes for any other woman. I feel lucky to have so devoted and constant a man at my side.

Although Maurice is not in the same financial league as Ari, he is more than well-heeled—he's probably a multi-millionaire many times over. His entire fortune is centered around Africa and the diamond industry. I've been asked what kind of diamond company Maurice owns. I can best explain it this way: If a man wants to buy a

thousand-dollar engagement ring for his fiancée, Maurice's company isn't interested. But if the stone the gentleman wants to buy for his lady is worth one hundred thousand dollars or over, his company will deal with him. I've been told (not by Maurice; he is too modest) that he has an "inside track" to the DeBeers Consolidated Mines, which controls the diamond industry in South Africa. He even sent my son John to intern in Africa to see if he wanted to be in the diamond business.

Maurice is a philosopher who equates the financial situation in Africa with the one in Israel. He says he has devoted his life to proving it is possible to do business—indeed, big business—with Africa. I admire his brilliance, his depth, his success, and his strength. What Maurice sets out to do, Maurice does, including winning and retaining my heart.

Our romance began quietly. I first met him at the White House. He was a friend of Jack and an influential figure in select Washington circles. Jack and other chiefs of state looked to Maurice for advice on how to deal with African leaders. He and his wife Lily were guests at the spectacular, candlelit dinner Jack and I gave on the lawn at Mount Vernon, overlooking the Potomac, for the president of Pakistan, Muhammad Ayub Khan.

We maintained our friendship throughout my marriage to Ari. After his death, our relationship changed. It was business at first, as he took my savings and turned me into a multi-millionaire. It progressed to a close friendship, and then, gradually, to a love affair. When my sister's husband, Stas Radziwill, died, Maurice flew over to London with me for the funeral and never left my side.

I considered myself fortunate indeed when Maurice became my financial adviser. I had been in a panic in the mid-1960s, when New York City was teetering on the verge of bankruptcy, and I could have lost millions of dollars. I turned to Maurice for help. After the city recovered, he continued to oversee my finances, and parlayed my twenty-six million-dollar settlement from the Onassis estate into anywhere from one hundred to two hundred million dollars, making me a very wealthy woman. Because of Maurice, my children and I will never have to worry about money again. To a child brought up as a "poor relation," as I was in the Auchincloss household, Maurice's skill and dedication on my financial behalf were a gift for which I shall always be grateful.

Outside our financial meetings, we began dating three or four times a week, and frequently speaking on the phone. Soon, we became inseparable. We went together to the theater, top-of-the line restaurants, the ballet, and art museums. When Teddy was running for president, Maurice escorted me to fund-raising events. We also enjoyed quiet time together, and on Martha's Vineyard, we often had dinner on trays in front of the TV, like any old married couple. Many times, we sailed on his yacht along the eastern seacoast, and once took a relaxed, unhurried one hundred-mile voyage from Savannah, Georgia up to Hilton Head Island, off the coast of South Carolina. His yacht wasn't the *Christina*, but then, he had no whale scrotum on it, either, like the covers on Ari's barstools.

Early in our relationship, he often visited me in Hyannis Port, where I still keep the home on the compound Jack and I had shared. Maurice and I spent a lot of time vacationing in the rambling white house and cruising the gray-blue waters of Nantucket Sound in my eighteen-foot sailboat. Because I am, in some ways, an old-fashioned woman who likes her man to act as head of the family, Maurice always sat at the helm of a motorboat, pulling me behind him on water skis. Sitting there in his bathing trunks, he looked just like an ordinary middle-aged man. Nobody gave him a second look. After all, who, on seeing him, would have dreamed he owned all those diamond mines? For that matter, they didn't recognize me either. All people could see was a bikini-clad, athletic-looking woman with a bathing cap pulled low over her head as a disguise and, in cool weather, a nondescript sweatshirt.

Maurice and I have a romantic relationship. Sometimes, I feel we are as enamored of each other as teenage lovers. We walk down the street arm in arm, hold hands in theaters and at the movies, cuddle in dark corners of restaurants, and kiss between courses. I am always interested in his thinking, as he is in mine. We never run out of things to talk about.

That reminds me of a story I heard about the duke and duchess of Windsor. They used to sit in restaurants and tell each other fairy tales in French so no one would know they had nothing to say to each other. Needless to say, Maurice and I never need to tell each other fairy tales, in French or any other language.

From Black Jack on, I always fell for domineering men. Jack was not quite as forceful as his father, but was nevertheless an authoritative husband who always told me what to do and made sure I did it. Ari gave me the freedom to do as I wished (so long as it coincided with his wishes), but at the same time, he ruled his extensive empire like a dictator. Maurice, on the other hand, is a *gently* domineering man. He runs the household in a quiet, unassuming way, but there is no question he's the man of the house, and that's the way I want it. He often disagrees with my suggestions, and makes no bones about it. I usually yield to his better judgment.

I realized how much I cared for Maurice when he suffered a heart attack. To be with him full-time, I moved into his room at Lenox Hill Hospital. I anxiously hovered over him, tirelessly quizzed the doctors and nurses about his health, and read up on how to take care of patients who had experienced a cardiac arrest. Then I took him back to my apartment and supervised his recovery.

People say that being with Maurice has changed me—that I am now a much simpler and more genuine person. I have also heard it said that, in contrast to my glamorous White House years, I am now a simply dressed, unassuming human being. They are probably right. What Maurice and I enjoy as much as anything on Martha's Vineyard is going for hamburgers and ice cream cones at the local snack bar, watching the glorious sunsets on the beach, and visiting country fairs, where we walk from booth to booth like everyone else. Perhaps I need the simple pleasures of life to relieve the stress of being an icon.

In contrast to my two marriages, Maurice and I share the

intimate, loving relationship of two mature people. He is my teddy bear—a warm, homey, loveable teddy bear. We have similar values, don't vie for power, and are as comfortable together as a couple that has been married for many years. We have a better and healthier relationship than any I have ever had. Maurice and I adore each other and care as much about each other as we do about ourselves. Isn't that a good definition of true love?

The one fly in the ointment—and it's certainly no minor one—is Maurice's relationship with his wife, Lily. They met when he was seventeen, and married when he was only twenty. He could discuss anything with her, including his business affairs. Lily is a strict Orthodox Jew who refuses to give Maurice a divorce, and she's now a marriage counselor at the Jewish Board of Guardians.

Maurice would have continued to live with her, but once the media caught on to me and Maurice, she grew sick and tired of seeing another photo of us every time she opened a newspaper, so she asked him to leave. When a journalist asked her what she thought of Maurice dating me, Lily answered, "I never comment on my personal friends." Then, she added snidely, "I suggest you ask *her*." Although Lily is furious with me and thinks I stole her man away, she and Maurice separated on friendly terms and have remained married. I don't mind being the patsy, as long as it keeps him happy.

He first moved out of their apartment into a comfortable suite at the Stanhope Hotel, right across from the Metropolitan Museum of Art and just down the street from me, and then, three years later, into my condominium. The last thing I want is a bitter court fight. Otherwise, we might marry. But you don't have to marry a man to be close. He made his choice, and I know I am the one he loves.

As I read over this, it occurs to me that Maurice is the only one of my three live-in men about whom I have no criticism. Should I have married him or someone like him in the first place? Some people know who they are early in life. Others take a bit longer. It has taken me until late in life to find both a career and a man right for me.

All of which raises two big questions: First, should I have married

Jack? I loved him very much (and still do), and we had some happy years as a family in the White House. I had the honor of being married to a wonderful president, being first lady of the greatest country in the world, and meeting the most important statesmen and artists of my times. If I hadn't married Jack, the history of the United States would have been a bit different, and I don't think for the better. And I wouldn't have had my two wonderful children. So yes, I have no question that I did the right thing by marrying Jack.

Was it a mistake to marry Ari? No, I don't think so. If I hadn't married him, I wouldn't have had the protection and security I needed at that time in my life. My children and I wouldn't have been able to escape to Skorpios whenever we had to. Then, too, if I hadn't married Ari, my children and I would have remained "poor relations" all of our lives, which I wouldn't want to inflict on anybody, let alone my darlings.

Chapter 20

ON DEATH AND DYING

So my horse stumbled over some stones and I "simply" went over the fence without him. *Simply?* I'm beginning to think there is no such thing as a simple fall. A young man I know fell in the street after tripping over the root of a tree and suffered seemingly minor bruises. He died a few days later from the bursting of some organ or other. I believe that, with me, it was the fall that did the original damage.

Maurice was opposed to a woman of sixty-four riding and jumping fences. He was afraid I would fall, become paralyzed, or worse. But I didn't listen. I wanted to do what I wanted to do. A little fall from a horse didn't frighten me.

It was November 1993—the thirtieth anniversary of Jack's murder—and it's possible I wasn't as alert as usual. I was competing in the jumping horses category at the Piedmont Club in Virginia when the horse in front of me knocked some stones off a wall. My horse, Clown, cleared the fence, but stumbled over the stones, tossing me back over the fence. I lay there inertly, but was conscious enough at first to hear a woman scream, "God in heaven! She landed so hard, she must have broken her neck!" A witness told me later that I was utterly lifeless, with my head twisted to one side and my black protective hunting cap, mandatory in the sport, ripped right off me, chin strap and all. I was unconscious for a good half hour while a crowd anxiously waited for an ambulance to arrive. By that time, I had returned to consciousness and was trying to stand up. The attendants rushed to help me.

"I'm just fine," I told them. "I'm sorry to be such a bother."

While I was unconscious, I had a dream, or perhaps it was a hallucination. But whatever it was, it seemed so sweet, and I would have liked to have stayed in it forever. In the dream, Jack came flying down from heaven with his arms outstretched. He landed gently, the way the good captain of *Air Force One* landed. "I've come for you, Jackie," he said. His face looked so real I reached out my hand to stroke it.

"Oh, Jack, I'm so happy to see you, but why did you take so long to get here?"

"I couldn't help it, sweetheart," he answered—he never called me sweetheart. "There was a long line in heaven of people waiting to come get their loved ones. I had to stand in line with the rest of them. I guess up there they don't care that I was president of the United States." He folded me into his arms, and it felt just like it did when he was alive. Then we shot up through the clouds to the heavens. Before we got there, however, I regained consciousness, and was sad to discover it was only a dream.

The ambulance took me to Loudoun Hospital Center, near Middleburg, where I was put under observation for twenty-four hours. I was in some pain, but it wasn't too severe. The Irish captain of the ambulance squad couldn't believe it. He shook his head and, rolling his r's, said, "It is a mir-a-cle! For a woman her age to come through such an accident without terrible injuries is nothing but a mir-a-cle!"

While I was in the hospital, the doctors observed a slight swelling in my abdomen, which they considered a minor injury that had become infected. They prescribed antibiotics, and the problem cleared up—or so we thought.

That Christmas, Maurice and I were sailing in the Caribbean when I noticed that my lymph nodes were swollen. Soon after, I developed what seemed like a bad cough. Maurice and I were vacationing, so I hacked away until I came home and could visit my internist. He was puzzled enough by my symptoms to refer me to Dr. Anne Moore, a renowned cancer specialist. She had biopsies of my lymph nodes taken and gently informed me that I had the beginnings of non-Hodgkins lymphoma.

"No, Doctor, you're wrong," I said immediately. "It's impossible. I'm a healthy woman. I've always taken excellent care of myself. I exercise every day and—"

"I'm sorry to have to tell you, Ms. Onassis, but I believe the diagnosis is correct, although of course you're free to get a second opinion." I got up and walked out of the office without responding.

I got a second and then a third opinion, but, unfortunately, wherever I went, the diagnosis remained the same. I was told that I had a particularly aggressive form of cancer, which most likely would metastasize to other organs shortly. If I were to have any chance at all of surviving, the doctors said, I had to undergo chemotherapy immediately. I couldn't make up my mind whether to do so or not. Having cancer still seemed impossible. Me, Jacqueline Bouvier Kennedy Onassis, a woman who never missed a day's exercise, and who had watched what I had eaten all my life! If the diagnosis was correct, I was going to be furious—I had done all those push-ups, and shoved away all those delicious French pastries, for 60 years, while some fat slob who sits and watches TV all day long, lives to be 107.

"How could this be happening?" I asked a priest. "How could God let it?" He had no satisfactory answer.

So I asked my oncologist, Dr. Moore, "How could such a terrible illness happen to so healthy a person?" She responded that, while nothing is known for sure, there are a number of possible causes for non-Hodgkins lymphoma. For years, both Jack and I were shot up, sometimes daily, with Dr. Max Jacobson's "feel-good" amphetamine cocktails, which have been linked to a number of cancers. If only I had known, Dr. Jacobson and his goodies would have been the first to be struck from our list of pleasures.

Then there was my terrible forty-five-year addiction to smoking, which, at the very least, must have compromised my immune system. Believe me, I tried many times to give up cigarettes, but it took something as dreadful as the cancer diagnosis to make my efforts stick. Looking back, I should have made Jack lock me up and tie me down until I promised to quit.

Then the doctor mentioned the black dye hairdressers had used for twenty-four years to color my hair. Dr. Michael Thun of the American Cancer Society believes that women who use black hair dye for twenty years or more have a four times greater chance of becoming ill with non-Hodgkins lymphoma than those who do not use it at all. That possible cause would have been a bit harder to eliminate. How long could I have remained America's most glamorous lady had I let my hair go gray? Then again, had I introduced the trend, it might have set a whole new pattern in the United States for graceful aging. Gray hair is better than no hair, although it's a bit late in the day for me to try it now.

After a while, my confusion cleared, and I grew to accept the diagnosis. My spirits even improved, as I thought, *So what if I don't lick the disease? Even if I have only five years left, life doesn't owe me much. I've been one of the luckiest women in the world.* I decided to make the best of the situation and proceed with the chemotherapy, along with steroids. I even gave up my three-pack-a-day cigarette addiction, which I had never been able to do before.

But if I had cancer and might die, there was one thing I needed to do first. Without telling him about the diagnosis, I asked Maurice to take me to lunch at Le Cirque. I've always loved desserts, but never let myself eat more than a bite or two because of my obsession about getting fat. Now, I wasn't going to worry about that anymore. I thought, *The hell with it! If I 'm going to die, why should I deprive myself?*

When the waiter brought over five or six desserts, I gorged myself on the first one, a delicious seven-layer cake, and sensuously savored each delicate layer on my tongue before swallowing. No French pastry had ever tasted so good. "You're not going to eat any more of them, are you?" Maurice said, starting to send the others back.

"Oh, no, you don't!" I shouted. "If you take any one of them away, I'm going to stab your hand with this fork!" Then I proceeded to devour every last one of the desserts. When I finished, I picked the crumbs up off the table cloth and ate them, too. Then I licked the icing off my fingers. The desserts tasted so good, it was almost worth dying for them.

Feeling replenished, I called Caroline, John, and Maurice into my comfortable library at home, and told them the diagnosis and my decision. All three began to sob.

"There, there," I said. "Don't cry. I'm a fighter, and I fully intend to beat this thing." I burst into tears.

I asked my loved ones to keep my illness a secret. They tried hard, but after a while, it became impossible. The side effects of chemotherapy—bloated face, skin blotches, nausea, and, worst of all, hair loss—were worse than the treatment itself. I could always read a book while I was getting the infusions, and often forgot where I was. But there was no escaping the tearful image that looked back at me in the mirror. My habitual sunglasses, along with my babushka, wigs, scarves, and long coats, hid the evidence for a while, but the paparazzi are canny when it comes to invading my privacy. They have their ways of digging out what I most want to keep secret. Hadn't they had years of practice, swarming around me and my private doings? Now, they were so omnipresent I wouldn't have been surprised to have a flashbulb go off while I was taking a shower. They didn't even have the decency to allow me to be sick in peace.

For example, a photographer tried to take a picture of me on one of our walks in the park. I looked so dreadful I couldn't stand for the world to see me in that condition. So good, kind, ordinarily restrained Maurice lunged at the photographer, as if to choke him. The surprised paparazzo dropped his camera and dashed down the Central Park bridal path without looking back. Maurice and I laughed all the way home.

I have always been a practicing Catholic who regularly attends Mass and confession. Conventional displays of piety, however, such as the correct way to pray the rosary, proved not much help to me, especially at this time. When I was a child, my mother sent me to a convent, run by a colony of nuns called the Society of the Helpers of the Holy Souls. The Society's headquarters was on the Upper East Side, and the nuns were used to instruct daughters of the Four Hundred, the elite of New York society.

They taught me much religion—the catechism, and how to sew, care for the poor, give first aid, and pray for the souls of people in purgatory. They insisted I sit up straight at all times. Unfortunately for my future as a devout Catholic, the slightest departure from their rules brought a hard wallop with a long, wooden ruler across the back of my neck or on my wrist. It still hurts when I think of it.

The nuns' cruelty left me feeling ambivalent about a church that permitted such treatment of innocent children. The conflict exacerbated after the Vatican threatened to excommunicate me when I announced plans to marry Ari. Since then, I have developed my own version of Catholicism. The aesthetic splendor of the Catholic Church—its great cathedrals, art, and music, and the mystery of the Mass—have always moved me. I believe that beauty, love, goodness, and mercy lead to salvation. But I find most comfort of all in the Catholic doctrine of the resurrection of the body, and fully expect to meet Jack in heaven after I die.

After I gradually began to accept the fact that I would probably die soon, if not in the immediate future, I took out the stacks of letters wrapped in blue ribbons that I had saved from a lifetime of correspondence and sat by the fireplace I loved. I tugged at the ribbons, and a brittle, yellowed letter more than forty years old dropped into my lap. Tiny pieces of the aged paper dropped all around me. I read it, with tears streaming down my cheeks. It was a personal and loving letter from my father.

"Nobody else can read this," I said, tossing it into the flames. "It is too private." I read another letter, smiled, and tossed it into the fire, too. One by one, I decided which ones to save and which to assign to the blaze. I have a great respect for history, but I also needed to determine how much I wanted to reveal about myself after my death. For example, many of the men I had gone out with had written me indiscreet letters. I thought it only right to protect these men, as well as their wives and children, from undue publicity.

Then there is the matter of my own children. There are things about my private life I never told them, and do not want them to learn after my death. So into the fireplace went whole batches of mail. When I finished burning the letters, I sat gazing into the fire for a long, long time, until only faintly glowing ashes were left.

Maurice couldn't have been lovelier to me. He put his business on hold and spent most of his time searching out the greatest medical experts and advice in the field. Nor did he stop researching alternative and experimental treatments. There are two forms of lymphomas, he discovered: Hodgkins disease and a dozen other forms grouped together as non-Hodgkins. People with non-Hodgkins-type lymphomas had a median survival rate of seven and a half years, and my chances for survival were only fifty-fifty. I admired his honesty when telling me that. I refused to try the alternative forms of treatment he had investigated, though. I had boundless faith in my physicians, and felt that if they couldn't help me, it was highly unlikely that some little experimenter could.

When I needed chemotherapy, he made all my appointments for me under an assumed name at New York Hospital, and didn't bring me into the hospital office until he made sure no other patients were there, thus providing me the anonymity I craved. When a CAT scan was required, he would even carry my breakfast for me in a little black bag, for me to eat after the treatment was over. He involved himself in every aspect of my fight against cancer, even the psychological. In his research, he had discovered that cancer patients were often ashamed of their illness and went to great efforts to hide it. He encouraged me to walk in Central Park and not to try to hide my condition from

public view.

My children weren't at all interested in Maurice until I got sick. But when they saw the tender and considerate way he treated me, they were touched. It made me feel good that all three began to feel close to each other.

I had decided that I would work as long as I was able. So, after Christmas, I stood up straight and tall and dropped into my Doubleday office. My colleagues tried to hide their shock when they saw me, but it crept in through their frozen smiles. No wonder! My skin had lost its glow, my features had begun to sag, and my face had become pinched and haggard. I had to hold onto the wall to get to the restroom. Sometimes, I didn't make it without falling. After I shook off their helping hands a few times, people pretended not to notice and looked the other way.

When I brushed my hair, clumps of it fell out. The wigs were hot and itchy, so sometimes I wore a turban. "Who knows?" I said. "Maybe I'll start a turban trend." I decided not to let the reactions of my colleagues bother me. Thanks to Maurice's psychological and emotional support, I was able to think, *This is the way I look now. I want to work, and anybody who can't take it can stay home.*

Though it was one of the coldest winters in New York history, I went into the office as often as before. My one concession to the illness was to take a cab every working day to Doubleday's Park Avenue headquarters, which were three blocks north of my beloved Grand Central Station. This former jogger and water-skier couldn't have walked the three blocks from the station, let alone the thirty-seven from my home.

I was grateful for the happiness in my life. My greatest joy was my grandchildren. Every afternoon, after I finished working, my devoted daughter brought Rose, Tatiana, and Jack to visit. I would think up delightful adventures for them, like treasure hunts in my apartment. I keep a chest in my bedroom with all sorts of wonderful treasures I've collected from my trips around the world. As soon as the children came in, they would dash into the bedroom, dump out the contents of the chest, bedeck themselves head to foot in jewelry, and make up exotic costumes of old scarves and other odd pieces of material. Then we would go on a fantasy adventure around the apartment, checking out ghosts and fairies hidden away in closets. When the game was over, we would sit on the living room floor and have a tea party. One freezing winter day, we went to the park and had a snowball fight. I'm delighted to say that I gave as good as I received. I was also pleased that, at one point, I was able to grab onto a steel rope and pull all three children across the snow. There was life in the old mare yet!

Even when the temperature dropped down to the teens, Maurice and I took our daily stroll in the park. My dear son John, who had rented a room at the Surrey Hotel to be nearer me, would take my arm and usher me across Fifth Avenue almost every day. We talked hopefully about the future, his and even mine. I held out hope that he'd be elected president one day.

Maurice and I went to the movies as long as I was able. I enjoyed (and was horrified) when we saw Steven Spielberg's Academy Award-winning film, *Schindler's List*. I watched every riveting minute of the movie because I was pretty sure it would be the last one I would ever see.

In the middle of March, 1994, I received some horrendous news—the cancer, it seems, had spread to my brain and spinal cord. Again, I couldn't believe it at first, but then gradually grew to accept the fact that I was indeed going to die. To the devastating chemotherapy treatments, Dr. Moore and her team of prominent cancer specialists added radiation therapy. They might as well not have bothered.

I was so miserable that I consulted Father Richard McSorley, a priest at Georgetown University who had advised me thirty years earlier on how to handle my grief, and I made no bones about the fact that I was contemplating suicide.

"I'm of no use to anyone now, including Caroline and John," I told him. "What do you think, Father? Would the church forgive me if I killed myself?"

The priest was sympathetic, but informed me that the Catholic

Church does not condone suicide under any circumstances.

"Then will you pray that I die?" I asked him.

"If you like," he answered. "It's not wrong to pray for death. But as for you taking your own life, it is absolutely forbidden. Committing suicide is a mortal sin that leads to eternal damnation. If you kill yourself, Jacqueline, you will forfeit any possibility of entering heaven and being reunited with Jack."

I take tremendous comfort in the Catholic belief that people whose sins are forgiven by God during life will have their bodies resurrected after death. I have always tried to be a good person and expect to be reunited with Jack in heaven. The priest's advice put an end once and for all to any thoughts of taking my own life.

I was soon happy that I had listened to him. Before long, blossoms began to appear in Central Park, ushering in a glorious spring. I have always loved spring as the beginning of new life, but this spring was different. Every leaf, every bud, every new blade of grass was a sign that life goes on. I told Maurice, "I'm almost glad I got sick, because it's opened my eyes to everything around me. I enjoy things I never noticed before. I've learned how to really live."

A friend once callously asked, "How do you feel about dying?"

I gave her the answer she deserved: "If you've got to go, you've got to go."

On April 14, I collapsed in my apartment and was rushed in an ambulance to New York Hospital. I was operated on there for a perforated ulcer, a common side effect of chemotherapy. On the hospital bed en route to the operating room, I remembered that I had a Doubleday appointment with author Peter Sís. "Please call Peter and tell him I won't be able to keep the appointment," I told the nurse walking beside me. "He'll be worried about me."

Maurice repaid me in kind for the help I had given him after his heart attack. He stayed at my side every possible moment, and his kind presence was always comforting. In his soothing manner, he continued his affection throughout my illness. When he wasn't holding my hand, he was stroking my forehead or holding his arm around me. I pushed away the unpleasant thought that it was too bad I had to wait until my last years to have the steady attention of a loving man.

By early May, the pain was unbearable. I suffered from pounding headaches as a result of the brain cancer. Every breath I drew was agony—it was a side effect of the steroids. The strong narcotics administered to kill my pain nauseated me. And the image of millions of malignant cells literally eating me alive terrified me and kept me up all night. In addition, I was losing my ability to think clearly—me, to whom intelligence was more important than bread and butter. My usual upbeat front broke down, and I called John and said to him, "I have to tell you. I can't take it anymore." He pleaded with me, saying that I had felt that way before and was wrong then. With my strong will to recover, I surely would feel better again soon. I agreed to try for a few more days.

On May 15, confused, shaking, and slurring my speech, I returned to the hospital. There, I was diagnosed with pneumonia and put on antibiotics. Dr. Moore told me that the cancer had spread to my liver, and there was nothing more she or her colleagues could do for me than to treat the pneumonia. When my cancer was first diagnosed, I had the staff draw up a living will, which said that no heroic measures were to be administered to keep me alive when my death was a foregone conclusion. Being at the brink of death did not make me change my mind. I was not interested in lingering, stuck full of tubes in a hospital, surrounded by doctors and nurses. I did not want to spend my last days lying on stiff, bleached hospital sheets in an ugly, germ-proof room, kept away from loved ones and treasured belongings.

I have always wanted to do things my own way. I want to die in my own way as well. So I told Caroline, John, and Maurice how I wanted to die. I told them I want to die at home surrounded by the three of them, with my favorite books by my side and *Alleluia, Beatus Vir Qui Suffert* chanted by the Benedictine Monks of Santo Domingo piped through my apartment.

I want scented candles lit at my bedside.

I want to lie on my favorite floral sheets, wear my most flattering nightgown, and cover my bald head with a beautiful scarf.

I want my loved ones to speak of treasured memories we share while I can still hear, and read to me from my favorite poets: Emily Dickinson, Robert Frost, and Edna St. Vincent Millay.

I want a few of my closest friends, like Bunny Mellon and Peter Duchin, and my sister, Lee, to come say goodbye.

I want my priest, Monsignor Georges Bardes of St. Thomas More Church, where Mass was celebrated for the twenty-fifth anniversary of Jack's assassination, to administer the last rites of the Catholic Church. I want him to hear my last confession: "Bless me, Father, for I have sinned." For I have.

Before I leave this earth, I will make my loved ones promise that they will have me buried next to Jack at Arlington National Cemetery.

And I will smile goodbye, glow in their love for me one last time, and close my eyes forever.

INDEX

BIBLIOGRAPHY

Adler, Bill, ed. *The Eloquent Jacqueline Kennedy Onassis: A Portrait in Her Own Words.* New York: William Morrow, 2004.

Andersen, Christopher. *Jack and Jackie: Portrait of an American Marriage.* New York: Avon, 1997.

———. *Jackie After Jack: Portrait of the Lady.* New York: Warner, 1999.

———. *Sweet Caroline: Last Child of Camelot.* New York: William Morrow, 2003.

Anthony, Carl Sferrazza. *As We Remember Her: Jacqueline Kennedy Onassis in the Words of Her Family and Friends.* New York: HarperCollins, 1997.

Aronson, Marc. "Robert F. Kennedy: Crusader." Available at http://www.marcaronson.co m/archives/2007/04/robert_f_kenned_1.html.

Bergouist, Laura (text) and Tretick, Stanley (photographs). *A Very Special President.* New York: McGraw-Hill Book Company, 1965.

Birmingham, Stephen. *Jacqueline Bouvier Kennedy Onassis.* New York: Grosset & Dunlap, 1978.

Blair, Joan and Clay Blair, Jr. *The Search for JFK.* New York: Berkeley, 1976.

Bly, Nellie. *The Kennedy Men: Three Generations of Sex, Scandal and Secrets.* New York: Kensington, 1996.

Bouvier, Jacqueline and Lee Bouvier. *One Special Summer.* New York: Delacorte, 1974.

Bradford, Sarah. *America's Queen: The Life of Jacqueline Kennedy Onassis.* New York: Penguin, 2001.

Bradlee, Benjamin C. *Conversations with Kennedy.* New York: Konecky & Konecky, 1975.

Buck, Pearl S. *The Kennedy Women: A Personal Appraisal.* New York: Pinnacle, 1972.

Bugliosi, Vincent. *Reclaiming History: The Assassination of President John F. Kennedy.* New York: W. W. Norton, 2007.

Burleigh, Nina. *A Very Private Woman: The Life and Unsolved Murder of Presidential Mistress Mary Meyer*. New York: Bantam, 1998.

Collier, Peter and David Horowitz. *The Kennedys: An American Drama*. New York: Summit, 1984.

Cooper, Ilene. *Jack: The Early Years of John F. Kennedy*. New York: Dutton Juvenile, 2003.

Davis, John H. *Jacqueline Bouvier: An Intimate Memoir*. New York: Wiley, 1996.

DuBois, Diana. *In Her Sister's Shadow: An Intimate Biography of Lee Radziwill*. Boston: Little, Brown & Co., 1995.

Duheme, Jacqueline, John Kenneth Galbraith, and Vibhuti Patel. *Mrs. Kennedy Goes Abroad*. New York: Artisan, 1998.

Exner, Judith. *My Story*. As told to Ovid Demaris. New York: Grove, 1977.

Francisco, Ruth. *The Secret Memoirs of Jacqueline Kennedy Onassis*. New York: St. Martin's Griffin, 2006.

Frischauer, Willi. *Jackie*. London: Joseph, 1976.

Gallagher, Mary Barelli and Frances Spatz Leighton. *My Life with Jacqueline Kennedy*. New York: Paperback Library, 1970.

Goldman, Eric F. *The Tragedy of Lyndon Johnson*. New York: Dell, 1974.

Hall, Gordon Langley and Ann Pinchot. *Jacqueline Kennedy: A Biography*. New York: Frederick Fell, 1964.

Heller, Deane and David Heller. *Jacqueline Kennedy: The Complete Story of America's Glamorous First Lady*. Derby, CT: Monarch, 1961.

Heymann, C. David. *A Woman Named Jackie*. New York: Signet, 1989.

———. *Bobby and Jackie: A Love Story*. New York: Atria, 2010.

———. *RFK: A Candid Biography of Robert F. Kennedy*. New York: Dutton, 1998.

Kennedy, John F. *Profiles in Courage*. New York: Harper and Row, 1965.

———. *Why England Slept*. New York: Wilfred Funk, 1940.

Klein, Edward. *Farewell, Jackie: A Portrait of Her Final Days*. New York: Penguin, 2004.

Koestenbaum, Wayne. *Jackie Under My Skin: Interpreting an Icon*. New York: ume, 1996.

Ladowsky, Ellen. *Jacqueline Kennedy Onassis*. New York: Park Lane, 1997.

Leamer, Laurence. *The Kennedy Women: The Saga of an American Family*. New ork: Ballantine, 1994.

Leaming, Barbara. *Mrs. Kennedy: The Missing History of the Kennedy Years*. New ork: Touchstone, 2001.

Lincoln, Evelyn. *My Twelve Years with John F. Kennedy*. New York: Bantam, 1965.

Lowe, Jacques. *Jacqueline Kennedy Onassis: The Making of a First Lady: A Tribute*. ew York: Stoddart, 1996.

———. *Remembering Jack: Intimate and Unseen Photographs of the Kennedys*. New ork: Bulfinch, 2003.

Maier, Thomas. *The Kennedys: America's Emerald Kings: A Five-Generation History f the Ultimate Irish-Catholic Family*. New York: Basic, 2003.

Merry, Robert W. *Taking on the World: Joseph and Stewart Alsop—Guardians of the merican Century*. New York: Viking, 1996.

Moon, Vicky. *The Private Passion of Jackie Kennedy Onassis: Portrait of a Rider*. ew York: Harper Design, 2005.

O'Donnell, Kenneth P., David F. Powers, and Joe McCarthy. *Johnny, We Hardly new Ye*. Boston: Little, Brown, 1970.

Oppenheimer, Jerry. *The Other Mrs. Kennedy: Ethel Skakel Kennedy: An American rama of Power, Privilege, and Politics*. New York: St Martin's, 1994.

Perret, Geoffrey. *Jack: A Man Like No Other*. New York: Random House, 2001.

Pitts, David. *Jack and Lem: John F. Kennedy and Lem Billings: The Untold Story of n Extraordinary Friendship*. New York: Carroll & Graf, 2007.

Pollard, Eve. *Jack's Widow*. New York: William Morrow, 2006.

Reeves, Thomas C. *A Question of Character: A Life of John F. Kennedy*. Rocklin, A: Prima, 1997.

Shaw, Maude. *White House Nanny: My Hears with Caroline and John Kennedy, Jr.* ew York: New American, 1965.

Shulman, Irving. *"Jackie"! The Exploitation of a First Lady*. New York: Trident, 1971.

Smith, Sally Bedell. *Grace and Power: The Private World of the Kennedy White House*. New York: Random House, 2004.

Sorenson, Ted. *Counselor: A Life at the Edge of History*. New York: HarperLuxe, 2008.

Spada, James. *Jackie: Her Life in Pictures*. New York: St. Martin's, 2000.

Sparks, Fred. *The $20,000,000 Honeymoon: Jackie and Ari's First Year*. New York Dell, 1971.

Spoto, Donald. *Jacqueline Bouvier Kennedy Onassis: A Life*. New York: St. Martin's, 2000.

Stebben, Gregg and Austin Hill. *White House: Confidential: The Little Book of Weird Presidential History*. Nashville, TN: Cumberland, 2006.

Steinem, Gloria. "Lee Radziwill: And Starring Lee Bouvier," *McCall's* (February 1968): 79, 134-140.

Suarés, J. C. and J. Spencer Beck. *Uncommon Grace: Reminiscences and Photographs of Jacqueline Bouvier Kennedy Onassis*. Charlottesville, VA: Thomasson Grant & Howell, 1994.

Summers, Anthony. *Goddess: The Secret Lives of Marilyn Monroe*. New York: MacMillan, 1985.

Talbot, David. *Brothers: The Hidden History of the Kennedy Years*. New York: Free Press, 2007.

Thayer, Mary Van Rensselaer. *Jacqueline Bouvier Kennedy: A warm, personal story of the First Lady illustrated with family pictures*. New York: Doubleday, 1961.

———. "Jacqueline Kennedy: Life at the White House," *McCall's* (February 1968): 15-17, 120-130.

West, J. B. and Mary Lynn Kotz. *Upstairs at the White House: My Life with the First Ladies*. New York: Warner, 1974.

Wills, Garry. *The Kennedy Imprisonment: A Meditation on Power*. Boston: Atlantic-Little Brown, 1981.

Wolff, Perry Sidney. *A Tour of the White House with Mrs. John F. Kennedy: The historic 1962 televised broadcast produced by CBS News*. Chicago: Marshall Field, 2004.

ACKNOWLEDGEMENTS

I would like to thank my publisher, Bruce Bortz, and his assistant, Harrison Demchick, for believing in *Jackie O: On the Couch* from the beginning. Without their faith in me and my book, it might never have seen the light of day.

I would also like to thank my cousin, Sylvia Weiss, and Kathryn Lance for their editorial assistance in earlier versions of the book.

I particularly want to offer my gratitude to my son, Jonathan H. Bond, CEO of *Big Fuel Advertising Agency*, and his assistant, Danielle Gilardi, for their extraordinary help in publicizing *Jackie O: On the Couch*. I greatly appreciate their expertise, with full awareness that it is easier to write a book than to successfully publicize it. I also would like to take this opportunity to thank *Big Fuel* for kindly allowing me the use of my son's services.

While I have read more than 100 books and many articles about Jackie Kennedy Onassis, and am grateful to all their authors for the huge amount of information which contributed to the content of this book, I would like to give special thanks to Vickie Moon for the knowledge I gained from *The Private Passion of Jackie Kennedy Onassis*, which supplied many of the ideas in my chapter, "Horsewoman Extraordinaire," and, especially, to Laura Bergouist for the moving material in *A Very Special President* that I used in my chapter, "The President and his Son."

And last but not least, I extend my heartfelt thanks to my friends and colleagues, Sandy Langer, Jill Morris, Carol Calhoun, and Karen Lane, who, as members of the Writers Group, listened with fascination week after week to the chapters of *Jackie O: On the Couch* as they rolled hot off my printer. I will be forever grateful for your encouragement and interest.

ABOUT THE AUTHOR

Jackie O: On the Couch is the first of Alma Bond's *On the Couch* series, and is Dr. Bond's nineteenth published book. She received her Ph.D. in Developmental Psychology from Columbia University, graduated from the post-doctoral program in psychoanalysis at the Freudian Society, and was a psychoanalyst in private practice for thirty-seven years in New York City. She "retired" to become a full-time writer, but now maintains a small practice in addition to writing. Her last book, *Margaret Mahler, a Biography of the Psychoanalyst*, received two awards: Best Books Award Finalist, USA Book News; and *Foreword Magazine*'s Book of the Year Finalist.

Her Maria Callas book, *The Autobiography of Maria Callas: A Novel*, was first runner-up in the Hemingway Days novel contest.

Her sixteen other published books include: *Camille Claude: A Novel; Old Age is a Terminal Illness; Who Killed Virginia Woolf?: A Psychobiography; Tales of Psychology: Short Stories to Make You Wise; I Married Dr. Jekyll and Woke Up Mrs. Hyde; Is There Life After Analysis?;*

On Becoming a Grandparent; America's First Woman Warrior: The Story of Deborah Sampson (with Lucy Freeman); and a children's book, *The Tree That Could Fly*.

She presently has another book in production, *Michelle Obama: A Biography*.

Dr. Bond also wrote the play, *Maria*, about the life and loves of Maria Callas, which was produced off-off Broadway and is currently touring Florida.

Dr. Bond is a member of the American Society of Journalists and Authors, the Dramatists Guild, and the Authors Guild, as well as a fellow and faculty member of the Institute for Psychoanalytic Training and Research, the International Psychoanalytic Association, and the American Psychological Association.

Dr. Bond is the widow of Rudy Bond, the acclaimed stage, screen, and television actor, and author of *I Rode a Streetcar Named Desire*. She is the mother of three children, Zane P. Bond, Jonathan H. Bond, and Janet Bond Brill, all of whom are published authors, and she is the proud grandmother of eight, none of whom has published a book . . . yet. But as a wise friend of Alma's put it, "In her family, it's pretty much publish or perish."